WHERE HAVE WE COME

Saz Vora

In a gentle way you can
shake the world

Saz
2021

A beautiful love story. It is modern and global in thought, yet fiercely Indian at heart.
Nik and Reena are unforgettable characters. They will stay with me for a long time to come.
Sarah Ismail, Editor, Same Difference.
www.samedifference1.com

A thought-provoking story that explores the complex emotions of giving birth to and the losing a child extremely sensitively. Saz recounts her personal journey tackling topics such as generational conflicts, economic privilege, cultural issues and gender politics with the backdrop of Bollywood. She has a unique style of blending striking themes with her favourite songs, giving the readers a gentle feel of life and laughter after dealing with heartbreak and loss.
Highly recommend these enjoyable reads.
Dr Pushpinder Chowdhry, MBE, Festival Director,
UK Asian Film Festival
www.ukaff.com

About the Author

Saz Vora was born in East Africa and migrated with her family to England in the 60's to the Midlands, where she grew up straddling British and Gujarati Indian culture. Her debut duet My Heart Sings Your Song and Where Have We Come is a story in two parts about love, loss and family, the second book in the series is based on true events that has shaped her outlook on life's trials and tribulations.

Please visit her website, where you can read her blog and sign up to her newsletter where she will share, missing scenes, recipes, playlists and all things book related.

Website **www.sazvora.com**

BY THE SAME AUTHOR
My Heart Sings Your Song Book One
University Reena & Nikesh Duet

Note from Saz

The spelling used in this book is British which may be strange to American readers, but NOT to those living in Australia, Canada, India, Ireland or the United Kingdom. This means color is colour. I hope this is not confusing and will not detract from your reading experience.

The Gujarati words used in this book can be found in the Glossary at the back.

WHERE HAVE WE COME

Copyright © 2020 by Saz Vora

www.sazvora.com

Book Cover design by Mita Gohel

Author photograph by Gulab Chagger - creativeplanets.com

ISBN: 978-1-8381465-1-1

First edition. March, 2020.

10 9 8 7 6 5 4 3 2 1

Dedication

For Chetan.
To Papa I miss you so much.

Where Have We Come
Book Two

"You're my moon, you're my sun, you're the star of my eyes."
Translated lyrics from "Chanda Hai Tu Mera Suraj Hai Tu" Lata Mangeshkar, Anand Bakshi

To enhance your reading experience, you can listen to my soundtrack on Spotify

Where Have We Come

One

January 6th, 1990 – four years later

UMI ARRIVES WITH A TOTE BAG and gives me a hug.

"You've grown so big," she pushes me away, the bag rubbing against my side.

"I know," I say, stroking my belly.

"So what time is Anne-Marie coming?"

I tell her Anne-Marie is working today and won't be coming until her shift finishes. Her eyes dart towards the clock. "Let's have tea and cake," she says and heads for the galley kitchen that runs at the back of the open-plan living area of our renovated Victorian workman's cottage.

I sit at the round table as Umi collects the teapot, teacups, saucers and plates from the kitchen cupboards. She pulls out a Marks and Spencer Victoria sponge and brings the plate to the table, saying, "I've missed cake."

"Don't they eat cake in Thailand?" I ask.

"Not Marks and Spencer Victoria sponge. Don't get me wrong, the food was amazing." She cuts a huge slice, takes a bite and walks back to the kettle.

She takes my hand. "So, what's wrong?"

"I wish the dreams would stop. I don't know what's wrong with me."

Umi and I don't have any secrets. She has been through my highs and lows and knows all about my anxiety attacks.

"I should have stayed here," she adds.

"No," I reply, looking at her concerned face.

Umi had been to Thailand for Christmas, after another breakup with Peter. They had already broken up twice before and somehow drifted back together. Umi is ready to take their relationship to the next level. Peter isn't in the same space. She was devastated when they broke up this time and booked the holiday on a whim, wanting to get as much distance from Peter as possible.

"Did you have a good time?"

She looks glorious, her naturally curly hair shining and her beautiful skin glowing from exposure to the sun. I wonder what is stopping Peter from committing to her.

"Yes, I loved it all. Massage, spas, swimming, being waited on. I'm glad I went, but we're talking about you. Still the same dreams?"

"Yes, the little girl is so beautiful and mischievous. I feel I know her."

"I went to see a clairvoyant, and she told me you were going to have a girl."

My jaw drops. "Are you serious? When did you start believing in that mumbo jumbo?"

"I just needed some help to move on," she says, her voice hushed.

"I'm sorry. He does love you. He just isn't ready yet."
I pull Umi towards me, her eyes dim with sadness.
"What shall we eat tonight?" she asks me, raising a thin smile.
The doorbell interrupts us.
Umi goes to answer it. We had been catching up on my Christmas break. Usually, Nik and I go away for winter sun, but this year as the baby is due in the second week of January, we hadn't had a choice but to stay in London. We'd gone to my family for Christmas Day and had spent New Year at Shakti Bhavan. The rest of our holiday had been spent watching our favourite films, eating our favourite foods and making the most of our time together before the baby arrives. We planned to spend one last Saturday night separately, Nik with his friends and me with mine.
This morning I woke up with the taste of bile in my mouth and had thrown up; the anxiety dream of losing the little girl was too vivid. When Nik was getting ready to go out, I'd been fearful of the separation from my husband, and he'd taken me in his arms and had said, "Let's cancel. Everyone will understand." I had pulled myself together and told him I was just hormonal and wanted to spend time catching up with Umi. When he left, Nik kissed me longingly, raising his wicked eyebrow. "Are you sure we don't have time for a quick kiss and cuddle?" I'd laughed and my stomach flipped as I looked into his sparkling eyes.
"Hello, Ree."
Anne-Marie is in the small entrance hall, her strawberry-blonde hair tied into a messy knot. She pulls off her round silver-rimmed glasses and wipes them with a tissue. "How are you today?" she asks me

and then turns to Umi, "Wow! Umi, you're glowing. Did you meet someone interesting in Thailand?" she teases.

Umi chortles, "Not everyone goes to Thailand for that. You're early; we weren't expecting you until seven-thirty."

"I finished my work sooner than I thought, and I've left Ree's number with Bill if they need me." She sits down on the sofa next to me and says, "So do you think this will be our last girls' night in, Reena?"

"I guess so, until the baby's at least six months old and sleeping through the night," I reply.

"So, where have they gone for their boys' night out?" she asks me.

"They're at Gino's so not far … just in case." I rub my tummy and see panic momentarily in her eyes.

"He's not due until the seventeenth. The due date's still the same?" she quizzes.

"Yes," I laugh, "I'm only teasing," although my body is practising lately as I've had some powerful Braxton Hicks contractions for the past two days.

"Let me say hello." She kneels down in front of me and speaks into my tummy.

"Hello, baby. It's your masi here. How are you today?" An elbow pokes my belly button, and we watch in amazement at my rotund belly.

"Did you see that?" Umi whispers. "Can't believe she responded like that." Her eyes twinkle in awe. "How long has this been going on?" she questions us.

"Quite a lot," I tell her. "You should see my belly when Nik sings; the baby spins round and round."

"It's my turn." She pushes Anne-Marie aside and kneels down to speak at my belly.

"Hello, darling. I'm your favourite masi; I'm looking forward to meeting you."

A lump moves by my rib cage. We all laugh at the way my baby reacts to the sound of his aunties. When I had my check-up with Sally on Tuesday, I'd told her I was worried about the baby's lack of movement and she'd told me the baby's head had engaged ready for the birthing process, so the loss of sensation of a tumble dryer in my belly was nothing to worry about.

Umi crouches down to stare into the under-counter fridge. "What soup do you want? Mushroom or cauliflower?"

"I don't mind, whatever," I reply.

"I want cauliflower, Umi. Are you going to make Reena's recipe, or have you found something else?"

"Reena's recipe, obviously, with some tweaks."

Umi quickly collects the chopping board, knife and pans; she knows my kitchen well, as I know her kitchen. We have spent many hours cooking together. Before she met me, Umi couldn't cook a thing. I had taught her the basics, and now we compete against each other on producing exciting and delicious food from simple ingredients.

While Umi cooks, Anne-Marie sets the round country-style dining table for three; she opens the bottle of Shiraz and takes out the wine glasses from the cupboard above the sink.

"Are you having a glass tonight?" she asks me.

"No, I don't feel like a drink tonight."

She looks in the fridge, "Ginger ale or Perrier?"

I opt for ginger ale, and she pours my glass and hands the glass of red wine to Umi as she sweats the onion and ginger on the stove. The smell of ginger and a hint of curry fill the house. "I'm starving." Anne-Marie takes a deep breath in to take in the aroma.

"Do you have bread in here?" she asks me as she opens the freezer door.

I tell her where it is. I have been batch cooking and stocking up the freezer for the last two weeks. Nik had teased me, saying that we'd be eating frozen food for the next six months and reminded me that Anumasi and Motaba would quite easily prepare and send us food.

A hot crusty loaf and a bread knife have been placed on a breadboard on the table. Umi lifts the pot off the stove and brings it to the table. "Right, it's ready. Let's eat," she says.

We tell Anne-Marie about the first time we had created the recipe. It was when I had come down to stay with Umi over the Easter break in our first year. I had wanted to explore London and be near Nik. We'd spent all day at Portobello Market shopping for second-hand clothes. "We bought a bottle of wine and thought we were so grown up and woke up with a huge hangover afterwards," Umi adds.

After dinner we discuss the names we've shortlisted for the baby. The list for boys' names is longer than girls'. Nik and Umi are adamant the baby is a girl. I was confident when I had my twenty-week scan that we were having a boy, although my certainty has wavered as the dreams of the little girl have become more frequent lately.

* * *

"I CAN SLEEP ON THE SOFA BED if you want me to stay?" Anne-Marie asks, as she gets ready to leave at ten o'clock. "I'm off tomorrow and Monday."

"No, don't worry. Umi's staying tonight and Nik will be back soon." I hug her holding back a yawn.

When Umi comes upstairs to the old guest bedroom, she smiles and says, "It's beautiful; when did you do this?"

I tell her Nik and I spent the holiday decorating.

"What did his motaba say?"

"Oh, the usual superstitious tosh."

"Tosh!" She lifts her eyebrows.

"Yes, I'm trying not to swear; the baby can hear everything," I say, pointing to my bulging tummy.

I eventually fall asleep. The Braxton Hicks contractions are extreme and, at times, the pain is unbearable. I practice the release of slow breaths through my mouth to ease the pain and find it uncomfortable to settle.

My mouth fills with bile; the contents of my dinner gush out as if through a tap. I steady myself and climb down to the bathroom, turning on the landing lights. My body is getting rid of what I had consumed in preparation for birth.

I am still sitting with my head in the toilet bowl when I hear Umi.

"Ree, what's the matter?" I look up, and she says, "Oh, is the baby ready to come?"

I nod. She brushes the hair away from my forehead and sits on her haunches, "Let's time the contractions." She raises her left wrist. The contractions are coming every five minutes.

"Where's your list of phone numbers?"

I point to the little address book by the phone. She brings the phone to me, and I speak with Sally first. She instructs me to stay calm and head for the hospital. Umi calls the labour ward and then she calls Gino's.

"It's time. The baby's ready to come. Get Nik and the guys to come to the hospital; I'm taking Ree."

Two

THE BIG HAND IS ON ONE and the little hand is on eight on the wall clock.

"Where is Nik?" My mind goes back to another time.

My stomach feels as hard as a rock; the pain is unendurable. For the past three days, I had been experiencing lower back pain, and the Braxton Hicks had been more frequent. But the baby wasn't due for another two weeks, so I'd ignored it, marvelling at how the raspberry tea I had been drinking was helping my body prepare for the birth of our first child.

"Come on, Ree, breathe. You can't hold your breath; you have to breathe through this."

The face of my best friend fills with concern. It's not often you see concern on Umi's face. She is a repository of calmness and strength. I didn't expect her to be with me as my birthing partner, but if I had to choose anyone else apart from Nik, it would be her.

My stomach decides to expel the last remnants of this evening's meal. I hate the bitter taste that fills my mouth; being sick reminds me of my panic attacks. It suddenly dawns on me that my body is expelling my baby.

"I can't do this on my own, Umi. Where is he?"

"He's on his way. Any minute now he'll rush through those doors," she assures me, pointing to the double doors of the birthing room. As my eyes focus on the doors, they burst open and Nik and the guys rush in. Nik is by my bed in seconds.

"My love, look at me. Breathe; deep breath in, now slowly out. Concentrate on the breathing." I feel like I'm the only one here with him.

We have practised this many, many times at the classes. As I breathe through the pain, I concentrate on what we'd learnt at the NCT classes and the Lamaze technique. I had opted for a pain relief-free labour. Sally, our midwife, had suggested it to me.

Nik had been apprehensive about the whole process and had tried to convince me that pain relief was a good thing. I stuck to my guns. I was not going to have an injection to numb the pain and reminded him of the many women around the world who gave birth without pain relief.

"Whoa, there's too many of you here."

Sally, a tall, slim, chestnut-haired woman stands with her arms out to block our friends. She is in her late fifties although, if you met her, you'd think she was younger. She was my primary contact and had become a firm supporter throughout the pregnancy. I guess she made more of an effort with me because I didn't have a mother to ask all the questions that had plagued me. It was Sally who monitored my pregnancy at our GP surgery, and as I had opted for as natural a birth as possible, it was Sally who I called when I knew the time had come.

Peter has broken away from Sally's outstretched arms and is looking into my eyes.

"Reena, you're unbelievably beautiful when you sweat."

I laugh. He smiles at Umi as he turns to walk out of the room.

Sally's soft, melodious, Gaelic timbre interrupts our laughter.

"Right, let's check the baby, shall we?" She places a trumpet-like instrument to my bulging stomach. It has become as hard as a rock again, and it feels like a metal bar is beginning to tighten around my waist. Her eyes lock with mine, and she smiles and confirms all is well.

"Breathe, Reena. Remember to breathe through the contractions," she reminds me, and I exhale through my mouth as the pain ebbs away.

"Can I get Reena into the water? It helps relax her," Nik asks quietly.

"Let me get a reading from the machine first, Nik."

Sally wraps a black elastic belt around my bulbous belly. In her hand are a set of plastic discs four centimetres in diameter attached to wires. One disc is placed just below the bulge near my pelvic bone and the second disc is placed on my lower back. The monitor by the screen comes to life with a beeping sound. Both Nik and Umi move towards the graph and stare at it in awe.

"Is that the baby's heartbeat?" Umi asks Sally.

"Yes, look at it. So strong. Some people can tell whether it's a boy or girl from this."

"Can you tell, Sally?" Nik's expression is full of love and awe. I think he's actually fallen hook, line and sinker for the person whose heartbeat he's just seen.

He takes my hand and kisses it, gazing into my eyes.

"Look at that, Ree. That's our child; I knew she'd be strong."

"He is strong, Nik. I'm the one who gets kicked all the time," I smile.

As the due date of our firstborn approached, we had been picking names. He was confident we were having a daughter, as was Umi. They'd ganged up on me and kept taking turns in referring to my belly with a girl's name. Recently he'd been calling my bump Maya. We weren't supposed to choose our own name: Motaba had already quashed the idea when we brought it up in conversation during a recent lunch at Shakti Bhavan. She had told us it was bad luck to give a child a name that wasn't selected by the alignment of the stars. Nik and I disagreed with her and were going to pick a name we wanted.

He puts his mouth to my stomach and says softly, "I love you, Maya. Can't wait to meet you." The machine pushes out the reading.

"He's going to get a complex," I reprimand, through gritted teeth.

He chuckles, "I'll go fill the bath," and he walks towards the bathroom.

Nat King Cole's melodious voice sings on the CD player, "When I fall in love."

Nik bends from the waist and bows as he waits by the end of the bed. "Your bath has been drawn, my lady."

He helps me get off the bed, lifts me into his arms and walks to the bathroom. Umi asks if she should leave as she waits awkwardly by the bed.

I look back at her with panic in my eyes. She acknowledges my angst and follows.

The water in the large bath covers my belly, helping with the pain, and a calmness washes over me. I love water, swimming in it, washing in it, hearing it; it reminds me of happier times in my childhood. Nik and Umi grab stools and sit next to the bath. Umi is making a note of the timing of my contractions. I sip ice-cold water from a glass proffered to my mouth by Nik. The contractions get closer and closer.

* * *

SALLY STANDS AT THE BATHROOM DOOR and commands, "Time to get out of the bath and onto the bed."
Nik stands behind my head, his arms around my breasts. The water splashes everywhere as I'm lifted out of the bath. The tracksuit bottoms he has changed into are soaking wet.
"Now, let's dry you off. Can you stand?" he questions.
I nod in reply. My husband is tall and well built; his T-shirt clings to his broad chest. His sparklingly golden eyes stare intently for any sign of pain.
Umi hands him a soft white towel. He engulfs me in it, scoops me up and carries me to the bed. He pulls the nightdress sleeves up my arms and starts doing up the buttons.
Umi and Sally prop pillows behind me. The bed has been placed against the wall of the birthing room, and a clear-plastic baby crib with a white blanket has been put to one side.
"Let me get this round you," Sally continues in her soft lilting voice as she wraps the elastic belt around my stomach. The discs are positioned as before, and the monitor screen comes to life with a beeping sound and

a blinking wave graph. Sally adjusts the nodes panel and presses a red button to record the heartbeat. Out of a horizontal slot just below the screen, a piece of paper tape, similar in size to a till receipt, begins to come out. She examines it as it curls out and then her brow furrows. She quickly tears the paper out and asks Nik to help move me.

The head of the bed is electronically tilted to sit me up; the base of the bottom part of the bed is lowered, my bottom straddling the edge, legs bent at the knee and stretched wide, my companions holding a leg each. My breath halts as a steel clamp wraps around my full belly, and the chronic waves of pain come without any respite.

"I have to push!" I shout.

"Wait. Let me check how far you're gone." Sally is crouching between my legs. She lifts her head. "Go push, but wait for a contraction. Good girl. Now get your strength back."

"I can't do this. It hurts so much; Nik do something!"

"Yes, you can, my love. Come on, breathe. Umi, can you get some ice?" Umi rushes to a small thermos she has placed on the side table and brings out some ice.

"Oh God, there's something wrong. I know it."

"Everything's fine," reassures Sally.

"Please, get the baby out," I plead with her.

"One more push, dear. Remember, only with a contraction."

It is all too quick. The baby's head is crowning one minute, and the shoulders and the rest of it follow the next. I let out a primal scream as my insides tear.

Sally stops me from pushing. "Wait I need to loosen the umbilical cord." She holds up a pair of scissors and gestures to Nik. "Congratulations, it's a boy."

His face fills with a lopsided grin, and his head disappears as he cuts the cord. Sally places our son on the bed next to me and uses a clear-plastic tube attached to a rubber bulb to suck out the mucus in his nose and mouth.

He is dark blue in colour, and my first thought is, how strange, he's the same colour as Peter, neither of our families are dark skinned.

Nik leaps towards the emergency cord by the right side of the bed and pulls it. A taste of bitterness fills my senses. Something is wrong. Please, please don't let there be anything wrong, I pray silently.

The big hand is on two and the little hand is on three.

As the double doors swing open, I can hear a siren. Umi is pushed out as a male doctor and nurses fill the room.

I glimpse our friends waiting outside the room. There is an orange glow from the flashing light. Peter rushes to Umi 's side, grabbing her hand, guiding her gently to a chair, their faces full of shock as different equipment is brought into the room.

"What's the Apgar score?" the doctor barks at Sally.

"Three," Sally replies, glancing at Nik, brushing a finger under her eyes as she turns her face away.

My heart hurts like someone has just taken hold of it and is squeezing it like a lemon.

The baby is like a rag doll, his arms and legs floppy, and he hasn't made a sound. The doctor hurriedly wraps him in a blanket and starts rubbing him vigorously. He lays him in the plastic crib on the side of the bed and suctions the mouth again, checks the colour of the mucus, and puts a small clear-plastic mask over his mouth and nose; he attaches a large red rubber balloon to the end and starts pressing rhythmically.

Two nurses, one mousy haired and the other a dark-haired Chinese woman, arrive with a closed incubator and plug it into the wall opposite the bed.

I stare at our baby boy. His colour changes from dark blue to a pale brown, however his fingers and toes are still dark blue.

A red spotlight is placed in the incubator. The monitor that was by the bed is taken to it. They work together silently and mechanically, adding and attaching wires and tubes to the incubator. Our son has small pads put on his chest and back; lines of wire from these pads are connected to the monitor. On the screen, a faint green axis records a wiggly line with small peaks and troughs; underneath, in a box, the numbers change, and a little heart begins to blink. I inhale deeply, my lungs thankful for the oxygen.

On the wall clock the big hand is still on two and the other is on six.

Nik's face is pale. I feel nothing. Sally has come back to the bed and gives me an injection in my thigh. "We have to deliver the afterbirth, Reena. I want you to push one more time."

She moves back to the position she was in at the birth and gently pulls as the contractions come. The afterbirth is delivered and placed in a dish. She quickly examines it and hands it to a thin Afro-Caribbean midwife who had arrived to help at the birth. I wonder why I'm empty of all emotions.

Nik looks on at the foot of the bed, his arms hanging by his side. When our eyes meet, I catch my breath.

The golden shards have dimmed.

I had watched this scene so many times on television and in films: a new mother holding a sleeping baby in her arms, the father smiling with loving eyes upon his wife and child. I had imagined the same scene for us, but instead of joy, we feel numb.

I hear a soft mewing, the sound of a frightened cat. Nik grabs me in his arms, resting my head on his chest. I begin to shake uncontrollably.

"Nik, get on the bed and hold her," Sally orders sympathetically. He pulls me to him. I lean into his chest for comfort and warmth; my teeth begin to chatter. My hand rests on his heart. His body softens as he slowly and reassuringly strokes my dark hair, softly and gently.

A woman with a green mask over her face arrives at the foot of the bed; her name badge reads Ms Beckwithe. She examines my tear and explains that I will need many stitches. She fills a syringe with a clear fluid from a glass vial while she says, "Local anaesthetic helps numb the area. Now you'll feel a prick." I don't look at her; my head is back, and I'm focusing on Nik's eyes. Where have those sparkling shards gone?

I don't care if she uses an anaesthetic or not, I feel nothing. The pain in my heart has numbed all the physical pain, and I've lost the playful twinkling eyes that usually look at me. I close my eyes to shut out the room.

"Hold on. Where are you taking him?" Nik has leapt up off the bed to block the doors.

"Mr Raja, we need to take the baby to the Special Care Baby Unit. We have better equipment there to take care of him," the dark-haired doctor who has been checking the baby replies in a Midshire accent.

"You're not taking him anywhere. You can do the tests here!"

"Nik, please, let them do what needs to be done." Sally gently pulls him away from the door. His fists are clenched.

He reluctantly steps aside to watch the incubator wheel out. Our son has a large tube in his mouth hooked up to a ventilator; plastic pads are all over his body. His eyes are closed. He still looks like a rag doll, his arms and legs splayed outwards. The nurses follow, pushing a trolley that holds the power pack.

As the trio pull out into the corridor, Nik says quietly, "Go up with them. I want to know what they are doing."

Jay nods as he stands up, releasing Anne-Marie's hand.

Ravi adds, seconds later, "Hang on, I'll come too."

Peter is sitting with his arm around Umi, and asks, "Can we come in?"

"Wait for a few minutes."

The door to the room closes. Nik rushes back to the bed. The thin-faced Afro-Caribbean midwife returns my hand to Nik.

"Do you want me to sit behind you, my love?"

I shake my head.

The stitching is taking a long time. The doctor explained I have a third-degree tear and that it is quite complicated.

On the wall clock the big hand has moved to three and the little hand is on twelve.

As the doctor leaves, Peter pops his head through the

door. Nik nods at him, and both he and Umi come into the room. He shakes his head. "No news yet. Jay and Ravi are still up there. Do you want to go up? Umi and I will stay with Ree."

"No, I want to help Ree get ready. Then we are both going up to see our son."

Peter frowns and nods.

Sally opens the door slightly, and she asks softly if she can enter. Nik looks to me for confirmation. I nod in reply, unable to talk from the lump in my throat. She comes to the bed and strokes my face; her eyes are red and watery. "Come on, let's warm you up. Can you bear to have a shower?" Her voice breaks.

Nik helps me out of the bed. My legs are like tree stumps, and I stumble. He lifts me up in his arms, and I cling to his neck.

"I'm going to have a shower with my wife," Nik informs the trio as he walks towards the bathroom. Sally rushes ahead to turn the shower on. She tells Nik as we approach the entrance that she will fetch some more towels.

There is a large walk-in shower in the huge bathroom. Against the wall there is a blue plastic seat that can be pulled down. Once we are inside the bathroom, Nik pulls at my nightdress, his other arm holding my waist. He pushes his tracksuit bottoms off his pert bottom, and he steps out of them. He keeps his T-shirt and boxer shorts on. He picks me up and cradles me in his arms, carrying me into the shower.

As the water washes over me, I let my tears wash over me too. I begin to sob, long wretched sobs. I gulp for breath and swallow water and cough. Nik pulls me away from under the showerhead and watches as the tears roll down my face. He slides me down in front of him, we fall into sitting on the shower floor. His kisses are soft and gentle, full of tenderness and pain.

"I know, I know, Ree. Please, please don't cry," he whispers as he continues to kiss my face. I hold onto him tightly, telling him I can't stop. He brings me closer to him, while we let the warm water wash over us. Our knees touch as we sit opposite each other, our hands clasped together. His face is full of sorrow; the eyes have lost their sparkle. The tight restraint is clearly visible. My playful handsome husband has gone. My eyes dart across his face, searching for the small signs of heartache. He pulls me on top of his legs. I am straddling him; our hearts touch. I draw his head closer, and he listens to my heart break. His long fingers slowly begin to massage my lower back. He knows this is what I need; his hands release the tension in my body. He stops, and I feel the air escape from his lungs. He finally gives up the pretence and sobs.

"What are we going to do?" His voice is thick with sorrow. Choking back my tears, I tighten my hold, and reply, "I don't know." We sit in the warm shower, hoping the cold numbness we feel will wash away.

Three

"WHAT ARE WE GOING TO DO, NIK?"

I repeat his question. I'm sitting on a stool as Nik fastens my maternity bra. The pain of not seeing my baby has heightened the pain sensors on my skin. His warm breath feels like tiny hot knives. My husband has a towel wrapped around his hip, and is helping me put on my nightdress; the fabric is like sackcloth, burning my skin. The pain is unbearable. I glance down at my belly and relief floods over me. I'm still pregnant. Confusion courses through my mind. Was it just a dream? I've had some vivid anxiety dreams lately, and I pray this is one of them. He kneels in front of me, taking both my hands into his and kisses my palms. I gaze into his beautiful eyes and my heart leaps. They are a muddy brown; what has happened to the bright golden sparks? He shakes his head knowingly and strokes my stomach gently. The nerves dull and every cell in my body screams with the ache. "Nik, where is my baby? Please. Take. Me. To. My. Baby." Each word comes out as a hoarse whisper; I want to scream, but my throat will not obey. My eyes flood with tears, and I let the rivers of sorrow stream down my face.

"I will … first let's get ready." He sighs softly.

He unwraps the towel around my head and begins to brush my long wet hair gently. The rhythm of the strokes helps ease the nerve endings. I close my eyes. Perhaps if I don't see where I am, I can drown out the memory. I flinch when he touches my face as he applies the cream.

"Sorry, sorry, my love. We're nearly done."

Did I really think that what I'd done was not going to have a consequence? Happy endings only happen in Bollywood films. I probably deserve this for my malicious act of destruction.

***

ON THE WALL CLOCK, the little hand has moved to four and the big hand is on three. Dick and Anne-Marie enter with a tray full of assorted mugs.

"How did you manage to get tea at this time?" asks Peter in astonishment.

"Dick used his English charm with the nurses. He flashed his oh-so-perfect teeth and twinkled those steely blue eyes. He was like a prostitute selling his body for a cup of tea."

Peter laughs out loud and glances guiltily at me. I smile back at him to reassure him I'm not upset. I'm relieved; I'm with some of the people I love the most. Nik had walked me back into the room and seated me on the sofa next to Umi. She is squeezing my hand tightly. Her eyes are red, the puffiness clearly visible.

Nik has gone back to the bathroom to get dressed, and we hear him shout, "Who's selling their body?"

"Dick!" they all shout back.

"No, I didn't. Anne-Marie's embellishing the story," he turns and explains to Nik as he emerges out of the bathroom. He has changed into a fresh white shirt and a pair of jeans he had packed in my hospital overnight bag.

"I only asked for some tea from the nurses at reception."

"Anne-Marie used her Irish connections to get these biscuits," he replies, holding up a packet of Bourbons.

"You're not going to believe me; one of the midwives is a neighbour of my brother, John." She hands a mug of tea to me. "Drink it, Reena. It's got lots of sugar," she commands. Nat King Cole sings "L.O.V.E." in the background.

"This one's for you, Nik." She turns and puts a mug into his hand as he walks to the sofa.

"I don't drink tea, Anne-Marie."

"It's coffee, and have a biscuit."

Dick hands me a biscuit. I shake my head; he thrusts it into my hand, and I try to take a bite. My throat is as dry as sandpaper and the piece of biscuit tears like a knife down my throat.

We drink our tea in silence, the packet of biscuits barely touched. I can feel the questions no one is willing to ask. No one in this room had imagined this. I think about the books and the classes Nik and I had attended. No one tells you about this; there is a path laid out for you to follow. The breastfeeding advice, nappy rash, croup, vaccinations, healthy eating, support networks, baby care. What happens to people like us? Do we get help or are we left to our own devices? I wonder what path we will be travelling.

The door to the maternity room opens and a tall thin nurse in a green hospital gown stands at the door. "Ready?" she asks us. "Come on, let's go see your beautiful baby boy. My head rests on Nik's shoulder; his body is tense and he is struggling to take a breath. He pulls me up, lifts my face to his and says, "Let's go meet our son." A small smile appears on his lips, and the creases on the edges of his eyes deepen. He gently kisses me on my lips. My legs are too heavy. I take slow shallow breaths. My body leans into him for support. Umi is still holding my hand. I glance up at her, and she smiles down at me, her dark eyes telling me that I can do this. We walk through the double doors and step into the Special Care Baby Unit. Ravi and Jay, one stocky and tall, the other wiry and small, are staring into a glass-encased room opposite a nurses' station, their eyes fixed on something inside. The nurse explains that this is the best place for our son. The ward is staffed twenty-four hours a day, seven days a week with experts who will aid in our son's full recovery. She tells us that she is in charge of his care this morning.

The duty nurse in a navy-blue uniform approaches us, disapproval on her face. "There's far too many of you in here. Mum and Dad only, please."

Nik raises a questioning eyebrow at Jay and Ravi, and they begin to explain what has happened so far. The nurse harrumphs and moves back to the station as we ignore her. My eyes keep drifting to the glass-encased room beyond. The nurse explains the rules to us, as we are led to a single door. The vestibule has a sink for washing our hands and a pile of green gowns.

As we emerge into the glass chamber, we see our friends. We have known each other since our university days, except Anne-Marie – she was my flat mate when I first moved down to London. Their eyes are fixed to a baby in the unit. There are several incubation units with monitors in this room; each has a small trolley laden with nappies, blankets and various stainless-steel bowls next to it. Each one is occupied by a baby, each of them wired to a monitor. The beeps reassuringly confirm a record of their heart and oxygen. They are tiny babies, some so dark and small that they are unrecognisable as human beings; they remind me of baby mice, their skin loose around their barely-developed bodies. We've seen a Special Care Unit before; I recall the day my brother called to tell me of the birth of his children, and the resulting difficulties we faced in finding an alternative wedding day. Our son is a giant barely fitting in the plastic box. The twins and the other babies are tiny in comparison. They have moved him closer to the glass window that is facing the corridor. The nurse directs us to his unit. His body is covered in round white discs and the wires connect to the monitor. My heart constricts, and a sob escapes from my mouth. Nik pulls me closer to his side. They have pushed a tube into our son's mouth, his eyes are closed, and his legs are splayed out. I watch his chest slowly rise and fall, his diaphragm forced to push out the air that is being pumped into him. I can't watch. My whole body is convulsing with sobs.

"Ree, you have to be brave. I need you to be brave, my love," he whispers in my ear. I take a long breath in and try to stop crying.

The doctor who had rushed into the birthing room introduces himself. He tells us our son needs assistance breathing. He explains that sometimes babies need help breathing in their early life. His smile is optimistic. He expands that apart from his difficulty in breathing, he does not have any other visible problems. Our son is ten days early, but is a good weight at eight pounds, two ounces and will recover very quickly. He apologises for the size of the incubator; our son is twenty-two inches long and just fits.

The nurse asks us if we want to touch our son and both Nik and I nod. Our eyes drift to him; the yearning to touch him and hold him has intensified. She clarifies we can't hold him like a healthy baby yet as they do not have an oxygen helmet for him, adding encouragingly that they will find one once he has had his scans later.

She lifts up a flap and allows us to put our hands in to touch our baby. My hand rests lightly on his chest, and I'm crying again, the ache of not holding him in my arms gnawing at me. I have grown him. I have felt him kick. I have laughed when he has hiccoughed. How can anyone ache so much for a new being? I want to protect him again. I wish he was still inside me protected from the pain he must be suffering. We are left standing by the unit, our friends looking on with eyes full of pain and love for our child.

When we emerge back into the corridor, we are sent to a room where Anne-Marie has taken our belongings. The private room is near the glass partition. It is painted in the same colour scheme as the rest of the unit, shades of yellow and blue. There is a single bed in the middle, and a baby cot, an armchair and a tall wooden bedside table. Nik guides me to the bed and asks me to lie down. He uses the pillows to prop me up. My body shivers again and Anne-Marie rushes off in search of more blankets. Dick and Ravi go in search of chairs.

Umi urges Nik to sit, and he perches himself on the bed, keeping a hold of my hand, his face full of worry. I can feel the thud of his heart as he takes a deep breath. Our carefree life slips away like sand, as we come to the conclusion that parenthood is tough.

The clock on the wall reads 5 a.m. I drift in and out of a fretful sleep, hearing snippets of discussions from the others as they find a way to help us cope with our situation. The door opens; Sally enters the room. Her puffy eyes glance at everyone and then she gives me a hug and I'm taken aback. I sympathise with her. It must be rare to have an uncomplicated labour result in a sick baby. I'm sorry to have burdened her with my bad luck. The bad luck that Motaba had warned about.

She pulls back, her expression full of warmth, and says, "Don't worry, he's breathing, and that's a good sign." She grabs Nik's hand and squeezes. "Have you had breakfast?" she asks.

Nik shakes a no.

"I'm not sure if I can get you all your breakfast, but let's see what we can do."

"No thank you, Sally," Umi tells her. She explains to her that they will head off to the canteen to give Nik and me time together.

"All right, tea and toast for Mummy and Daddy, then." Nik's eyes smile a little; this is the first time we've been addressed like that.

"Can I have coffee, Sally?" he asks apologetically.

"Sorry, Nik. Forgot you don't like tea."

A small Indian woman brings in breakfast. She swings the bedside tray over the bed, places the plate of buttered white toast on it and asks if we want milk and sugar in our tea and coffee.

Nik puts three teaspoons of sugar in my tea and hands me the cup. My hand shakes as I reach for it, and he raises the cup to my lips.

"It's hot, my love. Take a small sip."

I drink a few sips, and he breaks up a small piece of toast and offers it up to my mouth. I shake my head.

"No, you have to eat it," he commands, and I chew the toast several times. He lifts the cup to me again to help me swallow it down.

I tell him to drink his coffee before he offers me another piece of toast. It takes forever for us to finish our breakfast. The woman has come in twice to pick up the empties. Nik promises her he'll return them back to the small kitchen once we're finished.

"Let's get you down and sleeping." Nik takes the pillows out from behind me and instructs me to lie down on the bed.

"Are you sleeping too?" I ask.

He nods and takes the blanket resting on the back of the armchair, pulls the chair close to the bed, and holds my hand. I turn to face him as he sits back, resting his head on the high back. He closes his eyes and struggles to slow his breath, and I watch for his chest to rise and fall. He opens his eyes and says, "Close your eyes, Ree. I can feel you here," as he taps his chest.

*** * ***

I AM RUNNING AFTER A YOUNG child down a

corridor; he is laughing. "Stop, Diku. Please stop," I implore. He is too far ahead; the anxiety is rising, and I feel the panic in my throat. My stomach is knotted. I feel nauseous, afraid that I will lose him. I can't see him and continue to shout. "Please slow down; I can't see you."

I see him turn a corner ahead of me and run faster; his laughter bounces off the empty walls. I turn a corner, one, two, three, four in a circle and begin to lose hope. Tears are streaming down my face. "STOP, PLEASE STOP." Suddenly I'm in a corridor with countless doors. I can't hear his laughter. I haphazardly reach for a door to an empty white room. I try another and another but they are all empty. I move to the other side, and the door is locked. I force the doorknob with all my strength and open it to reveal a white room with a painting of a sunny meadow. I'm drawn to the canvas. I gasp in shock. I recognise the place, and it begins to come to life. The grass weaves in the breeze; a bird lands on the tree and the small boy is running towards it. I start to cry. I've lost him. He is inside the painting and I can't get to him.

I wake up with a start, tears streaming down my face. I search for Nik and begin to shout, "Nik! Nik! Nik!" He rushes into the room, leaps onto the bed and holds me. Umi and Peter follow him in. "It's okay, Ree. It's all right, my love." He comforts me.

I whisper, "It's the dream again." His body shakes; a teardrop plops on my head.

Four

Early morning, January 7th, 1990

THE BIG HAND ON THE CLOCK is on eight and the little hand is on six.

I am awake. Nik is no longer by my side on the bed. I turn to see if he has moved to the armchair and see Anne-Marie dozing in it.

"Where's Nik?" I begin to hyperventilate. "Is something wrong? Has something happened to the baby?"

"No, no, Reena. He's fine." Ravi is by my side, holding my hand, his eyes red-rimmed from the lack of sleep.

"Where is he?" I ask him.

"He's gone to make some phone calls. Everything's fine. I checked on the baby a few minutes ago."

We are the only ones in the room. Anne-Marie's small form is wrapped up in blanket on the chair. I wonder where everyone has gone.

Ravi squeezes my hand, his other hand rakes through his short-cropped hair, and he tells me to sleep.

I close my eyes, not to sleep, but to block out the reality of the day. The sun has risen, and shards of light come through the blinds. The door opens, and I hear voices.

"Don't you have homes to go to?" It's the nurse in charge. "You are not allowing my nurses to work efficiently, standing in your huddle."

"We'll go once we've seen the doctors," Ravi informs her.

The others creep quietly into the room and sit on the chairs, talking in whispers I can barely decipher. Nik and Peter are at the door.

"Well, did you get a hold of them?" Peter asks.

"I've spoken to Amit. They are on their way," Nik replies.

"And your family?" There is a pause as I hear Nik take a breath.

"My parents will land at three this afternoon, and I've told my motaba. She's coming as soon as she's made a few phone calls."

"We need to have Sunil here, Nik. He'll be able to get answers quicker," Peter's soft baritone urges Nik.

I lift myself up, and Ravi helps me to sit up. Dick rushes and asks if I want something to drink. I nod and he fills a plastic glass from the water jug. His warm hand holds mine until I finish my water. I look into his steely-blue eyes and see that they are puffy and red-rimmed too. His usually well-groomed blond hair is dishevelled.

Nik leans down and kisses the top of my head. "Hello, my love, did you sleep?" His eyes are full of concern.

I smile in reply and ask, "When are the doctors coming?"

Anne-Marie stirs; she rubs her eyes and reaches for her glasses, her Gaelic colouring more pallid than usual.

"They don't do the rounds on Sunday. I've spoken to the nurse, and she'll send a doctor over," Peter informs me.

There is a strained silence. The people in the room are more like my family than friends. They are also coming to terms with the night before. My karma has affected them too.

***

THE TIME ON THE CLOCK READS 9.30 a.m.

There is a knock on the door; a young red-haired man with a neat goatee beard and horn-rimmed round glasses enters. The tall nurse who had taken us to see our baby accompanies him. He is holding a clipboard in his hand.

"Can you all leave? I would like to speak with the baby's parents."

"We're not going anywhere," Anne-Marie barks at him.

He is taken aback but composes himself as he stares intently at his notes. His sharp eyes focus directly on me, and Nik takes my hand.

"Your son is very ill. His Apgar score was quite low, and he cannot breathe on his own. We have him on the ventilator, which is helping him. We have a scan scheduled this morning and will be able to tell if he has water on the brain."

"Wait, what do you mean water on the brain?" Nik asks, his hand raised.

"Sometimes babies have a small haemorrhage when they are born." The doctor explains.

"And what does that do to his brain?" Umi asks.

"It makes them poorly. It can disperse, and there might not be any lasting damage. That is all I can tell you at the moment, I'm afraid. We won't know anything until the scan."

The nurse tells Nik and me that we can go and sit with the baby any time we want. They both walk out of the room.

"Right, we need Sunil here. Call him, Nik," Umi demands, her dark eyes tearful.

"I'm going to go find that midwife who's my brother's neighbour." Anne-Marie is up on her feet. I'm surprised at her energy; she usually needs at least eight hours of sleep.

"I'm coming with you Anne-Marie," Ravi adds.

Jay is watching Nik intently, and Dick and Umi are both rummaging through my belongings. Dick finds my diary and starts making notes of the conversation we just had with the doctor. Peter asks Nik for Sunil's phone number and walks out to give them a call. Nik tells him that they are probably on their way.

"I don't care, Nik. I want to confirm that they know." His tall frame grows as he glares at Nik.

Nik is slumped on the chair; I can see the tension in his sculpted jaw as he fights to stay in the hospital. His instincts tell him to run away; anything that requires emotional decisions is very difficult for my husband. Jay's eyes gaze at him with sympathy, trying to catch his eye, and, when he fails, he stands and stares out of the window. Jay is the shortest in this group of men; he is wearing a white shirt and dark jeans, his usual go-to outfit for a night out.

Umi hands a Mars bar to Nik and tells him to eat it. He takes it without objection, opening the wrapper, and, as he splits it in half to offer some to me, she stops him with her hand. "No, eat it all. I have one for Reena, too." She hands mine to me. "Anyone else want some chocolate?" She pulls out a plastic bag full of snack bars she had put into my bag last night. Everyone takes a snack, grateful for the sugar rush.

"You two should go and be with your baby now," Umi tells us.

We don't object and get ready to leave the room.

"We're going to go out for some fresh air and wait in the reception area for your family," she informs us as we all walk out together.

We watch them walk down the corridor; Umi and Peter are holding hands, and Dick and Jay follow behind. When they reach the double doors, Anne-Marie bumps into Peter, her head barely reaching his chest. Ravi is just behind her; they have a brief conversation and all of them leave the Special Care Baby Unit.

We are alone to deal with our son. The loneliness and the daunting task of parenthood in a Special Care Baby Unit make our steps falter, and we stop by the door to the vestibule.

The unit has one blue wall and another pink wall. There are four incubators on one side and four on the other. Our son's incubator is placed against the blue wall, and it is closest to the glass partition on our side of the ward. Anyone who walks past can see him. The room is like a glass cube; on the other side, there is a replica corridor to ours, small isolated rooms, full of mothers whose babies are premature or sick, waiting anxiously to take them home.

A short, plump Afro-Caribbean nurse with a white cap stands up from the desk that is situated in the middle of the room. Two chairs are at the table each facing one wall of incubators. I check her nametag, Paulette. She introduces herself and smiles at us. "Okey dokey. Come on, Mummy and Daddy, let's get you settled around your baby."

As we turn, I see a tiny baby, the size of my husband's hand, with a plastic hood; she doesn't have a tube in her mouth. Paulette explains she is breathing with some help now and the helmet is providing oxygen. She informs us that she is eight weeks premature, which isn't unusual for this unit, but has a very low birth weight. There is a card bordered with baby ducklings above the crib, and Grace has been written on it with a black marker pen. I marvel at Grace; the strength of this tiny creature brings a ray of hope to my heart.

Nik pulls me to him. "Do you remember the twins?" he asks, and I nod.

Paulette is efficient and friendly, giving us information about the unit and pointing to a notice board imprinted with phone numbers that we can call. To confirm that it is possible, the phone rings; it is a low buzz, and the tall nurse, who we met earlier, picks up the phone. She speaks quietly into the phone.

"SCBU, Janet speaking."

"Hello, Thomas is fine and has had a good night," she adds.

Paulette asks, "Do you have a name for your son?" We both glance at each other. We have a name that is our favourite but are unsure about telling her. I'm not sure if it's the fact that we are scared he might not live for long or that we can still hear Motaba's words, 'You can't choose your baby's name without checking the planets. It's bad luck.'

"It doesn't matter." She gestures with her hand. "Let

me know when you make your mind up and I'll change the name." She points to the card on the wall above our son's unit. Baby Raja.

"I'll open both hand holes of the unit so you can hold him." She sees the change in my demeanour and touches my arm. "Don't worry, he won't get cold. Did you know there's research from New Zealand that says poorly babies recover faster if they are held frequently? When he's better, you'll even get to hold him in your arms with his tubes in."

Janet brings hard, wooden stools to our son's incubator. Nik helps me sit down on the tall seat, the pain from my stitches making me wince, but I don't want Nik to see the pain, so I clench my jaw tight.

As soon as I hold my son's tiny fist, I forget the pain. My heart is full of love. My eyes glance at Nik. His eyes are sparkling; his face is full of the joy of touching him too, and he smiles at me. Our son's skin is the colour of cream. He has a tremendous amount of dark-brown hair. He has deep folds in the skin at his wrists and under his knees. His face is the same shape as his father's, and I can see a tiny Raja nose. I urge him to open his eyes. Are his eyes the same as his daddy's, all golden and fiery? We both realise our heart has been lost to this tiny new member of our family instantly.

"Did you see that?" I ask Nik. Our son's leg moves when Nik tickles his feet.

Nik chuckles. "Told you he'd be a footballer, Ree," he replies through his smile.

My husband relaxes as the tension ebbs away. I glimpse our life as a family and vow to do anything I can to keep us together. I will not allow the insecurities that have built up about my luck and karma to prevent me from protecting my family.

Time slows down to make up for the time we had been deprived of our son's first few hours of life. Our hands are playing a dance of caresses with our child, and we periodically touch each other's hands too.

"Reena has a third-degree tear, girls. She has to sit on a cushion," Sally's Scottish burr interrupts as she approaches.

Paulette rushes to a cupboard and brings one to me. "Why didn't you tell me?" she asks.

"I'm surprised at you, Nik. You're always so attentive. Did you forget about the stitching?"

Nik's face drops, and he takes my free hand. "I'm so sorry, my love. Are you okay? I should have remembered." His chiselled face fills with pain. I can't bear to see him suffer.

"I forgot too, Nik. We were preoccupied with our son," I respond.

"You'll need to speak up and ask for things. These nurses don't know about you, Reena. They are here to look after your baby." I nod, and Nik assures Sally that he will put my needs first.

She smiles up at him. "I'm sorry, Nik, I shouldn't have spoken like that to you." She rubs her forehead, "It's been a long day." She gazes at the incubator and says, "Oh, he's a bonny baby, and he looks like you, Nik. Do you know what's wrong?"

We recount what we have been told.

"Paulette, have they done the scan?"

"No, not yet Sally. We're waiting for the machine to come up from maternity."

The clock on the wall says twenty past twelve.

"Go get your lunch, I'll wait here with your son." Sally

directs us out of the unit.

Nik helps me sit on the bed, putting a pillow under my bottom. The tray table is brought to my bed as a rotund, lilac-haired woman enters the room and places a tray on it. "Here you go, lovely. Baked potato with tuna and salad. Can I get you a soup? It's chicken and mushroom or vegetable?"

I ask for chicken and mushroom. She brings a bowl of soup with a bread roll and butter.

"Do you want soup?" I ask Nik.

"No, you eat it, Ree. I'll get something later."

I'm worried about him; he has a good appetite and all he's eaten is two slices of toast and a Mars bar. I take a couple of sips, and Nik sees me make a face.

"Not up to your standard?" He smiles.

I put it aside and tear off small pieces of the bread roll. No one can ruin that, I think.

The rest of my lunch is inedible; the baked potato is hard, the tuna is too salty, the salad limp.

A skinny young woman comes in and asks me if I want tea or coffee. I opt for tea and ask for a coffee for Nik. She explains that they prefer there are no visitors during lunch and dinner service. She tells us that as we've only come into the ward last night, she'll get a coffee for Nik.

Peter, Ravi and Anne-Marie walk into the room while we are drinking our tea and coffee. Anne-Marie has a plastic carrier bag in her hand and starts filling a metal fruit bowl with bananas, oranges and a bunch of red grapes.

"I've washed the grapes," she says, and she puts two packs of sandwiches on the tray table. "What do you want, ham and cheese or chicken salad?" She also gives us a packet of cheese and onion crisps each and hands a can of Coke to Nik and a small bottle of Lucozade to me. Nik grabs her hand, smiles and thanks her.

She brushes his thanks aside and says, "You're family, Nik. I'm not going to let you go hungry." They explain the others are waiting by the lifts to guide the family to where we are.

After lunch, I decide to go for a walk in the corridor to calm down. Lying and sitting in the room is claustrophobic. Anne-Marie volunteers to walk with me for support. Nik objects and says he'll do it. I snap at him and tell him to go get some fresh air.

"I'm fine here, Ree," he retorts. My legs give way a little and I lean on Anne-Marie; we are the same height. "See, you need me." His lips purse into a thin line.

"I don't want to argue with you, Nik. Just take a breather," I plead quietly.

Ravi puts a hand on his shoulder, "Come on, Nik. Come and watch me smoke."

Nik holds me tightly and kisses my forehead; I lean into him, feeling a sense of overwhelming sadness. He lifts my chin, "I will always love you, Ree. Always have, always will. Without you, my heart is empty."

He releases me and hands me to Anne-Marie. I watch him turn to the glass partition; he touches the glass and reluctantly walks towards the exit of the Special Care Baby Unit. Ravi grabs his arm and they both stride slowly out, their heads lowered.

Five

THE BIG HAND ON THE CLOCK is on two and the small hand is on four.

We are watching our son from outside the glass partition as a technician is scanning his head. The machine is the same type that is used during the ultrasound scans, the device they had used to check on him when he was in my tummy. The new nurse in charge of the unit explains the fontanelle has not sealed so they can get an excellent image of any fluid that may have leaked out of his brain. I start to cry uncontrollably. I can't stop the stream pouring down my face. Nik is holding a box of tissues in his other hand, supplying me with fresh ones as they deteriorate.

The technician prints out paper copies of the scans, walks to the desk in the middle of the room and hands them in at the nurses' station. They put them into a crisp blue folder.

We watch transfixed; our son's chest lifts up and down, the rubber balloon on the machine filling and deflating.

The doors swing open and my brother is running

towards me. He takes me in his arms and holds me tight, his heart beating, thud, thud, thud, thud. I'm relieved; he's here, my big brother. He'll make it better like he always does.

"So where is he, Nik?"

Nik points and he gently turns me and faces the glass partition. My heart tears a little as I hear his heart stop, one, two, three, four. He gasps, "I'm so sorry, Sis."

I lift my head from his chest and search for my father, but there is no one in the corridor.

"I ran up the stairs," he tells me.

"Does Daddy know?"

He confirms a yes; I begin to sob, stomach-clenching sobs. My father isn't going to handle this well.

Umi pushes the door and my father shuffles through. His gait is different; his face is ashen. With his greying hair, he reminds me of an extra in a zombie movie.

Nik rushes to him. "Daddy, everything's fine." He wraps a hand around my father's shoulder and brings him to the partition to show him our son. My father takes my hand.

"Daddy, look how big he is," I utter, pointing to our son. His eyes glisten, and he reaches inside his trouser pocket for his handkerchief.

Umi is by our side. "Naren Kaka, Amit, let's go sit in Reena's room."

My brother and my father wrap an arm around me from each side, and we walk back to my room.

Umi slips beside Nik and she enquires, "So, where's your family? They live closer than Leicester."

My big brother has instructed me to get back into bed; he is unhappy that I've been standing up and berates Nik for allowing it. My father is sitting in the only armchair and Nik stands guard next to my bed opposite the armchair. Amit has placed himself next to Nik and is asking us questions. Nik recounts everything we know so far.

"Where are your parents, Nikesh?" my father asks flatly.

I'm taken aback at the lack of emotion and the hint of malice in his voice. Tears glisten in Nik's eyes; he's confused as to why they are not here either. His head drops towards his chest. I reach for his hand.

"Nik's parents are arriving from Nairobi at three o'clock," Peter informs him, even though my father had asked in Gujarati.

There is a knock and the door swings open. Rita rushes to the bed, taking me into her arms, giving me a kiss on my forehead. She then pulls at her brother and gives him a long hug. His body starts to shake as he releases the tears that have been welling up inside him. Sunil asks Amit if he's spoken to anyone. They both go in search of answers, reassuring us that they'll come back quickly. Our son is twelve hours and thirty minutes old, and his family are here. I can finally breathe with ease, knowing that Nik and I will be okay.

Rita's hand is holding her younger brother's. She apologises to the room for their tardiness. She explains that Sammy, their son, had a rugby match at a club in Surrey.

"What time are Kaka and Kaki landing, Niku?"

"They're landing at three fifteen, Ben. Bhai's picking them up," he responds to her enquiry.

"Did you tell Bhai to bring them here?" she asks. He confirms with a nod. "Where's Motaba?"

He glances sideways at the clock.

My eyes sting; she should be here. If she cares for Nik, she should have been here this morning. I watch the two siblings as Rita quietly gleans information from her brother on the lack of Raja presence in the room.

***

THE ROOM IS BECOMING OVERCROWDED, and Ravi and Anne-Marie tell us that they are going home, asking to be informed of any changes.

Tiredness overwhelms me as the adrenaline depletes from my blood and I begin to drift off to sleep. I can hear murmured conversation. Rita is soothing my father.

I wake up feeling groggy; my head is throbbing, and the pain from my stitches is agonising. I search for Nik. Rita comes to the bed and takes my hand. She has tied her layered hair back into a bun.

"Hello." She sees the enquiry in my eyes. "I've told everyone to wait in the waiting room. Niku's with Kaka and Kaki. Do you want me to get him?" Her smile is weak; her pronounced dimples barely form on her cheek.

I shake my head, "Can I have a painkiller?"

She reads the chart at the end of my bed and nods, "I'll go and get the nurse." She opens the door to leave.

Shortly afterwards, Nik's mother and father enter the room.

"Jai Shri Krishna, Beta, how are you feeling?" Kaki asks, raising a smile; the dimples on her cheeks have disappeared, too. She sits down on the bed. Her expressive kind eyes are red-rimmed and full of sorrow.

Nik's father comes to the bed, gives me a kiss on my

forehead, takes my hand and assures me with his words. "Everything will be fine. We're here. You're not to worry about anything." He is identical in appearance to his son, except his father has greying hair and doesn't have the same striking eyes as Nik.

Nik smiles as his father says this and I can see him let go of responsibility. He sits down next to his mother, his head resting on the top of her head, and closes his eyes. She pats his hand gently and says, "I love you, Niku." Nik's father squeezes his son's shoulder.

The nurse comes in with a small paper cup, "Here are your painkillers." She picks up my chart and makes notes. "If it doesn't work, let me know. I can give you something else." Then she leaves.

"Lie down next to Reena, Niku. I'm sure she won't mind," his mother instructs.

He has become the young, carefree man he was yesterday again. He asks me if I'm okay with it. I nod and he slides next to me. They walk towards the door.

"Try and rest. We're going to watch over our beautiful grandson," she informs us. "We'll come to get you when Sunil and Amit are back," Nik's father adds, turning to us as he closes the door.

Nik caresses my back and helps ease the knots; his hands are warm and comforting. They work their magic and ease the pain I've been holding on to. My eyes water and the tears start to stream down my face again.

"I'm sorry, I can't stop them." I turn to face him.

He starts to kiss my forehead, my eyes, my wet cheeks, murmuring, "It's okay, my love, cry. Cry as much as you want."

I hold onto him, wrapping my legs around his, holding

his hand close to my heart, resting my head on his chest, listening to his heartbeat. "I wish our son was with us," I whisper.

"He'll be with us soon, Ree. I promise," he replies.

We lie like this for a long time. No one comes in to disturb us. Eventually I drift into a fitful sleep.

***

A COMMOTION OUTSIDE OUR ROOM wakes us up.

"Take that away. I have brought my daughter-in-law's dinner."

The door opens and the lady who had brought my lunch walks in and asks, "Do you want me to take this away?" holding up the food tray for my consideration. Nik peers over his shoulder at her, his eyes questioning. I can make out the figure of Motaba as she confirms, "Yes, yes, take it away."

I'm confused and don't know what to say. Nik's mother rushes in and stands by my side. "Reena Beta, let's get you up. Motaba has brought you some food."

Nik lifts himself off the bed and wheels the bedside tray table to me.

"Wait, you have to sit on this." Nik's mother is holding an inflated rubber ring that a child uses as a swimming aid. I gawp at her; she smiles at me and tells me it will protect my stitches and help with the pain.

My husband's arms are hanging by his sides, his eyes locked on Motaba, and she puts the black holdall she is carrying on the tray table. She doesn't make eye contact with him and moves towards me, giving me a small hug. "Jai Shri Krishna. I've brought khichdi, methi nu shaak, bajra no rotlo." She starts to take out the food. I watch my husband shrink and find myself questioning why she is ignoring him. Why has she turned up so late? Why won't she hug him? She told me to leave him because she couldn't see him in pain, so why isn't she comforting him?

"Let me do that, Bhabhi." Nik's mother starts to serve my dinner onto the porcelain plate that Sarladevi has brought with her.

Eventually she turns to Nik and takes him in her arms; his face rests on her shoulder and scrunches up, and he begins to cry.

"What took you so long, Motaba? We've been here for ages." Rajesh is at the door, voicing the questions that we all wish to ask. She releases Nik and turns to Rajesh.

"Jai Shri Krishna, Rajesh. I have some boxes of penda I want you to give to the people in the waiting room. Is Naren Bhai here?"

"Wait, you made penda? You do know the baby isn't well?" Rajesh, Nik's older brother, exclaims.

"Baby? I thought you told me you had a boy, Nikesh?" the beautifully attired women asks Nik.

"He's a boy. I just meant ... forget it. Yes ... " Rajesh sighs, "You have another grandson."

Rajesh's shoulders slump and I think of the terrible time Rupa Bhabhi and he had when their daughter Anousha was born.

"Eat while it's hot." She turns to me. "Nikesh, I have food for you, too. Pushpa, can you make a plate up for Nikesh. Sit down," she commands as she hands the plate to him.

She turns her attention to the room and her eyes settle on the bananas in the fruit bowl. She begins to rant at me, gesticulating at them. "Don't eat those. They are not good for you; you will eat only what I bring for you to eat. Do you understand, Reena? No bananas, oranges, grapes, apples. No fruit, it's too acidic for your system. You will eat the kaatlu when you want to snack, I'll make sure you have a thermos of raabh and badam nu dhudh for when you are thirsty. You can drink tea, but no coffee. If you insist on nursing your child, you will need to be careful about what you eat. I told you this when you were pregnant. Your child is ill because you ate the wrong food. Your education doesn't explain everything; we have rules and customs that go back centuries."

The spoon I am holding to my mouth stops in mid-air, and my eyes fill with hot, angry tears. How dare she say these things? She hasn't even asked after our son. Most people would be supportive at this time. Not Sarladevi. Wherever she goes, she has to do or say something to belittle me.

"Motaba!" Rajesh interrupts. "Kaki, can you take Motaba to see her grandson."

Nik's mother steers her towards the door into the corridor.

"I've said nothing that isn't the truth." I hear her as she enters the passage.

Nik's head is bowed, and I can see his shoulders shaking; he is sobbing silently. I put the spoon down on my plate and can't hold back my sobs. Suddenly he is holding me and caressing my head. "Don't listen to her. She doesn't know anything, Ree. None of this is your fault. Other pregnant women eat bananas all the time."

Rajesh has gone out of the room, and we hear Rita.

"What … why would she say that?" She enters the room. "Niku, Reena." She is by our bed, her hands resting on each of our shoulders. "Ignore everything Motaba has said. She's upset and can't deal with this sort of thing."

Rajesh sighs, "You know what happens to her … in these situations." He is sitting at the foot of the bed.

We both continue to cry. The tears roll down our faces freely and we make no attempt to wipe them away; they stay with us until we stop. The food has gone cold, and Rita takes our plates away. Rajesh goes in search of Amit and Sunil to find out what information they have about the scan.

* * *

THE CLOCK ON THE WALL READS 7.30 p.m.

Umi and Peter come into our room. We are still smarting at the pain of Motaba's words and are holding each other for comfort. Umi hands us a Mars bar each and tells us that everyone is gathered in the canteen to find out what the doctors have told Sunil and Amit.

Nik tilts my face to his and asks, "Are you strong enough to go?"

I nod, "Will they allow me to leave our son?"

"We've spoken to the nurse on duty. You can go out of the ward," Peter informs us.

Nik helps me put on my nightgown and slippers, and we take one more look through the glass partition at our beautiful son. The machine pushes air through a tube in his mouth. We watch briefly as his chest rises and falls. His legs are splayed out, his arms by his side, his hands fisted. I wish I could have him in my arms and could take him with me.

The canteen at Ealing Hospital is full of patients, visitors and staff mingling on large tables, getting their dinner. At a bank of long refectory-style tables sit our families, the Solankis and Rajas. As we approach, Dick and Jay come forward and flank us on both sides. My father is sitting next to Nik's, and they both have their heads bowed, whispering amongst themselves while the rest nurse their teas and coffees, staring silently into their cups.

There are two stainless-steel daba filled with nasto, chevdo and theekha gathiya placed in the middle.

They have left four wooden chairs empty for us to sit. Umi hands me the rubber ring, for which I am grateful. Peter places a box of tissues in front of us.

"Reena Beta, Niku, I've got you hot drinks." Nik's mother hovers around us, placing a tea for me and a coffee for Nik.

We sit in silence for an eternity as the hot liquid fills our bellies.

"Everyone finished?" Sunil asks. We all nod.

"Right, I've spoken to the maternity and the SCBU teams, and this is what we've found out."

Dick sets my diary in front of him. He must have picked it up at some point and kept it with him. He starts to make notes.

Sunil explains to everyone that the baby had a low Apgar score of three and has what is known as floppy baby syndrome, which is an indication of a problem with the brain or spinal cord.

"Although a low score of three at birth is not uncommon, your son had a low score at five minutes, hence the need to rush him to SCBU. This is something that cannot be predicted during birth or pregnancy. I want you to understand this: whatever happened during the delivery or the pregnancy had nothing to do with it." He stares intently at Sarladevi with his dark eyes.

Her glasses-encased eyes fall down to her lap.

"The unit has stabilised him and he now only needs assistance with breathing, hence the machine. His blood tests are normal, and they are investigating what type of damage, if any, there is to the brain."

Sarladevi's mouth tightens into a fine line. Nik's father has put his hand on top of my father's.

"Niku and Reena, you mentioned he reacts to your touch, so a spinal injury has been ruled out as this proves that the nerves are sending a signal to the brain. The scan they performed earlier has not revealed a cerebral haemorrhage."

"What's that?" Peter interrupts.

"A bleed outside the brain. This is very common when babies are born naturally; sometimes the pressure on the brain causes a slight bleed. However, that does not mean that he doesn't have an intracranial bleed. They will discuss that investigation tomorrow."

"Is the intracranial investigation easy to do?" Dick asks.

"Yes and no. It means they have to inject a chemical dye into the baby; there are side effects, and he could react to the dye. They will also have to sedate him, although as he doesn't have the muscle memory, they might not need to."

"Then they will take an X-ray," Amit adds, raising a small smile to reassure us.

"How severe is the brain damage?" Rita asks. She is

sitting next to her husband.

"We won't know until further tests. The brain is a marvellous thing. Do you remember Daniel who was at St Mark's with me? He had a severe stroke and couldn't do anything, but, after physio, he has all his functions back. The only thing visible from the stroke is that his left eye droops a bit," Sunil replies, clasping his wife's hand, his tone of voice calming.

"What if … " I begin to ask, and the words catch in my throat like glass shards.

"If he's disabled, we'll be the best parents ever, Ree." Nik wraps his arm around me and smiles.

Sarladevi's face darkens.

Nik's mother leans across the table and grabs my hand, "We'll deal with that when the time comes. I don't want you to worry about it."

"Haan, haan, he's so big and strong. Everything will be fine," Sarladevi interjects.

We sit in silence as the news sinks in. My mind wanders to how Nik and I had planned to bring the baby home tonight, our house set up for the new arrival, and tears roll down my face. I don't wipe them but let them drop on my lap unhindered.

* * *

I HAVEN'T EATEN ANYTHING since lunchtime, and yet I am not hungry. Nik's motaba has gone home telling me she will come in the morning with breakfast. She had tried to persuade Nik to go back home and rest, but he insisted on staying by my side. She sighed and said, "You'll become ill and will be of no use to your wife."

My brother is making me eat a little bit of the khichdi

and shaak, feeding me like a child, making jokes about how he used to bribe me to eat it when I was younger. Rita and Sunil are out in the corridor with my father, who has placed himself in front of the glass partition since we came back from the canteen.

Peter, Umi, Dick and Jay have gone home, making Nik promise to call them at any time of the night if we need them.

Nik is eating a Chinese takeaway that Peter had got him from Hanwell high street.

The nurse in charge comes in to check my charts and leaves a small plastic pot of pills. She darts her eyes at Nik and my brother and asks, "How long are you going to be here? Visiting time finished at 8.30 p.m. Mum needs to rest, and she can't do that if you're here."

"I'm not leaving my wife or my son," Nik barks, his chow mein-filled fork floating near his mouth.

She blusters, "What about the rest of them?"

Amit has been ignoring her and continues to feed me, "We will be off soon, but this is a private room. And we're not disturbing anyone." The authority and calmness in his voice is comforting, and I let myself relax. Even the frown lines and creases on the corner of Nik's eyes lessen. He has been holding that expression since Sarladevi's arrival.

***

Early morning, January 8th, 1990

OUR SON'S CHEST RISES up and down. If it weren't for the tube in his mouth, he would be like any sleeping baby, his arms out, his legs relaxed. I had dozed off after my breakfast of kaatlu and raabh. When I had woken up in the unfamiliar room, the tray with the breakfast detritus was still on the table and I willed myself to calm down. I was overwhelmed by sadness, and the familiar ache of a stone resting on my chest returned. The breakfast lady gently explained that Nik was in the unit.

My husband is inside the unit in a green hospital gown. He has dressed our son in a blue woolly hat and a white vest with a blue aeroplane design. The wires and nodes are barely visible. My vision blurs. A glimpse of the life we'd dreamt of plays in my mind: changing the baby, bathing our child, dressing our son. If only I hadn't done what I'd done. We would not be here. My thoughts take me back to a darker time, that dreadful day in August when I made a choice that still haunts me.

The double doors at the end of the corridor swing open and a stout, tall man wearing an orange turban and a cream silk full-length robe enters. I turn and read the clock behind the nurses' station. It is half-past eight; it is far too early for visiting time. In his left hand is a bulbous copper pot in which he dips his fingers flicking drops of gangajal as he walks. I have seen him do this before; he did the same ritual when Nik's brothers' children were brought home. He believes the water of the holy rivers Ganga and Jumana can purify the places that he visits.

There are six people with him including two women dressed in orange sarees, one dark-skinned and thin, the other very fair-skinned and plump. The men are exceptionally tall and broad; they are also dressed in orange. Out of their mouths emerges a rhythmic, "Hari ohhhm, Hari ohhhm, Hari ohhhm." Slow, soft, monotonous, it resonates against the walls.

The duty nurse, a very bony woman with hair tied back in a neat bun, rushes to prevent him from entering the ward, but, as his booming voice joins the mantra, "Hari ohhhm, Hari ohhhm!" she stops short. He waves her aside and walks briskly towards me.

Guruji's plump rosy lips curl up with disdain. His mouth and nose are covered with a white mask. He is upset; he doesn't want to be in the hospital, and he certainly doesn't want to be in proximity to me, a woman who has just given birth.

I recall how he had told everyone present at the house when Ram and Ashi came home that a highly respected Brahmin like he would have to chant many prayers and incantations to purify himself. "However, as Sarladevi follows her Dharma seriously, I could not say no to her."

I'd overheard Rajesh say, "Yes" under his breath, "And she pays for your ashram in India and sponsors all of your trips around the world."

"Jai Shri Krishna. Why are you standing here, Beti. Shouldn't you be with your child?" His sharp, black eyes bore into me.

"Jai Shri Krishna." Nik has stepped out of the unit still wearing his hospital gown. He pushes his way through the flock of disciples and tells the broad-faced man, "He's in there, Guruji." He pulls me to his side and points to our son. "Why have you come to the hospital, Guruji?" Nik adds, his words a whisper.

"Where's the door to the unit?" he asks briskly as he turns to look for it. One of the women who had been following him rushes to open the door. Paulette steps out of the vestibule.

"Hello, can I help you?"

"No, no, step aside. I want to see the baby." The Guru glares at her with condescending eyes, his English immaculate.

Nik steps forward, apology and embarrassment written all over his face, as he blocks the gang by placing his palms together in submission and bowing his head to the man. "Sorry, Guruji. You can't go in; only parents as you can see." He points at himself, "And even we have to wear hospital gowns."

My eyes drift back to the glass enclosure. A young couple are leaning into an incubator; inside is a very dark-skinned baby that we know as Grace. Her chest is rising up and down. She is wearing a giant disposable nappy and a pink woollen hat suitable for a doll and nothing else. Her dark colouring is from the fine down of hair which covers her whole body.

"Hari ohhhm, Hari ohhhm, then I will pray from outside. Tell me, which one is your son?"

Nik and Paulette gawk at each other in disbelief. She turns abruptly and walks back into the vestibule. He quickly rushes towards the entourage as they march back to the glass partition in a single file with the Guru at the head. I step back.

The Swami chants a prayer in Sanskrit and his followers start singing a song. As the song reaches a crescendo, the duty nurse forcefully shouts, "Can you keep quiet, please? My ladies are trying to sleep!"

The Guru throws a disparaging look towards the seated nurse, ignoring her. He turns abruptly and walks briskly towards the exit door.

"Your motaba has already told me the time and place.

What I want to know is who else was present?"

"What do you mean, Guruji?" Nik is hurriedly walking alongside the man.

"How many people, Beta? Were you there? And who else? I want to know how many male or female, the colour of their skin; it will help me create his charts."

"Let me think." Nik rubs his forehead.

"Three women: Umi, Sally and one other, me and Reena."

"What colour skin did they have?"

"What?" he asks, shock audible in his voice.

"I want to know the colour of their skin. Were they black, white, fair-skinned, dark-skinned?"

"Oh, Sally is Scottish, and the other one was Afro-Caribbean."

"So, one white woman, one black woman and Umi?" asks the Guru in Gujarati. Nik confirms with a nod. "I have much to do. I'll get the birth chart to your motaba as soon as I can. Take courage my child." He rests his hand on Nik's head briefly.

Nik stares on in disbelief as the man and his troop march out of the ward. He turns to come back to where my feet have taken root. He sprints to my side, holding me in his strong arms. "Ree, my love, what's the matter?" he asks with concern.

Aching sobs resonate throughout my body; it heaves up and down, like the swell on a rough sea. Nik takes off his robe, hands it to the duty nurse and guides me back to our room. He pulls himself on the bed and makes me lie down with my back resting against his chest. I feel his tears drop on my shoulder. He is also shocked and upset by the visit from the man and the need for Motaba to find a fault in our son's birth.

Six

Mid-morning, January 8th, 1990

MY HEART IS FULL OF THE JOY of playing with my son; his hair is black and slightly curly, and he is wearing a pair of white dungarees and a white T-shirt. The heat of the sun is warming my back as I watch him on the climbing frame. The children's playground is empty; I find myself wondering where all the children have gone.

"Stop, Diku." He is climbing too high, and I'm afraid I won't be able to bring him down. "That's enough!" I shout. "Come down right now!"

His beautiful face smiles down at me, "One more, Mummy."

"No, that's enough. Come down."

I feel a tug on my sleeve and see a young girl, she must be eight years old.

"Do you want me to bring him down?" she asks me.

Her face is familiar; she is wearing a white broderie anglaise dress, and her hair is tied in two pigtails.

"It's okay, he'll come down soon."

I search for her parents, but there's no one nearby.

"Where's your mummy or daddy?" I ask, concern in my voice.

"Aren't you my mummy?" she asks.

My eyes swivel back to the climbing frame, and he's not there. I desperately scan the children's playground for him. The bitter taste of bile fills my mouth and my stomach clenches.

"Diku, Diku, where are you?"

The little girl pulls at my hand. "Please, are you my Mummy?"

Suddenly it dawns on me that the little girl is like me, and her eyes, the colour of gold, remind me of my husband. My head spins and the children's playground shrinks away to a cavernous white room. I can hear two children laughing in the distance.

"Where have you gone? Stop, this is not funny! Come back to me! PLEASE COME BACK TO ME! PLEASE! PLEASE!" I scream frantically.

***

"REE, MY LOVE, YOU'RE SAFE."

I'm in Nik's arms; my face feels wet. I take deep breaths and look into his eyes, red and full of sadness, as I try to get oxygen into my lungs.

"The same dream?"

"No," I sob. "This one was different." I don't want to tell him that I dreamt about a girl as well as our son. The pain and anxiety of this dream brings back memories of a painful time.

Nik pulls my head to his chest and soothes my hair. "This is not your fault, Ree. What has happened is not our fault. We have to be strong."

There is a knock on the door. Nik's father enters; he has a large bag in his hands.

"Good morning, Beta. Did you get any sleep last night?" he asks both of us, his voice full of concern. He must have heard my scream. He takes off his coat and starts to empty out the contents of his bag on the tray table. "Breakfast." A thin smile is on his lips.

Nik climbs out of bed and brings the table closer. "Do you want to sit on the armchair, Ree?" and he puts the rubber ring on the upholstered leather armchair.

Nik 's breakfast is hot parotha and gaur keri nu athanu, and my breakfast is gaur no sheero and roasted papad. I eat the sheero expecting it to taste horrible but am pleasantly surprised that it is flavoured with dried ginger and the salty, savoury rice papad go well with it. To drink we have a thermos of masala chai for Nik and more badam milk with cardamom and nutmeg for me.

"Do you want some tea, Kaka?" I ask Nik's father.

"No, Beta. I'm fine at the moment … What time will the doctor's round start?"

"Not sure, Kaka. I'll go check after breakfast," Nik replies.

The big hand on the clock is on ten and the little hand is on three.

Nik's father explains his mother will come with our lunch later and we will get more visitors in the evening. He has been given clear instructions from Sunil to make notes on what the doctors have to say. I point to my diary telling him Dick has already been using it and he should make his notes in there, too.

"Shall we go see my grandson?" Nik's father asks once

we have tidied away our plates.

Nik and I are in the unit, and his father watches as we show him how our son reacts to our touch. His eyes are glistening, but he smiles as he watches. Nik is changing his nappy; I am frantic, my mind screaming for me to interfere. Today our son is wearing a pale yellow Babygro. I glimpse a white coat in the corridor on the other side and tell Nik the doctors have finished their visits.

"Yes, I know, Ree, but let's stay a little longer." He smiles down at our son, relishing the time we are spending with him. We hold hands in the incubator and take our son's hand. I will him to open his eyes. I'm desperate to see his eyes. Are they like mine or has he inherited his father's beautiful eyes?

Nik's father waves at us, and we head for the vestibule. White coats disappear into the first room on our corridor.

While I wait my thoughts wander to when we first came to visit the maternity ward as part of our neonatal classes. We had been shown the regimented cubicles, each occupied variously with crying, sleeping, nursing, talking: the idealistic images of mother and child. Instead, the mothers in this ward are locked in isolated rooms, alone, waiting for answers as to why they don't have their babies, their days filled with pain and anxiety.

Nik is waiting outside the glass partition with his father, quietly talking, asking him what Sunil needs from the doctors.

A Middle Eastern woman in a white doctor's coat and a bright-green headscarf enters the room and introduces herself as Saida Hussain. She has a dark-haired man and a mousy-haired woman standing next to her, both holding notepads, pens poised.

She picks up the clipboard hanging at the end of the bed and says, "I'm afraid your child is very sick; he is having difficulty breathing and may have suffered severe brain damage due to oxygen deprivation during your very long and complicated labour." While she studies the notes again, Nik and his father have entered. Nik's face has changed from the serenity that had washed over him during our time with our baby to a thunderstorm as she continues in her accented condescending tone.

"What complications? Do you know what actually happened or are you just passing the buck?" he questions her angrily.

Dr Hussain jumps out of her skin. She hadn't noticed Nik's quiet entrance. The aggression in Nik's voice changes her demeanour; the transformation is striking. She stares up at him and is startled by his appearance. His eyes have a look he gets when he is on the edge of anger, a fire in them, which can strike a scorched knife through your heart. Her hands shake as she sheepishly rustles through the notes. Making herself as small and as invisible as possible, she turns towards the door, and the group of doctors walk out without saying another word.

"What was that?" Nik is fuming; he has already turned abruptly towards the door. "I'm going to sort this out. How dare they do this!"

The tears start to flow, washing my face with burning, salty tracks. He has gone off, leaving me to cope with the shock alone.

His father grabs my hand and pulls me to him. "Let him do this, Beta. He needs it."

I can hear Sarladevi's voice, "Well, what did you expect? It is your karma."

Karma: the Hindu concept of cause and effect. The action of your past that will, in the future, create a reaction. My Hindu upbringing has a different definition of karma to the one that Nik's motaba holds; her karma is of one's fate, written in the stars, sins brought from your past life. My views are that human beings can create their own destiny, so if you sow goodness you reap goodness, and if you sow evil, you reap evil. I had done something terrible, something that would take hundreds of good deeds to atone.

When Nik comes back into the room, he smells of tobacco. My initial reaction is to be cross because he has taken up smoking again. He had finally stopped before Christmas, and he still struggles to beat the urge. But I understand he needs to do this at this moment. It is becoming more and more painful for me to sit on my bottom, and I am lying in bed, unable to bear it.

"Ree." He is feeling my head. "You're burning up. Kaka, can you call the duty nurse, please?" he says.

The tall redhead puts a thermometer in my mouth while taking my blood pressure. She makes a note on my chart and then turns to my husband and father-in-law.

"Can you leave the room? I want to examine Mum's stitches."

Nik hovers by the door, reluctant to leave. I nod to him,

and he steps outside.

"I'm going to give you some antibiotics, and I'll ask Miss Beckwithe to come to see you. Stay in bed lying down. No sitting up: you need to allow the stitches to take."

She nearly bumps into him as she opens the door. He is by the bed in two long strides, and he takes my hand. I tell him I have an infection from the tear and have been told not to sit on my bottom.

"I'm so sorry, Ree. I shouldn't have allowed you to sit, even if it is on the ring."

"Allowed? I'm a grown woman, Nik."

He pulls the armchair closer to the bed, sits down, takes my hand and brushes my knuckles with sweet, tender kisses.

"You're an amazing woman, Ree, so brave and strong. Try to sleep. I'll wake you when Jijaji arrives." I frown at his words.

"I called him after the doctor's misdiagnosis. We need proper answers. I'm not going to allow them to get out of doing the best they can for our son or for you. Now sleep." He makes me turn onto my side and rubs my back, his warm hands releasing the tension and anxiety, and I drift off to sleep.

***

WHISPERED CONVERSATION BRINGS me back from my sleep. It is challenging to follow entirely, but I glean nuggets of information: second opinion, transfer, appointment with the obstetrician. I stir, and Nik's head lifts up. He offers me a drink and a tablet from a plastic cup on my bedside table. The clock on the wall says twenty minutes to eleven.

"Did you speak to the doctors in the unit?" I ask, as I rise up on one elbow.

"They are still deciding on the X-ray. Jijaji will be here soon, and he and Kaka will find a consultant to talk to about our options. Are you hungry?" I shake my head. "You have to eat, Ree. You didn't eat much for breakfast. Do you want me to get you a sandwich?" My eyes dart to Nik's father.

"Don't worry about me. I won't tell if you don't," he conspires with me.

"Kaka, can you get Reena a chicken salad sandwich on brown bread and Lucozade."

I say, "Thank you, Kaka," as he steps out into the corridor.

Once he returns, I eat the sandwich to please him; my appetite has left me.

When Sunil arrives, he and Nik's father head out to the nurses' station to find a doctor or anyone who is in charge.

Peter and Dick arrive just before twelve o'clock; they have brought with them some extra clothes from our house in a large leather holdall.

"Thanks, guys. I'll go freshen up; can you stay here with Ree?"

He's rummaging through the bag. "Did you bring my wash bag?"

Nik is looking dishevelled: he has two-day stubble, and his clothes are crumpled.

"Yes, it's in there," Dick confirms. "I've brought some day clothes for you, too, Ree," he turns to tell me. "We can leave the room while you change into them."

"No, wait for me to come back, and I'll help you, Ree," Nik says. The sparkle in his eyes tell me not to disobey him.

"Come on, my love, it's your turn to freshen up."

He is dressed in a crisp, white shirt and dark-blue trousers and has shaved and combed his hair. He has put on some aftershave, the musk and sandalwood that I love. He turns to Dick and Peter.

"Can you keep guard outside?"

I had a showered in the morning and had changed into a fresh nightdress and tied my hair back into a loose plait. He pulls out a pair of black leggings and a loose red cotton shirt that I'd made to wear as my bump grew. I reach for the buttons on my nightdress, and he stops me, "Let me do that." He slowly opens my nightshirt, keeping his smouldering eyes on mine. He pushes back the shirt; it falls off my shoulder onto the ground, and his eyes slowly scan my body. "You are so beautiful and have your breasts got bigger?" He raises his left eyebrow, and a slow, wicked grin appears on his face. He takes me in his arms and kisses me with longing. I lean into him and return the kiss. His hands rub my back and caress my shoulders. I want the warmth of his body. Since the birth of our son, we have been surrounded by people, our intimacy compromised.

"Can you sit on this ring for a minute for me?" He lowers the bed, kneels in front of me and pulls one leg and then the other up. He fumbles at adjusting the elastic to fit my shrinking waist. He pulls the shirt over my arms and shoulders and starts to button it up from the bottom, planting a kiss on the tops of my breasts before he closes the buttons at the collar. He reaches in my bedside cabinet and pulls out my make-up bag.

"Not sure if I'm any good at this, but I could have a go." He grins at me.

"No, thank you." I pull at the bag, smiling back at him. I take out my lipstick and put a thin layer on my dry lips and add a touch of Vaseline. Dark circles have formed under my eyes, and I hastily put my make-up mirror away. He makes the bed and opens the door.

Nik's father, Sunil, Peter and Dick enter the room.

"Can you lie down on the bed, Reena? We'll stand around the bed as we talk so you don't have to strain your neck," Sunil commands in his soothing baritone. "Kaka and I have spoken to the doctor in charge of SCBU, and want to tell you what they think. It's not good news."

Nik takes my hand, and his shoulders slump. His father steps closer and wraps his arm around his shoulders to comfort him.

Sunil begins to explain the opinions of the doctors on our son's wellbeing and mine.

"Firstly, Reena's health: she has an infection in her stitches and will need to take some powerful antibiotics. They are also going to prescribe some sleeping pills as she needs to rest to heal quicker. Miss Beckwithe will come to see you later. If at any time you can't bear the pain, Reena, you have to tell someone; they can give you stronger pain relief. I believe this will help you rest, too."

"Will the antibiotics stop me from nursing my baby?" I ask.

"No, they'll prescribe something safe for you and the

baby and ... "

"What about the sleeping pills?" Nik interrupts.

"I was just going to say that sleeping pills are also safe. The consultants on the unit have decided not to do the X-ray; they believe the baby has had a severe intracranial bleed and will not be able to survive without life support. They have asked if we want to switch off the machine."

"Why don't they want to do the X-ray?" Nik asks angrily. "They don't know for sure." His father pulls him closer.

"They see this all the time, Niku. Some babies are happy while they are supported by their mother's blood supply, but they can't sustain life outside. It is a known fact, and with your son, there are signs he won't survive."

My mind is numb. I fix my gaze on the ceiling and focus on the uneven paint. I feel nothing, I think nothing. The cloth of my soft cotton shirt, itches and burns against my skin. I turn my head and the world reflects my mood.

"NO! They are not going to switch off the machine without any further tests!" Nik is controlling his anger; his grip has tightened on my hand.

"I agree," Dick says. "Many people in a coma recover fully, and you said the brain was a wonderous thing."

Nik's father confirms he would want more tests, and we should get a second opinion.

"Is that how you feel too, Reena?" Sunil asks.

The lump in my throat is choking me. I swallow hard and nod, tears streaming down my face.

"I'll ask for a transfer to Hammersmith Hospital; they

have the best neonatal unit in West London, and they have an outstanding paediatric consultant who specialises in brain damage."

He turns and walks out of the room. Nik falls further into the armchair, all his strength gone, his head in his hands. Dick takes my hand and sits on the edge of the bed. Nik's father is sitting on the arm of the chair, his arm wrapped around his son's shoulders. Peter's arms hang down by his sides as he turns towards the window. Everyone is dealing with the shock. At one day, ten hours and thirty minutes old, our son's life is dependent on the doctors agreeing to a transfer.

The food trolley rattles on the ward. As the small blonde enters the room to deliver my lunch, Nik's mother comes with fresh food from home. Her eyes are red and puffy; Nik's father rises from the chair and places his arms around her shoulders. She leans into him and smiles up. They exchange a look full of sorrow.

"Jai Shri Krishna, Reena Beta. I've brought you lunch. I have extra for everyone else," she explains as she glances at the people in the room. "Mug, baath, I know you don't like khichdi." She smiles at me.

I tell her I'm not hungry, but she urges me to eat because of the medication. She dishes out food for Nik and me on plates, and hands the bag to Peter and Dick. "Take this to the canteen; we'll join you soon."

As they open the door, Sunil walks in. "You'd better stay while I explain," he directs Peter and Dick. "They've agreed to the transfer, but it won't happen until tomorrow morning. Miss Beckwithe will discharge you from this hospital then, too, but you'll have to come back for check-ups. I have spoken to your GP and Sally will also come to check on you at Hammersmith. I've arranged a time for a meeting with Dr Hussain and your obstetric consultant, Mr Carr, to examine the readings during your delivery for Friday morning. I'm on duty that day, so you'll need to take Rita with you."

Dick is writing everything in my diary, adding to the notes made by Nik's father. We sit quietly absorbing the information he has given us, no one wanting to break the silence, reflecting on how much has changed in the last two days for all of us.

"At least they've agreed to the transfer," Nik's mother says softly, squeezing my hand. Nik is slumped in the armchair, his head resting on his father's shoulder. I stare at the plate of food on the tray table.

"Sunil, Beta, come and have some lunch. Let Reena and Niku eat in peace."

Sunil's sympathetic eyes ask for permission.

"Thanks, Jijaji. We'll see you after lunch." Nik nods at him, lifting his head.

We eat our lunch in silence; it tastes like sand, but I make myself eat, knowing I will need to build my strength for the days to come.

Seven

January 9th, 1990

THE CLOCK ON THE WALL READS six o'clock; the unit is quiet. Nik is sleeping, his arms wrapped around me on the single bed. The duty nurse was not happy when she had come earlier to check my temperature. I had implored her with my eyes not to make too much noise.

Yesterday had not begun well. Early in the morning, we had been subjected to a visit by Guruji, the man who is a significant influence on Nik's motaba. The doctor's round proved to be an exercise in misinformation and Nik had stormed out, and, finally, we'd been told our child had very little chance of survival and the hospital was no longer willing to do more tests. I was in shock for most of the day, crying at the slightest news, unable to function properly. Even sleep wasn't a respite for me, falling in and out of feverish nightmares. The heat of the ward was making me flustered, and the fact I didn't have the energy to even take light exercise was adding to my frustration. As Nik had started to smoke again, he was more out of the ward than in, finding any excuse to step outside, leaving me alone with my thoughts.

Nik's mother had spent the afternoon by my side, gently cajoling me to drink and eat. She had been subjected to one of my dreams, the screaming, the crying, the panic attack. She had held me and said, "Talk about your dreams, Reena; it might help you understand them."

The dream was similar to the one I had when I first became pregnant. My early dreams were of children playing in summer meadows, but as the pregnancy had progressed, the visions have become more about the panic of losing them. I had convinced myself it was an anxiety dream. Carl Jung said that dreams were telepathic visions, so was my subconscious telling me a dark prophecy? How could I tell her what my dream was about? I had taken one grandchild away from her, and because of my choice, she might lose another.

By the end of the day, my anger and guilt had become resentment directed towards my husband. Motaba had come with my evening meal of methi na thepla and chai without masala. I was pleased, finally, after knowing me for over five years, she had remembered I didn't like masala chai, but she made a point to tell me that it was Anu Masi who had made it especially for me.

Last night she sent Nik and everyone to eat in the canteen. As she sat with me, she told me again that I should have given Nik up, that our son's fate was written in the stars and we should accept our destiny and our son's.

My rage had increased as she stayed with me; the blaming eyes, scornfully telling me of my bad luck. When Nik came back to the room, he had halted at the door. She stopped abruptly. Instead of reprimanding her, he hunched his shoulders in defeat. She continued her tirade, telling us to wait for the Guruji and our son's janam kundli to select a name according to his horoscope. He took her hand and promised we would wait.

Later in the evening we were told again, by the new duty nurse, that the transfer could result in our son's death. The news hit me like a sharp dagger.

It started with a small disagreement about having a shower before bedtime and had turned into a full-blown argument on our son's name. I wanted to name him before the transfer. He repeated Motaba's words, "Let's wait for his horoscope."

I yelled at him; I dreaded the possibility he could die without a name. He told me I was irrational; I blamed him for our son's illness. I reminded him of his reaction to the pregnancy test. I told him of his lack of support for when I was left alone to make a decision about another pregnancy. He stared at me, his eyes dirty brown and full of hurt, and he walked out. I didn't stop him but watched from the door of my room as he left the ward. Instead of sorrow, I had anger gnawing in my soul. My mind kept replaying the day I found out I was pregnant.

***

IT WAS A HOT DAY IN MAY, and I was busy working on our next research project for a documentary. I'd retched at the coffee in the morning and had detected a metallic taste when I had my usual breakfast of toast with peanut butter and sliced bananas. It was only after I had drunk a gallon of orange juice by lunchtime that I'd made the connection.

When I returned home that evening, I felt nervous and had delayed the test, using any excuse, paperwork, ironing, cleaning. When Nik arrived, he was surprised to see me cleaning the kitchen floor on my hands and knees and had commented on my sudden domesticity and asked if I was angry about anything at work. He knows there are only two reasons for me to clean: sadness or rage.

After dinner, I finally built up the courage to check and waited, locked in the bathroom, for the results. Nik was on the telephone talking to Jay about an import–export exhibition they were scheduled to go to in a couple of days. When I came out with the test in my hand, Nik had turned, and his eyes focused on the white stick.

"I'll call you tomorrow." His voice was stern; he had slammed the phone down. "What is that, Ree. Is that what I think it is?" he'd said, the fiery shards showing their anger.

"I … I'm pregnant, Nik. We … we're pregnant."

He didn't say anything; his eyes drifted to the white stick and my stomach, and then he asked me why I was angry. I told him I had misgivings about getting pregnant. I was in line for a promotion at work, and I said to him that having a baby now would jeopardise it. I was angry the job would go to Max. He had furiously paced the length of the room, cross for me, cross for himself. He kept saying it was all too soon, that we had not been married long enough and we were too young. He reminded me of how we'd discussed what we wished to do for the next few years and pregnancy was not an option.

"We can't, Nik ... I can't," I'd replied, filled with sadness. I could not go through the hurt I had felt the last time and was not willing to do that again.

"We should think about our options," he had said. "I can't do this, Ree." He grabbed a bottle of wine and had gone upstairs to the guest bedroom, wanting to create distance between us.

For the first time in our marriage, he slept in the guest bedroom. He held his position and blamed me, science, God, the universe, for putting him in this situation. I was angry at his childish behaviour and had told him that if he wasn't man enough to take responsibility then I would do it on my own.

Deflated, my mind thought of the time I was left to make a decision that still festered like a boil on my conscience. Nik was behaving like a child, his promise to never hurt me forgotten.

The frustration of being apart gnawed at both of our hearts when Nik went on business trips. We would argue about the slightest thing, but this time he had sulked for days, barely speaking, taking refuge in his work. Finally, on Sunday morning, he'd taken me in his arms and said he loved me. I had told him we needed to support each other, that's what marriage was, a union of two people who were committed to cope with any crisis that came our way.

While he was gone, I waited anxiously for his usual phone calls; he spoke of new clients and the business most of the time and avoided the topic. He always ended his calls with, "I love you, Ree. Always have, always will. Without you, my heart is empty." Those words gave me some comfort that perhaps our marriage wasn't in trouble, and maybe my husband needed some time to adjust.

I, too, had to reassess my life. It was the wrong time for me. I was enjoying my job and was getting quite good at it. I had started to work as assistant producer at Tony Sheene Associates in Soho a year ago, and Tony had already allowed me to work on some productions. Television production was not a business suitable for working mothers; the hours were long and unpredictable. The women who did well in the industry were either single or childless. If you were a woman you had to work twice as hard and twice as long to get anywhere. You needed to be manlier than a man to succeed, as Jane Cawthorne, my mentor, would say repeatedly when I moaned about the hours and the injustices I'd experienced.

He had come home with flowers and heart-shaped diamond earrings to apologise for his behaviour and promised he'd get the matching necklace upon our child's birth. He had told me we would find a way for me to have a career and a child. We cried for the child we had lost and laughed about the child we were going to have.

∗∗

HE CAME BACK LAST NIGHT at ten o'clock, smelling of drink and tobacco, apologising for leaving me, and promised he would never leave my side again. "I love you. I should have been more grown-up and said I'd marry you that day."

"It was the right decision, Nik. We were too young."

"No, I was too young, you took all the responsibility and suffered because of it."

"I came back, Nik. I love you … you said that it isn't

our fault."

"I know, but I can't help thinking that our sins have come back to haunt us."

He had voiced my fears, that it is our karma. I hated to revert back to some higher being who was punishing us. My belief in God was all about love and compassion, not retribution and revenge.

Eventually, he told me he was scared that if we chose the name without consulting his horoscope, we would lose our son. He paced late into the night about the injustice. I watched as he built up the courage to fight and change back to the man he had been on the day of our son's birth. For a brief period, he had relinquished his responsibility to our families.

I pleaded with him to come and sleep with me. I told him I'd wait and he let out a soft sigh. I felt his chest rise up and down, as his heart quietened, and I eventually fell asleep, wondering *why it is so essential for Sarladevi to make everyone bend to her will.*

* * *

IT'S EIGHT-THIRTY, AND OUR SON is going to be transferred to Hammersmith Hospital's Specialist Neonatal Unit today; I am also leaving Ealing Hospital, too.

When I step into the corridor, my eyes rest on Nik's parents, holding onto each other, their bodies hunched as they watch their grandson.

Nik's mother turns, her arms open to embrace me, and his father says, "Jai Shri Krishna, Beta. How are you today?"

"Jai Shri Krishna, I'm good, thank you Kaka, Kaki. Where's Nik?"

"He's gone to get the baby carrier from the car, just in case we need it. I hope you don't mind, he gave me the house keys yesterday," she replies.

"No, no, it's your home, too," I reassure her.

I recall the words that Nik's motaba had said when we'd told her about the house.

'She thinks she's clever, taking my son away from me! But she'll come running back when she needs our help.' She might be right. Can we cope alone if our son is so ill? A glimmer of regret gnaws at my thoughts; perhaps I have deprived this wonderful couple of spending time with us. I have begun to love his parents; they are supportive and always kind. However, I couldn't live with Motaba. She has made me feel unwelcome since my first visit to Shakti Bhavan. The way she talks to me, continually reminding me I'm not good enough to be part of the family. It was Nik's father who had told Nik to move out; he had seen how I struggled to live at Shakti Bhavan. I used to wander through the enormous house, never finding a spot I could call my own, always feeling like an imposter who'd stumbled into a palace.

Our little house in Ealing was a first wedding anniversary present from his parents. I love it. I can manage it by myself, cooking and cleaning for us; I am comfortable there. It is very much like the home I grew up in. Nik and I visit Shakti Bhavan for weekends and events; we still have our rooms in the big house. I've left most of my Indian clothes and jewellery there and, when we visit, I pretend we're on holiday.

With the announcement of the arrival of the baby, there had been another disagreement. Even Nik felt it would be wise for us to move back. He had pointed out the advantages of having babysitters on tap, food ready for when we came home, the lack of chores at the weekend. The Raja nanny, Jessica, would look after our child as she had done with the others. I agreed reluctantly to move back in, but only after my maternity leave was over. I wanted us to be a couple with a baby, like the photographs I'd seen in the parenting magazines. I wanted a bit of normality.

'Why do you think we have these traditions? Mothers need help in the first few months. You're not a poor villager who can't rest. You're a Raja daughter-in-law,' Nik's motaba had said to me.

I'm not sure if this will ever be an option for us now if the baby is as handicapped as they say he is. *Would Sarladevi be pleased to have us or would she prefer we stay away?*

I watch our son breathe imperfectly; his lungs controlled by the machine. His father has changed him. He is in a bright-blue footless Babygro with yellow ducks. His head is covered with a yellow hat with two cloth ears.

"Go, go, have your shower," Kaki instructs, waving her hand towards the bathroom. "I'll take this bag to the room, and you can have breakfast. I've brought porridge, Naren Bhai's recipe." She speaks quietly to me, watching him, too. Her eyes moisten.

I squeeze her hand and say, "He's a fighter. Can't you tell?"

She raises a small smile, "He is that Reena. He is that," and she hugs me.

When I walk into my room, Anne Marie and Umi have arrived and are sitting on the bed. I hug them both.

Nik stands up from the armchair to take my wash bag and towel.

"Nik called us yesterday. We're here to go with the baby to Hammersmith." Umi smiles.

"You and Nik are going to go home and sleep," Anne-Marie adds.

"No, that's not what we discussed. I'm going with the baby, and you're taking Ree home to rest," Nik interrupts.

"Yes, that was yesterday. We've decided you both need to rest, Nik." Anne- Marie's green eyes glint; she points her finger at both of us. Nik pulls me towards him.

"You look like shit, Nik … " Umi adds, "When they run all the tests, you'll need to have your wits about you. So, you'd better rest when you can. Today's a good day. They're not going to do the X-ray until later."

"Let the masis take care of him, Nik." Anne-Marie lightens the mood.

He relaxes; she's used the Gujarati word for maternal aunties, as they have since they discovered I was pregnant, and reluctantly agrees, unclenching his jaw. I offer them some porridge, and they both pull faces.

There is a knock on the door. The clock on the wall reads half-past nine.

A woman with mousy hair and blonde highlights walks in and introduces herself.

"Hello, I'm Suzanna, but most people call me Su. I'm from Hammersmith Paediatrics. You must be Mr Raja." She holds her hand out to Nik and considers the women in the room. She sees that I'm sitting on a rubber ring and smiles, "You must be Mummy?"

Nik shakes her hand, "Hi, I'm Nik, and this is my wife,

Reena."

"Great to meet you." She has a New Zealand accent and rolls the r in great. "Are you the baby's aunties, ladies?" she asks as she turns to Umi and Anne-Marie. They introduce themselves and Su begins to explain that she will be accompanying our son in the ambulance. She also tells us we will need to bring a bag for overnight stays as the unit has family rooms for parents.

"It's not the Ritz, and you'll have to share the bathroom, but it's in the same block as the unit, and there's a small kitchen. We give our families somewhere close so you can come to see your son in the unit anytime, night or day."

As she explains the X-ray procedure, the duty nurse walks in and asks if I'm ready to go to express my milk.

Su interrupts, "Sorry, Sister, it might be difficult for Reena at the moment as she hasn't held her baby. Can you wait until after the X-ray? We'll let you hold him, and it will be much more comfortable," she informs me. I agree to wait.

"Are you sure you want to do this, Ree?" Nik squeezes my hand.

"Yes, I do … I … " I pause to choke back tears, "It will help other babies. You were at the class when that woman came in and told us how it helped her premature daughter."

"Yes, there's lots of research on breast milk and premature babies," the duty nurse confirms. "We're always grateful for mothers who supplement our breast milk bank." Her teeth smile, but her eyes are sad.

At ten o'clock two burly men in dark-green overalls arrive outside the neonatal unit. Nik and I are stroking and holding our son's hands. I had given up all hope of keeping my tears back and am crying salty rivers, large drops forming under my chin. When I glance across at Nik, he, too, has tear tracks on his cheeks and is fighting the urge to take me into his arms to comfort me. We both know that switching the machines is a risk. Sunil had explained all the risks; his heart could stop or the brain would sustain more damage. His explanation was candid.

Paulette is on duty when the paramedics arrive; she asks us to step back.

"Don't worry," she adds.

Nik envelopes me in his arms, and we watch on as she and Su work wordlessly on moving our baby out of Ealing Hospital SCBU to a temporary incubation unit. They both smile at us when the procedure runs without a hitch. At the glass partition my best friends wait: one tall and dark-skinned, with straight black hair, the other short with skin like porcelain, her curly strawberry blonde hair cascading around her face, and they, too, raise a smile.

The transportation unit has a smaller machine to control the rate of air, which they place under the trolley. Paulette wheels the unit out of the room and Su follows afterwards, handing her coat to one of the paramedics. We step out in our gowns.

"Niku, Reena, we have the initial for the baby's name," Nik's mother says as she comes to the opening onto the corridor. I sigh, Nik holding me closer as she tells us the letter. We both let out a long breath and say "Amar" together.

"Isn't that the name you'd chosen already?" Anne-Marie asks. She and Umi have been standing behind his mother.

"Yes." We both grin at each other.

"Lovely name. Means immortal." Nik's mother smiles back with tears in her eyes and wraps her arms around both of us.

"Can you wait for a moment?" Nik's father asks Su.

"Not too long." She lifts up the small oxygen tank, indicating to the dial that measures the amount of oxygen.

Nik's mother takes out a small silver pot and opens it. "Can I?" She gestures to Su; one of the paramedics lifts the lid. She puts a red sindoor tilak on our son's forehead and leans in and calls his name, "Amar, Amar, Amar."

"Great name, Amar Raja," Paulette says. "Let me add it to his folder." She writes AMAR, showing it to Nik to confirm the spelling. She hands the folder to Su.

We walk with the paramedics to the exit door of the ward and Su turns to us and says, "I'll do my best to keep Amar safe. See you at Hammersmith Paediatric Care."

"We'll follow you in my car," Umi tells her, and they both hug us and leave.

We are left in the ward; my thoughts are with our son, and I long for the promise of holding him later today, hoping and praying his journey is safe and he will survive.

"Let's take these off." Nik is pulling at my gown. I move to the vestibule and he helps me. He takes me in his arms and remarks as he lifts my chin, "Sorry, my love. Can you believe that his horoscope initial is the same as the name we chose. The universe is on our side, my love, Amar – Immortal."

"Do you really believe that, Nik?" My eyes are full of questions.

"I have to, Ree. I don't think I can function if … we are being … " His words choke.

"Punished," I whisper and weep uncontrollably.

Eight

WE HAVE VACATED THE PRIVATE ROOM and are in the waiting room. Nik's father had taken our bags to the car earlier in the morning. I am unable to speak; the separation from my son is intolerable.

"I've left some food for you in your fridge, Beta," Nik's mother tells us. "Eat, shower and then go to sleep. You've got plenty of time to rest."

"We're going to the hospital and will see you later," Nik's father says as we walk to our cars.

The house feels cold and empty as we step into the small hallway of our Victorian workman's cottage, even though the heating is on. Our hopes and dreams are shattered; no one had mentioned the gut-wrenching ache that comes from coming home without your baby. Nik's arms are wrapped around me, our coats deposited in the cloak cupboard. We are stuck, afraid to open the door to our living room and to the new life that lies before us. He turns me around and lifts my chin, a silvery trail of tears running down his face.

"He's strong, Nik," I reassure him with a kiss, wiping his tears with my fingers. I open the glass hallway door.

The answering machine on the telephone table is blinking, and my breath catches, the confidence I had mustered leaving me in an instant. Nik leads me to the cream sofa and sits me down. I hold on to his hand as if my life depends on it.

"Ree, let me listen to the messages."

"You have four new messages," an automated female voice tells us.

"Hello Reena and Nik. I heard the news, call me. When can we come to visit?" Beep.

"This is British Gas. You've missed the engineer. Please call to make another appointment." Beep.

"Hello. Amar Raja's a great name. When can I come to see him?" Beep.

"Hello, Nik, Ree. We got here safe. Amar is settled. I'll call you at four to wake you up. Eat and rest. Love you guys." Beep.

Nik's shoulders fall as he hears the last message; he has been standing by the machine, his fists thrust into his trouser pockets, his back to me. He turns and gives me a thin smile. "Right, I'm going to get the stuff from the car. Do you want to eat first or have a proper bath?"

I tell him I'm desperate for a bath and he tells me to wait as he wants to wash it first.

Nik is leading me upstairs to the small landing. We both gaze at the daylight streaming into the room on our left before we enter our bedroom.

Our king-size bed has moved nearer the sash window, and a wooden baby crib on a stand is next to my side of the bed. Nik smiles at me. "Suresh has been here."

It is the crib that their son, Ram, slept in before he

moved to his cot. Before that Tarun and Anousha had used it, the Raja grandchildren's first bed.

"Lie down for a bit. I'll come back to help you down." He runs down the stairs to our bathroom.

The small mattress has been covered with a white sheet, and a white crochet blanket has been left folded inside it. On top of it there is a cream envelope. I open it and read the note.

Dear Reena and Nik,
Ram loved sleeping in this crib. Do you remember him crying with the colic, but as soon as we put him in it, he seemed to calm down. I hope and pray your son will be home soon and enjoy being in the crib too.
We'll wait for you to tell us when we can come to visit; Motaba's given us strict instructions not to disturb you.
All our love, hugs and kisses

Ashi and Suresh

"Why aren't you resting?"

I can't stop crying, my wretched body shaking. Nik takes the note and reads it. I watch as the creases in the corners of his eyes deepen. "Strict instructions?" He flops to sitting on the bed and puts his head in his hands.

We had been wondering why his siblings hadn't come: the visiting times were quite long, and they do have a nanny to care for the children, whereas, my family live and work in Leicester, and cannot do the daily visits. Why would Motaba forbid them from coming to see the baby and us?

He pulls his hands away and takes a deep breath. "Can I share the bath with you?"

I take his hands in mine. "Look at me, Nik." His eyes meet mine. "Only if you scrub my back."

He laughs; he knows I hate the way he scrubs my back. "I promise to be gentle." He raises a smile. He pulls me to standing and takes my clothes off. He swiftly pulls at the belt and zip of his trousers and pulls them down as I unbutton his shirt.

"Your breasts are so big. God, Ree, I've always loved your body, but now it's exquisite." He touches my breasts, and I wince. "What's wrong?"

"They're just sore. I think I need to express some milk soon." We kiss, his lips are soft and comforting.

He grabs our nightgowns, and we walk down to the bathroom. The bathroom has a huge bathtub with a shower over it. It was one of the things we had insisted on when the cottage was being remodelled. I love soaking in the bath with Nik, and we have developed a habit of soaking in the tub after a long day at work, candles lit, sipping a glass of wine, unwinding and washing away the stresses of the day. The warm water has a relieving effect on my breasts and stitches. The tension Nik has been holding relaxes as I lean against his chest.

We eat our lunch in our nightgowns, sitting next to each other at the round table, holding hands as we eat. Nik's mother had left us ringda no oro, bajra ni rotli, mug ni dall and baath. After lunch we go to our bedroom; it feels strange coming back to sleep in our bed. We've become so used to sleeping in the single bed that we lie wrapped in each other's arms in the centre, leaving a vast space on either side. Our eyes close immediately.

"Ree, Ree, my darling, wake up. Wake up."

I open my eyes and feel the damp beads of sweat on my body.

I focus on his eyes and begin to whimper, "I … I'm unlucky … I'm bad luck." I dreamt about the Guru and his predictions again.

When we had told Motaba we wanted to marry, she had insisted on getting Jagdish Maharaj to do an astrological chart to find out if we were compatible.

I'd complained afterwards to Nik, asking him if our charts weren't aligned would he change his mind and not marry me? He'd laughed but had said it's a custom to please his motaba.

When the charts had been compared, the Guru had told her that we were incompatible and would have to perform certain rituals to strengthen our planets' alignments. I had dreamt of the words again.

'Your janam kundli shows that in your marriage you will bring pain and suffering.'

I dreamt of Sarladevi in the family mandir. 'I knew it when I first heard about your mother and grandmother dying when you were young. You carry a burden of unhappiness and bad luck with you. Reena, give up my son for his sake.'

He pulls the damp tendrils of hair away from my face and kisses me.

"I'm unlucky, Nik. My grandmother died. My mother died."

"Don't be silly. How can you be unlucky … where's the Reena Raja who doesn't believe in all that mumbo jumbo?"

"What if it is my bad luck? Maybe Guruji is right. Maybe being together has made our son ill."

"Don't ever think that, Ree. I'm the luckiest man alive

to have found you. Our son isn't ill because of you. I will never believe that. I love you."

I hold on to my husband and try to convince myself that it is all superstition, and none of it is based on scientific facts. But I think of the woman who does believe it, and who reminded me of the conversation the other day.

***

THE PHONE IS RINGING OFF THE HOOK. "Hello … thanks, Umi. We'll be there soon."

Nik pulls his arm out and leans over as I open my eyes. "Hello, sleepyhead. Do you want to stay in bed a bit longer? I need to pack our bags, so you have time." I close my eyes again, my mind numb, my body exhausted, and all is dark.

"My darling, time to wake up."

My eyes open to his beautiful smile; he is fully clothed, propped up on one elbow watching me.

He helps me put on some clothes that he has pulled out of the wardrobe.

As we step into the small landing, my eyes drift to the guest room that has been converted into a nursery. 'It's bad luck to decorate rooms and buy clothes before the birth of the baby. We don't do that in our family.' Sarladevi's words resound in my ears. My eyes fill with tears.

Nik takes me in his arms, kisses my head and whispers, "I love you, Ree, everything is going to be fine."

"I love you too, Nik," I say, choking back the tears.

The journey to the hospital takes twenty minutes from our house but it seems endless. I am using the rubber ring, and Nik has tried to avoid the bumps that send jarring pain through my body. As we turn into the narrow road between Wormwood Scrubs and Hammersmith Hospital, my heart sinks. It is full of potholes and only wide enough for one car.

Luckily, we only have to pull up once into the ditch to allow for a car heading out. The road winds round to a car park next to the grounds of the West London Stadium. Nik pulls up in a parking space. "Sorry." He squeezes my hand, "I have to get a ticket. Can you sit for a little while longer?" he asks. I nod, although my instinct tells me to get up.

He opens the passenger door and lifts me to standing. "Lean here while I get our bag." I wait against the car as he opens the boot and lifts out a holdall and a camera bag. I frown at him. "We haven't taken many photographs of Amar. I'm going to change that from now on," he says with determination. He takes my hand and kisses my head. "Ready? Let's go to see our son."

Hammersmith Hospital is an old Victorian building, red brick with white arched windows. We follow signs to the paediatric unit through a pedestrian tunnel that runs from the back to the front of the hospital. The tunnel is covered with pictures and murals to brighten the long dark passage.

We enter the neonatal ward through a set of double doors. This unit is different to the one in Ealing Hospital. The nurses' station is by the doors, and a smiling brunette in a dark-blue uniform greets us. "Hello, how can I help you?"

When Nik explains, she replies, "Ah yes, baby's being taken care of by grandparents," and she points to the end of the corridor to a glass partition and a door.

Nik's parents are standing over our son. He is inside a large clear-plastic cot that can accommodate a child up to the age of two. There is a large lamp above which radiates blue light. The cover has been pushed back, and they are both holding his hands. Tears prick at my eyes. Nik pulls me to him and smiles.

They turn their heads towards us, both raising a smile; he signals for them to stay as he pulls out his camera.

"Do you want to go in and take a closer picture?" Su asks Nik.

His jaw drops, but he quickly composes himself and says, "Yes please, that would be great."

"We don't usually allow more than two people at a time, but it's not busy today, and I can see you want some memories," she informs us.

"Is it okay with you, Ree? Can I leave you here for a bit?" Nik takes my hand to his lips and searches for my approval.

He enters the door on the side, emerges in a white apron and almost runs to his parents. He begins directing them; he makes them lower their heads so they are level with the cot. A short Chinese nurse brings another low chair to them so they can sit on each side of the unit, their faces level with his body. My heart is bursting as my husband collects memories of our son's third day of life and his first day in Hammersmith Hospital.

The room is long and thin; beyond this section is another area that is just as well lit. Su is standing next to me and explains that the front part is for babies and children with neurological conditions, the second section is for premature babies, and there is also another room which is for intensive care babies and children. She informs me how the unit works. Here they allow family and friends to visit their babies, but there is a limit of two people at a time. Opposite Amar there is a boy who is probably a year old with a bandaged head.

In total, this section has ten cots; all except one are occupied with children ranging from newborns to toddlers. Some of them are asleep, some are awake, and all are connected to different machines.

"Do you want to go and hold your son?" she asks and signals to Nik and his parents to come out of the unit. They head for the side door.

I walk into a small room with shelves full of cotton aprons in varying colours and a big open laundry bin. Nik's parents are beaming as they enter. Su walks up to the door and tells Nik to stay there.

"Did you rest, Beta?" Nik's father asks. The need to hold Amar has overwhelmed me, and I am unable to speak.

"He's very strong." Nik's mother takes my hand.

When I step into the sterile room, Nik is taking more photographs. Amar has a catheter in his right hand which is attached to a drip; he still has the oxygen tube in his mouth, but this machine does not have a red rubber balloon that inflates and deflates. The noise of whirring wheels turning, filling his lungs with air, and the beep, beep, beep of the monitor, create a cacophony of sounds that add to the anxiety of my heartbeat.

"Are you ready to hold your son?" she asks both of us, and Nik grins at her. I nod my head. "Jessie, can you come and help," she asks the other nurse.

Jessie is recording some readings in a chart at the unit

with the little boy with the bandaged head.

The chairs are moved to one side of Amar's cot, and Su places a soft cushion on one, "Mummy, sit here." She stands by the oxygen pipe and gathers it up; Jessie pushes the heart monitor and drip closer to where I'm sitting and picks up the attached tubes and wires. "Nik, can you put the camera down and pick up your son and put him in Reena's lap?" Nik is apprehensive. "Don't worry, nothing is going to go wrong," Jessie tells him.

My husband lifts our son in his arms for the first time in his short life, and my heart stops. He carries him close to his chest, his heart beating against our son's tiny heart and a tear plops on our son's chest. He takes short slow steps to me and puts him in my lap, taking his hands away gently as I hold him in my arm. My heart swells; the agony of waiting for this moment takes over, and I, too, release big fat tears that roll down my face. The two nurses move discreetly away. Nik sits down in the chair next to mine and holds his hand, and we both gaze at our beautiful son. If the tube weren't in his mouth, no one would know that he isn't a perfectly healthy baby.

Su comes back. "Do you want me to take some pictures?" she asks.

"Yes, please." Nik shows her what buttons she needs to press, and she takes photographs of us with Amar to add to our collection. We savour the moment, feeling like new parents holding our baby, in awe of the beautiful child we've created.

"Time for Amar's X-ray. We have to put Amar back in the unit," Su tells us.

Nik asks if he can do it and she says yes. I take lots of

pictures of Nik smiling as he puts him back into the plastic cot. We follow Amar as he is wheeled out of the unit. Sunil is standing at the glass partition as we come out. We are beaming from holding our son, and he smiles back at us. "Do you want to come with me to the X-ray, Niku?" Nik turns to me.

"Yes, you go, I'll wait," I say, pointing to the waiting room.

As I say this Umi's head pops out of the room. She rushes to us. "You seem happy?" she questions.

"Nik and Reena have been holding Amar," Sunil informs her.

"Oh, I missed it. I brought my camera."

Nik shows her his camera bag. "I've got photos."

The nurse from the reception desk hands me a key and tells me the rooms are directly above the unit.

"Why don't you girls go and settle in," Nik's mother says.

"I'll fetch you when he's back," Nik's father adds.

The parents' rooms are on both sides of a long corridor in the Victorian building; access to them is up a set of stone stairs on the right of the Specialist Neonatal Unit. The room we are staying in is on the right-hand side of the corridor. Umi opens the heavy door to reveal a small room with a double bed, a wardrobe, a dressing table, a small table and two chairs. On one side of the bed, there is a bedside table with a small bedside lamp. Su was right when she said it was not the Ritz; it was very much like student accommodation with basic but functional furniture.

"You lie down, and we'll put your clothes away," Anne-Marie instructs me. I'm happy to take the weight off my bottom, and lift off the covers and lie down on my side as my friends empty our bag.

Umi leaves the room to explore the kitchen and bathroom. When she comes back, she tells me there are four bathrooms with walk-in showers on this level and the shared kitchen with toast and tea-making facilities is on the right. Her voice drifts away, and all is dark.

My husband wakes me up. "Hello, my love." He is lying on his side, staring intently at me.

"What time is it?"

"Nearly six-thirty," he whispers. I sit up when I suddenly realise he's here with me and search his face for any signs of stress. "Everything's fine, Ree. He's strong. The X-ray went well. Bhai and Jijaji are with him."

"Lie down again. I want a hug."

I wince; my breasts have ached and tingled since I held Amar this afternoon. My cotton breast pads are soaked.

"Have you told anyone about this?" he asks me. I shake my head.

"Ree, you need to look after yourself. Why didn't you tell the nurses?" He sighs. "Where are your pads?" he asks as his eyes search the room. I point to the bedside table. He takes two out and hands them to me.

I open my shirt and feel the heat from my breasts.

He strokes the red blotches and kneels in front of me.

"Oh, my love, what are we going to do about this?"

"I just need to express some milk," I reassure him as the thought that this might not solve the problem seeps into my mind.

Nine

IN THE EVENING WE SIT with our friends and family in the canteen; we have food that Rajesh has brought from Shakti Bhavan and food from the restaurant.

Sunil informs us the neurology team will come to speak with us and will probably ask us questions about our families' medical histories. He stares intently at Nik's father when he says this, and I wonder if there is something that has happened before to a child in the Raja family that Nik is not aware of.

I know very little about my family's medical history and tell him so, and he reassures me that he'll speak with Amit when he gets home.

When everyone goes home, we go back to the unit to spend time with our son and Nik makes me find out where I have to go to express my milk. A dark-haired nurse with a short bob takes me to the maternity unit and shows me how to use the machine. I sit for an hour trying to express the milk, only to fill a small bottle with thirty millilitres of breast milk. When I show her, she says, "That's normal; your baby doesn't need much in the first few days. Try and have a lukewarm shower before bed to help cool your breasts."

"Please, please, give him to me. Please don't take him. Please."

I wake up gasping for breath, the dream still vivid, the faceless man walking faster and faster away from me, taking my child away from me.

The room is pitch black; my stomach lurches, and the telltale taste of bitterness enters my mouth. I sit up to stop the contents of my stomach from coming out and to search for something to be sick in, just in case.

The light comes on. Its yellow glow throws strange shadows in the room. I don't recognise the place.

"Ree, it's all right." Nik has a stainless-steel bowl in his hand. I don't understand where we are; my eyes scan the room in apprehension. He pulls me to him, "It's okay, Ree, we're in Hammersmith Hospital. I'm here. You're safe. I have you."

"He took him away, Nik." I gulp back a sob.

"It's only a dream, my love. No one's going to take him away."

He holds me and wretched sobs fill the silence of the night. My stomach remains clenched; I take several deep breaths to calm myself down. The ache of having Amar taken away from me eases as my heart returns to normal.

"Do you want to go and see him?"

We press the buzzer to the Specialist Neonatal Unit; the clock behind the desk says 5.15 a.m.

"Hello, have you come to see your baby?" the nurse on the desk asks.

We walk to the glass partition. The light above the cot has been dimmed and we gaze on our son; the nurse asks us if we want to go in.

"He'll need a nappy change." I change our son's nappy, while Nik watches, his arm around my shoulders.

* * *

I WALK BACK DOWN THE COLD hospital corridor from the maternity unit and reflect on the process to get another meagre thirty millilitres of breast milk from my sore breasts. The noise had been loud, the suction painful; I felt I'd just come out of a dystopian future, written by George Orwell. The plastic discs, the sterile bottles, the tubes. Whoever thought a soulless grey room with shelving full of boxes, a dark-grey metal machine and a padded chair was conducive for new mothers to express their milk must have been a man, or a woman who had never had children. I was upset my breasts hurt and angry my body had betrayed me. Even the simple job of providing my child with sustenance didn't come without a struggle.

I tell Nik that I will call Jane and Mary from our local NCT group who had left messages on our machine yesterday. I give Mary a call first and tell her the news. She is shocked, to begin with, but soon remembers other parents' networks I could contact from the NCT. She promises to drop off the numbers and details at the house. I thank her and find myself believing there is hope for us, too.

My courage fails me when I speak to Jane, and I bawl down the phone to her. I tell her about the Guru, about Motaba, about the sadness in my father's eyes. I tell her about my early fears, about not wishing to be pregnant, and how I am being punished. She listens, like she always does, quietly breathing through my outbursts, reassuring me this is something that happens, and I am not to blame myself.

When I return to the neonatal unit, Nik's father is watching and laughing, and I walk up to stand beside him. I yelp and his father takes my hand and smiles. My brother is with my son, and my husband is taking photographs and laughing at the three yellow fluffy ducks in various sizes; two of the smaller ducks are in the cot, and Amit is holding the biggest one.

My thoughts go back to another hospital and another anxiety-filled time when Amit and Smita's twins were born. Nik had come to visit with a huge Mickey and Minnie Mouse for Rishi and Rakhee. I smile as I recall the photographs of the tiny twins and their giant plush toys.

Amit waves the soft toy at me, grinning, and Nik turns and points, his face in mock shock at the size of it. I laugh out loud, and Nik's father hugs me, happy at my elation. Amit brings the huge duck out and gives it to me. I hold it in both my arms.

"Hey, Sis." He pulls me for a hug. Searing pain shoots through my breasts. He pushes me to arm's length; two lines appear between his eyebrows. "What's wrong?"

"Nothing."

"Something is wrong, I know that look, you're holding something back."

"It's nothing, Bro. I'm okay, taking my pills, dealing with it. I'm so glad you're here." I smile up at him.

Nik takes my hand and gives me a kiss on the head,

"She'll rest now you're here, Amit."

"Let's go to the waiting room. I've spoken to the duty sister and requested the paediatric doctor come see us at eleven-thirty," Amit adds.

"I'm going to get some tea and coffee, Reena. Do you want tea or shall I get your milk?" Nik asks as he gives my hand to my brother.

A tall, pale-skinned mixed-race woman with dark straightened shoulder-length hair enters and introduces herself as Ceri Thomas. She has a lilting Welsh accent and is softly spoken.

"I wanted to explain what we would be doing today to get a better idea of what is wrong with your son. We had blood tests and the X-ray yesterday. Today we have scheduled an electroencephalogram – EEG, an ophthalmic test and the ENT specialist planned for this afternoon. Once we have this information, Professor Rossi will see you tomorrow morning. We will also take the tube out of his mouth to find out if he has the swallow reflex, but I'm not sure if this will happen today. We hope to get as much as we can done today, so we have a better understanding of his condition."

While the doctor is speaking, Nik's father is writing in my diary. It has become a notebook, no longer my journal; my last entry was five days ago.

"Do you have any questions?" She stops, an open smile on her face, her hands clasped on her lap.

"What part of the brain has been affected?" Nik's father asks.

"We think the Vein of Galen has burst, but can't be certain. I don't want to speculate about what part has been affected, you'll need to ask the professor that."

"When is the EEG happening?" Amit asks.

"This afternoon. They usually come after lunch."

"Will it … will it hurt?" I stammer.

"No, none of the tests we are doing today are intrusive. The EEG is a set of wires that are attached to your son's head, and it measures the brain's activity."

* * *

AMAR IS HAVING AN EEG when I come down after my post-lunch nap. Amit had insisted I rest, telling me off for not taking care of myself. His words resound in my head. 'You're not looking after yourself. You need to eat and rest, Reena. You don't want to get ill. Nik has enough to worry about with the baby.'

Nik and his father are inside; small electrical probes are glued onto our son's head. I hear my brother's voice.

"Jane, so glad to see you."

I turn and watch as my mentor and friend, a tall woman in a navy-blue trouser suit, her handbag slung over her shoulder, walks confidently towards us.

"So, where's my godson?" she asks as she puts her arm around my shoulders, and I point just as a cloth tube is being put on Amar's head. I begin to weep, and I cannot control myself anymore as I sob into Jane's arms. She is a surrogate mother to me; she knows of my fears and misgivings. She passes me to my husband, who has come out to greet her. When I peer up at her, her pale-grey eyes gleam reassuringly as she says with calmness and authority, "Look at him, Reena. Everything will be fine. He's such a bonny baby."

"Come on, Ree. Kaka's going to stay with Amar. Let's go for some fresh air." I hesitate, my eyes drawn to our son. "The EEG will take two hours," Nik informs us.

We take the pedestrian tunnel to the park that runs on the right-hand side of the car park. Jane asks questions and Nik and Amit answer them; both of them know Jane well. She is part of our family. It has been Jane who has frequently come up to see us and cajoled my father into allowing his children to venture out. It was Jane who has eased his misgivings about me marrying Nik. I think about how great she would have been as a mother, but the man she loves is already married, and she has told me that she had made a decision not to have children or guilt him into leaving his wife and children.

The sky is grey, and the easterly wind is stinging, but the fresh air clears my head. I'd forgotten how much I like being outside; it grounds me and allows me to process my thoughts. I savour the biting wind on my cheeks as I hold my brother's hand. Nik leads with Jane, her hand resting on his forearm.

***

RAJESH GIVES ME A KISS on my forehead as I stand up to greet him.

"You're garam." He puts his hand on my forehead. "Niku, has Reena been to the maternity ward today? I don't want you to neglect your health, Reena." He frowns, "You have to rest. Go and have a lie down in your room. I'm here now. You don't need to worry."

Nik walks up with me to our room, and we discuss what he should ask the technician who is performing the EEG.

"Rest, my love, I'll wake you at five o'clock." He kisses me, and I taste the tobacco. I can't remember when he'd lit a cigarillo. I eventually fall asleep after listening to the noise from cars pulling up in the car park and the sounds of the ambulances.

I am woken by a hushed conversation.

"What do you think we should do, Jane?"

"I'm not sure, Pushpa. She needs someone to take care of her, and Nik can't at the moment. She's stubborn. She won't want to go with you."

"I've brought some cabbage leaves, they should ease the pain. But if the milk ducts get infected, she'll have to stop expressing milk."

I sit up to let them know I'm awake. "Jai Shri Krishna, Kaki. When did you come?"

"I've been here since five, Beta. We wanted you to rest longer. I'm worried about you. Niku told me that you might have mastitis. Do you want to show me your breasts?"

I ease my top off and unzip my maternity bra. When I look down, several red blotches are on my left breast.

"What is this white witch doing here?" Motaba darts a disapproving glance at her.

"Nice to see you too, Sarladevi," Jane answers through gritted teeth and smiles, showing her even white teeth. Even though Sarladevi had said this in Gujarati, I'm sure Jane understood what was said as we walk into the kitchen. She had been warming up my dinner, and Nik is sitting at the dining table. "Jai Shri Krishna, Reena. I've brought tindora nu shaak, chora ni dall, bajra na thepla and baath for you to eat. Sit down, and

I'll serve you. Pushpa, can you get a mug for the milk?"

* * *

January 11th,1990

WE HAVE BEEN WAITING for Professor Rossi to speak with us for over an hour, the appointed time has come and gone. The ENT department has sent another technician to perform a few more tests the neurologist has requested. My anxiety is heightened, and I am exhausted from lack of sleep last night.

Every cell in my body is frightened, the slightest sound is loud, my body is heated, and I cannot keep anything down. I have already expelled my breakfast and a snack of tea and biscuits.

Nik and I argued late into the night. I recoil at the way she delivered the news, not an ounce of compassion. 'Your son is not long for this world. All the planets are weak, and he has brought pain and suffering with him. Only if we perform the cleansing havan can the burden of his past sins be washed away. I've asked Jagdishbhai to find a date for the havan to take place. We will hold it at Shakti Bhavan; Amar should be present. Nikesh, can you tell me when he is coming home, so I can make the arrangements?'

She continued to tell everyone of all the other rituals we'd have to perform to help ease his troublesome life. I was numb and dumbfounded by the way she spoke to the waiting group. No one said a word, not even Nik's father, who I know does not support Sarladevi in all the rituals she observes.

Jane broke the silence. "What has she just said, Nik?" she asked.

"I've told my family that they have to do some prayers for Amar, Jane," Sarladevi explained.

"Yes, I can tell, Sarladevi," she replied, "But whatever else you said has left them devastated."

"Leave it alone, Jane," Amit interjected. "Let's go for a walk. Come with me, Reena." His eyes filled with sadness as he held out his hand. We walked back to the glass partition to seek comfort, watching Rajesh holding my son's hand as he watched over him. A small part of my brain recalled the time when he and Rupa had to endure the same outbursts from Motaba.

The distance eased my pain. I knew she meant I was the one who brought on the pain.

Before leaving for the night Nik's father had kissed me on the forehead and seemed deflated; they must have continued once we'd left and the lines in the corners of his eyes had deepened. I felt the resentment build up. I resented myself for allowing her to impose her prejudices and her old-fashioned rituals, and her for causing hurt by her callous words. I cried from the unfairness of it all. Nik tried to hold my clenched fists. "Please, Ree, talk to me. You've said nothing to me since you came back from your walk."

"Why did you let her say that, Nik?" I shouted.

"She has to do this, Ree. It's her way of coping."

"What about my feelings, Nik? Is she more important than I am to you?"

"No, you know you are the world to me," he replied softly.

"What about our son? Is he the world to you, too, Nik?" I asked.

"How can you say that? Of course, he is. I … love him

just as much."

I held my head, and I was back at Shakti Bhavan, the words of the Guru filling my mind.

'Together, you will struggle with your home life. I can see many hurdles that you will need to climb,' he had said, looking intently into my eyes, burning into my soul.

'Give her up, Nikesh, if you want an unburdened life. That would be the best option,' Sarladevi had advised us.

'I can't and won't. I've been searching for Reena all my life. She is my soulmate, Motaba,' Nik had said, holding me close to his side.

"Do you remember what she said about us, Nik?" He nodded, searching my eyes. "Do you remember what you said?"

"I do, but if there is anything that can be done to make Amar's life easier, I'm going to agree to it."

"Did wearing the ring and the fasting make our hurdles go away?"

"I don't know, Ree. Maybe we ignored it and didn't really believe it. Maybe we are too modern to understand the spiritual side of our life. I have to believe this will work. It is all I know." He sighed.

"I can't believe and don't believe there is a malevolent God who punishes you for your sins. What sins has our son committed, Nik? Tell me, and I'll agree with your havan. Tell me, Nik!" I'd shouted at him, my face so close to his that he closed his eyes.

He had stood up, his fists clenched. I felt he wanted to shout back at me, but he turned to the door and walked out, slamming the door behind him with so much force that the room shook. I lay seething with anger, the muscles in my jaw clenched from holding back the tears, my body ready for a fight. I was not going to allow Sarladevi Raja to dictate my son's future.

He came back in the early hours of the morning, smelling of alcohol and tobacco, slipping into bed quietly. "Ree," he whispered.

I changed my breathing, pretending I was asleep. Nik turned his back to mine and fell asleep straight away. He didn't even snuggle up to me as he usually did.

Ten

I WAKE WITH A START, my hair stuck to my forehead, my nightdress clinging like a shroud. My muscles ache as if I have been fighting.

He isn't in bed. His damp towel is drying on the radiator. When I walk past the kitchen, he isn't in there, either. He's probably going to avoid me today like he usually does when we have a fight. *When will he grow up?* I am not going to make it easier for him this time. I can sulk too.

I eat my breakfast of brown toast and drink my hot milk. I was also told to drink dill water to help with breast milk production, but as soon as I finish the glass of water, the contents of my breakfast fill my mouth. Nik is walking up the corridor and follows me into the bathroom. My eyes water and the contents of my stomach end up in the toilet bowl; he rubs my back, his hands are warm. I long for his touch. I want to push him away. He makes me lie on the bed.

"You're not too good today."

"Didn't sleep much last night," I tell him.

"I'm sorry, my love. I shouldn't have left you last night." He apologises, lifting my palms to his soft lips.

I think, *yes, you shouldn't have, you should have stayed with me, comforted me and told me everything was going to be okay.* But you ran to Jay, and he did what he always does, ply you with drink. I don't say it out loud, but he knows from my eyes and sits, deflated, on the bed.

He comes with me to the maternity ward and helps with the cups and tubes as I try in vain to express milk from my sore breasts. We don't speak much. We continue to function as a couple, but I hold my anger and resentment towards him and his family.

When we come to the ward, I am relieved to see I have the majority of supporters on my side today, as if we are on two different corners of a boxing match.

Dick went to the canteen and brought back some teas and coffees for us. Professor Rossi enters, proffering her hand to everyone. I pull my hand away from Nik and his eyes fill with hurt as I sit in between Jane and Amit. Dick places himself in the corner of the small waiting room.

Professor Rossi sits opposite us and begins to explain the results of the test performed on our son.

She is a plump woman with huge breasts that burst out of her white coat, her black hair cut short and layered; she wears no make-up, and a pair of rectangular black-rimmed glasses hang from a gold chain around her neck. She speaks immaculate English, as most people who have learnt it as a second language do, using words that are hardly spoken in everyday use. She has the confidence of someone who is used to being listened to.

She explains that the MRI shows Amar had a severe brain haemorrhage that had begun in the centre of the brain where there is a major blood vessel. The EEG confirmed he is not experiencing any unusual electrical activity that prevents him from responding. She tells us the eye tests show damage to the retina and he is blind. It was too soon to diagnose whether he could hear. She speaks precisely and pauses briefly after each point.

"I am so sorry to inform you that your son's life cannot be sustained without the machine."

My life falls apart. My world becomes dull and the colour drains in front of my eyes. A gaping hole grows in my heart. I listen to the questions Jane asks but don't comprehend them; the words slip out of my mind as they enter. My eyes dart from one face to another, my heart thumping so loudly my eardrums ache. My skin feels so sensitive I feel my clothes burning against it. I resist the urge to rip them off.

All of my hopes and dreams shatter; my reluctance to embrace the pregnancy gnaws at my conscience. The decision I made about another pregnancy sits like a heavy mill stone on my chest.

How can I still be alive? I think, shouldn't my heart stop, how much more can it take before it gives up and allows me the relief from the pain? I wish for oblivion. Then I think it can't be true, it's just another one of my vivid nightmares, and I'll soon wake up, Nik holding me, caressing my hair. He stands up, takes my hands and pulls me up, holding me. I can't stand his touch and flinch, and he loosens his hold.

"If you'd excuse us, Professor Rossi, my wife and I need some time to process this."

Jane hands him our coats, and he takes me out of the ward. We walk down the pedestrian walkway; the people coming towards us are blurred.

The bitter cold stings at my face as we enter the rear car park. Nik takes out a cigarillo and lights it as we walk to the park.

Time stops as we stand under a tree, my head resting on his shoulder, as he blows the smoke away from my face, and we watch the people in the park. Everyone is either pushing a pram or has young children with them. Taunting us with the life that has been ripped from us by the words that reverberate in my ear. 'Your son's life cannot be sustained without the machine.'

Dick walks up to us slowly, his eyes bloodshot from crying. He pulls me towards him and gently hugs me, knowing my body is in pain, both physically and mentally.

I glance to where Nik is standing, his arms hanging limply by his sides. Dick lets go of me and hugs Nik, and his body convulses as he cries. A sob escapes my mouth. Both men are by my side each holding me by my waist. I finally let go and cry for the loss of the life I'd begun to imagine for us.

***

RAJESH HAS URGED US to keep him alive and promised he would find a private care home for our son, but Nik and I have already discussed what we'd have wanted if we were in the same situation and want our son to have the same fate. Within a few hours, nurses have moved Amar to the back of the unit to a long thin room. The blinds are pulled down, and the lighting is subdued. The rules are relaxed in this section. Everyone is allowed inside, waiting and watching Amar, his life only possible through the aid of the machine. They have taken off the drip to enable us to sit with him in our laps. Nik is recording every minute of his short life. We are all aware that these photographs will be our only memory of Amar Raja.

I spoke to the maternity ward, and they've advised I stop expressing. My breasts suddenly decide to fill up and expel milk at the slightest thought of my son. I've had to change twice, my breast pads struggling to cope with the volume.

The nurses have shown us how to move the machine and oxygen tank to allow us to hold him in our arms. My arms are aching from his weight as I hold him. I marvel at how heavy and tall he is; his face has developed a double chin, and I wish he would open his eyes just once so I can see if he has my eyes or his father's. In my dreams, he has always had his father's eyes. Nik is sitting next to me on the sofa, holding his hand. He starts to sing, the song by the Carpenters that he's sung since he felt Amar's first kick, "Close to You", telling him we want him to be close us. The nurses gather at the entrance, enchanted by the voice. Tears roll down his face as he continues to croon to our son, and I, too, allow tears to roll down my face. Our family hold hands as they watch.

We both have a troubled sleep. I wake to a sobbing noise and realise Nik is crying in his sleep. I push and pull at him to wake him up, but he is so deep in his nightmare that it takes all my strength to bring him back to me. I panic: what if he never wakes up? What if this is what happens when people say that they died of a broken heart? Eventually, I leap off the bed, turn on the lights and lift myself above him, kissing his face, hoping he will open his eyes. When he opens his eyes, he seems like a small boy, and, I think, *this is what Amar would look like if he could live and have bad dreams.*

"I had a bad dream," he says and takes me in his arms. He kisses me for comfort and to wash away the sadness.

We hold each other until we both fall asleep again, leaving the bedside lamp on, fearing the darkness and the unknown demons that haunt our dreams. I wake with a start, shouting, my pleas unheeded, tears rolling down my face.

"I have you, Ree. You're safe," Nik tells me, locking his eyes onto mine. They are dull and dark. Where have the golden shards gone? I inhale and smell the tobacco and musk of his scent and close my eyes again.

He whispers, "Sleep, it's still dark outside."

We both fall into a deep dark abyss.

***

THE NEXT DAY THE WARD is full of our friends and family who have come to visit our son before his life-support machine is switched off. I recall the duty nurse at Ealing complaining about the number of people in the waiting room, but here they haven't once told us off for blocking the waiting room or the ward.

All of Nik's family have come. Ashi and Suresh are visibly upset at the news, and she grabs my hand.

"I'm so, so sorry, Ree. I've wanted to come since Sunday. It has been agony waiting to see you. I should have come earlier."

Jaish and Anil are subdued and quiet, which is odd, considering they are usually the loudest and most jovial of all the family. I wait for my family to come. Amit has called Smita and told her to bring the kids and my father as soon as she can. Everyone is allowed to hold Amar, and photographs are taken. Nik is trying to keep busy; he is creating a memory album. Most of the shots are of our family and friends holding Amar and smiling, but their eyes are full of sadness. Dick has brought his guitar, and he and Nik sing songs, softly in hushed voices, not wanting to disturb the other babies and families in the unit.

"Jai Shri Krishna, why are you singing these English songs? Put on the Bhagavad-Gita. We want his soul to rest in peace. If you do this, he clings to the material world," Motaba chides as she steps into the darkened room.

They stop in mid-flow and stand up, hurt by the comment, unable to tell the woman these are the songs that he has heard when he was safe in my tummy. The songs he kicked and danced to; his favourite songs.

"Why did you stop, Beta? Dick? That was lovely." My father has come. He gives Sarladevi a nod, "Keep singing, boys. My grandson has listened to you for most of his short life." Dick picks up his guitar and asks my father what song he should play.

"I think some Nat King Cole. Isn't that his and his mama's favourite, Reena?"

Dick plucks the chords, and Nik begins to sing again. I pass my son to Sarladevi. She holds him with trepidation, and then her face softens with a smile and she says, "He is just like your papa, Nikesh. I hadn't noticed before." That photograph is one of the few that has smiling eyes and a smiling face.

Nik's voice softly sings "Smile", the song that brings hope to lovers with broken hearts.

The rest of the day and evening is filled with people coming to see Amar. Jay arrived after five and had taken Nik away. I sit with Smita, dreading the time as it passes slowly, expecting my husband to come back drunk, unable to support me when I need him most.

"So, where is he?" Umi asks, disapproval in her voice.

"He's gone with Jay."

"And you let him? You are incredible, Ree. Why would you let that guy do this to you?" She is pulling her hair up into a messy knot.

"Leave it, Umi. He needs some escape from all this." I use my hand to gesture at the room.

"And you don't?" she asks, her eyebrows raised.

I purse my lips. *I need to escape, too, but I feel responsible for what is happening to our son.*

At six-thirty, I hear a familiar voice in the corridor. I have come back to the waiting room to escape the gnawing anxiety and pain that has built up since Nik left with Jay. My stomach is full of clenched fists bombarding it, and the bile has risen again as I wait. This is the second day I have not been able to keep any food down.

"Where's Reena?"

"She's in here." Anne-Marie pokes her head out.

Gino walks in with Nik behind him. "I've brought him back to you, Reena. Don't ever allow him to go out with that idiot again."

Nik looks sheepish, and his eyes lock on mine. I take a sharp breath; his eyes are brown and bloodshot, the yellows and the ochres have disappeared completely.

"I've tried to knock some sense into your stupid husband's head. He's responsible for your wellbeing and your son's. Isn't that right, Nik?" He turns to confront him. Nik shuffles towards the vacant space that Smita has just created next to me, his head bowed. "I'm sorry, my love. I thought we were going for a cigarette break." He is clasping both of his hands. And then he weeps, his sobs wretched, his breath laboured, and we wait for him to quieten down. Gino has sat down by his side and put his arms around his shoulders for comfort. I rest my head on his shoulder, silently crying, not allowing the enormity of what is happening to sink in. Otherwise, I will also lose all control. I have let my mind go numb and focused only on the task at hand, making sure everyone has a personal connection to remember Amar.

We had agreed with the duty nurse that the machine should be switched off at night and Nik and I would be the only two people present. When we'd told everyone, there had been complaints from my father and Nik's parents. Telling us we were too young to deal with the situation alone, that they should be there to help us. I was adamant we would do this alone, as a couple. To placate our parents, we agreed to call if we couldn't cope. Motaba had clung to Nik for a long time, and she had turned to hug me. I was shocked by her tenderness. She had never hugged me with the warmth I felt in all the years that I had known her. I'd watched her hug her children and Ashi, who she had known most of her life, but she never hugged Rupa Bhabhi or me.

"Put on the Gita and give him gangajal," she'd said to me when she released me.

We wait for everyone to leave. I still can't keep any food down. My body's adrenaline level has risen. Usually, I run and hide, but today I'm ready to fight. It feels strange to have this sensation. I wonder, is what motherhood does to women? I've heard many stories of a mother's acts of bravery to protect their children.

Thursday, January 11th, midnight

AMAR IS IN MY LAP. Nik sitting by my side, holding his hand, cooing and singing softly. Su is on duty tonight, and she talks us through the process, reassuring us that he will not feel any pain when the tube is taken out of his mouth. At five days, twenty-two hours and forty-five minutes, the oxygen supply is pulled out of our son, and we gasp at his arms flaying, the movement jagged, the first time Amar has moved his arms away from his side.

The portable music player is reciting the Gita in the background and Nik adds a drop of gangajal into our son's unobstructed mouth. He has a tilak on his forehead and is wearing pale-blue dungarees with leaping sheep embroidered on the bib. I hold him in my arms, willing him to take a breath and defy everyone. "Be strong," I urge him. "Fight for your life. Fight to stay with us."

"Yes, fight to stay with us, Diku," Nik confirms. Nik takes my chin and makes me look into his eyes, the eyes that have lost their golden shards. "No matter what happens, we'll cope. I promise everything will be all right." He kisses me tenderly.

The rhythm of Amar's chest slows, the laboured breaths from the machine cease, and he takes a deep breath. We both hold our breath, and he exhales, a long slow breath. I look at the clock; the time says quarter past twelve. I close my eyes, not ready to see him leave us.

I feel his breath as my hand rests on his back; he inhales slowly, feebly, and releases wobbly exhalations. A gurgling sound comes from the back of his throat. My eyes open to confirm the rise and fall of Amar's chest. The breaths are tiny and feeble, but they are there. He is breathing on his own.

"Su! Su!" Nik stands up abruptly.

Su rushes in and uses a stethoscope to listen to Amar's heart. She walks out, brings back a small machine with a tube, puts it into his mouth and suctions out the liquid that has accumulated. She turns to us and says, "He's strong, but it's still too early to build up your hopes." She turns him onto his side in my arms. "Try to keep him on his side. I'm going to call for the doctor on duty."

We watch our son breathe unaided for the first time in his short life and grin at each other. Nik turns my face up to his and kisses me and then kisses our son. I rest my head on his shoulder, and I feel like a mother for the first time. We are a family. It might not be the life that we'd planned, but our son is alive, and we are the parents of a severely disabled child.

Nik has gone to the kitchen to get us a hot drink and have a cigarette break. When he comes back, he is smiling and holding his mother's hand. I read the clock; it is only four o'clock in the morning.

"We couldn't sleep, too worried about you ... sometimes even the doctors are wrong," she says as she sits down next to me.

A few minutes later, the grandfathers enter; my father is carrying a tray of mugs. Nik takes it from him. I hand our baby to his grandmother and rush up to my daddy.

He kisses my forehead and says, "He's as stubborn as his mother. I think we've got another fighter in our family." I laugh and then burst into tears. "What's the matter, Reena?" Nik's father touches my shoulder.

"Nothing, I'm so glad you're here." I wipe my nose with the disintegrated tissue I've been using.

When we go back to our room, I cannot hold my body upright anymore, and I collapse onto the bed. I begin to cry. Nik pulls me to him, his arms comforting, and we both cry tears of apprehension. We had been prepared for Amar to leave this world, our life almost back to how it was without a child.

"Our son is a fighter just like his mother," he murmurs as he kisses me on my forehead. "It's going to be interesting."

Even though we don't speak of it, we know we are both thinking of his diagnosis and the fact that we have no idea how to take care of a child with a disability and we have no idea what the quality of his life is going to be.

"We'll manage," I say in reply and we fall asleep from exhaustion.

***

SUNIL HAS ARRIVED at 10.00 a.m to accompany us to see the obstetrician and Dr Hussain at Ealing Hospital. I'm apprehensive about leaving our son; he still isn't out of danger, and I want to be nearby. I ask him to cancel, but he tells me that it's best to keep it as I need a check-up.

"But, what if … " I wipe my nose.

Nik has his arm around my waist. "Nothing is going to happen while we're gone. Kaka, Kaki and Daddy are here."

"We'll be back before you know it. Reena, I've arranged to speak with the paediatric doctor after lunch. It won't be long." Sunil adds.

I'm upset and angry with the obstetrician, a man in his late fifties with greying hair, who believes natural childbirth is an abomination and, if he had his way, all mothers would be strapped to monitors throughout their labour. Dr Hussain does not give an apology for her actions and blames everything on her junior who had misinformed her. When Sunil asks to examine the monitor readings, they both bristle and decline, until he insists, saying he would rather see them today and not waste their time again.

"I'm never coming to this hospital again," I tell Nik, as we leave his office, making sure the people in the waiting room hear. They know I am angry and don't say a word as we walk back to the car. Eventually I let go of my anger with a sigh.

"Amar's heart monitoring shows no sign of stress, so the haemorrhage must have happened at birth," Sunil informs us. He had taken notes and tears the sheets out of his notebook and passes them to me. "Put these into your diary," he adds and starts the car.

***

WE GRAB SANDWICHES for lunch as we head back to the ward. The duty nurse greets us and tells us that Amar is doing really well and that we have visitors in the waiting room. Ravi has brought Rohini to see

Amar. She is a thin small-boned woman with almond-shaped eyes, shy in nature, who clings to her husband when they are at any social event.

"Hello, Reena and Nik." She stands up. "I've bought a gift for your son." She reaches for a blue gift bag and hands it to me.

"It's good news, right?" Ravi asks Nik.

"Yes," we both reply, smiling at him. He and Rohini have been trying to have children since their wedding night without any success.

"Have you been to see him yet, Rohini?" I ask.

"No, we were waiting for you. It would be nice to have a photo of us together," she replies quietly.

I put down my lunch and take her hand, and we walk ahead, our husbands following.

"Ravi told me he was big, but he's a giant." She grins at us. "Can I hold him?"

My father hands Amar to Rohini. Once he's in her arms, her eyes glisten, and she adds, "He's beautiful."

I suddenly feel sympathy for her; we have been urging Ravi to think about IVF. He is reluctant; I'm not sure if it's the cost or the fact that the success rate isn't high, and he doesn't want to subject his wife to the pain. The grandparents leave the room after taking a photograph of us. We sit and talk about how our life has changed.

***

BY THE TIME IT'S TWO O'CLOCK, all the older siblings and their partners have arrived at the hospital, and the parents have been sent home to rest. We have agreed between us that Amar will not be left alone and a schedule for a vigil is drawn up. Smita and Rupa are with Amar when the paediatric doctor arrives to explain why our son is still with us. It is the same doctor who had come to speak with us previously, and she begins to explain the new diagnosis to us. Instead of sitting opposite her, we spread ourselves out in the small waiting room. Amit is writing up the notes and sits with Rita who silently prompts him. The doctor clears her throat and begins to explain the new diagnosis.

"We know the medulla oblongata has not been affected by the damage caused by the vein of Galen bursting. So, your son is very similar to someone who is in a coma; all the bodily functions, breathing, swallowing, heart, blood pressure, consciousness, and sleep and awake states are working. I want to get a genealogist to take some information about your family history to rule out anything we've missed genetically. In the meantime, all I can say is that he is still very poorly, and we will be monitoring him closely throughout the weekend. He will stay in the room he is in, and you and your family are free to come and go."

"If you're saying he's in a coma, does that mean Amar can wake up from it?" Rajesh asks her.

"I'm saying it's like someone who is in a coma. There is extensive damage from the haemorrhage; we can't tell if he is okay. Some research shows babies like Amar recover some function, but still have a severe disability. I'm sorry I can't say any more. The best person to ask is Professor Rossi; she'll come to explain the next steps to you on Monday. I'll try and schedule any additional tests we need as soon as possible bearing in mind it is Friday and most of the departments are closed over the weekend."

We thank her, and everyone presents anecdotal evidence of recovery from a coma, pinning our hopes on this being the case with Amar.

During the afternoon we all sit with our son, listening to music from Nat King Cole, the Carpenters, The Beatles, a compilation of our favourite music that we'd listened to when Amar was in my tummy. Sunil had informed us that music was an essential tool for children with disabilities. The nurse brings a small electric blanket and wraps him in it, reassuringly adding, "Some babies need some extra heat in their early life; he's just a bit cold. I'll come to check on him in an hour. He should be nice and toasty by then."

Amit and Sunil exchange a concerned look; my heart clenches, my eyes sting, and I begin to cry. Nik gets up from the sofa and swiftly pulls me to his side. "It's okay, Ree. We just have to take it a step at a time."

The anxiety that had somewhat diffused is back; the contents of my stomach threaten to come out, and the thought of losing him again is too hard to bear. Everyone looks away as I hold Amar and the tears continue to run down my face unhindered.

* * *

A DOCTOR WITH A CLIPBOARD enters the room and introduces herself as Seema Sharma; she informs us that she has come to collect our family's medical history. Everyone has gone to the canteen for a break and Nik, Rajesh and I are the only people in the room. Amar's temperature has returned to normal, and the electric blanket has been taken away. She sits down on one of the chairs.

"I've got a form I'll have to work with so please bear with me. I have baby's name. Can I ask who the parents are?" She has a Midlands accent.

Nik tells her, and she fills in our names, our ages, our ethnicity on her form.

"Are you related in any way? First cousins, second cousins?" We both shake our heads. "Do you have anyone in your family that has a genetic disorder?"

I explain my mother is not alive and that I have no contact with her only remaining relative, her brother.

"Do you have siblings?"

I tell her I have a brother.

"Does he have children?"

I inform her of the twins. She frowns and asks how early they were and whether they had any health problems. She asks if my father is healthy. I tell her yes, thinking that the chest infections from his tar-coated lungs are not applicable in this case. When she asks about my mother, I cannot reply.

Nik takes my hand. "Reena was only three when her mother passed away. Her mother died of an overdose."

She apologises and turns her head to Nik.

"The same questions apply to you, Nikesh. Anyone with a genetic disorder?"

Nik answers with a no.

"Sorry, I need to butt in here. Nikesh and I share the same father. But we don't share the same mother."

"So, you are Nikesh's older brother. Your mother is not Nikesh's mother?"

"Yes, that's correct."

"So, your father remarried?"

"No, my father and Nikesh's mother are not married."

"What are you saying Bhai … that Papa and Kaki had an affair?" Nik's eyes have fiery embers in them.

"No that's not what I said. Kaki is not your mother, but Papa is your father."

"Why would you say that about Papa, Bhai! He's not here to defend himself." He stands up, his fist clenched, his shoulders hunched.

"Can you excuse us, please?" Rajesh turns to the genealogist, who is sitting in her chair.

"Sure, I'll come back later." She throws a sympathetic glance at me.

"How … how do you know this?"

"I've been told this, Niku. Reena can you fetch Ritu?"

I'm reluctant to leave Nik and hesitate. I stand up and lock eyes with Nik. "Nik, please, sit down, Nik."

His eyes focus on mine, and he sits down on the sofa. I hand him our son and kneel in front of him, holding his hand. "I'm just going to fetch Ben. I'll be back soon." He nods, and his eyes fall on our son's face.

"I love you."

I walk towards the exit door of the ward, numb from the shock of what I've just heard. I concentrate my entire mind on the job of fetching Nik's older sister.

I meet them as they are coming up the pedestrian tunnel. Amit rushes to me. "What's the matter?"

I shake my head. "Everything's fine. I've come to fetch Ben."

Rita frowns, her expression changing when she obviously remembers the genealogist is due to visit. She shouts back to the others as we walk briskly back to the ward. "Can you wait in the waiting room until we fetch you?"

Rita sits next to her younger brother and puts her arm around him. She beckons me to sit down and clasps my hand.

"What does Niku know, Bhai?"

"Only the basics, Ritu. I thought we should tell him together."

My husband is incredibly still; he is stroking our son's cheek with his finger.

"When we were younger, Papa spent most of his time in the Nairobi office. It was there that he met your mother. They had an affair, and she became pregnant with you. Kaki lost a child about the same time you were born and because your mother's family didn't want to keep you, Papa and Motaba went to fetch you, and you came into our family. You're still my little brother, Niku," Rajesh implores.

"Just like you're my little brother," Rita adds.

"When did you find out?" Nik's voice is choked.

"Papa told us when he had his first heart attack," Rita answers.

"Everyone knows I'm a bastard!" The anger is palpable.

"Don't you ever use that word about yourself. You are Nikesh Raja. Your father's name is on your birth certificate. My father's name is on your birth certificate."

"Have you seen it?" He glares accusingly at them both. They reply yes together.

"Kaka has shown it to us. He has other documents that you can read through," Rajesh expands.

"Who else knows? How many people? I need to know," he quizzes them; his voice has risen slightly.

"Motaba, Kaka, Kaki, me, Bhai and Sunil. Just the six of us. No one else, Niku," Rita answers his question calmly, although I sense Nik's birth has been discussed recently with other people.

"Where is my mother? What country does she live in? Who is she?"

"Your mother isn't alive, Niku. I'm sorry, she died a long time ago." Rita rests her head on his shoulder.

His head turns to her. "Can you take Amar? I need to take a walk with Reena."

We walk back to our room to fetch our coats, and Nik asks me, "Do you mind if we get away from here? I know you don't want to be far from Amar, but I can't do this … here." His eyes are full of hurt; at least he hasn't run away from me this time.

The strong painkiller I took this morning has numbed the pain of my stitches, but I soon realise they don't work on sports car seats. He slides into the driver's seat and we head back to the place we can truly call our own.

Eleven

THE HEAVY SCENT OF FLOWERS fills our nostrils as we open the front door; there are several bouquets on the display unit, coffee table and the dining table. I see a stack of colourful drawings, too, and smile.

I walk him upstairs to our bedroom. I pull down the blinds, and I start to take off my clothes. He watches, his eyes dark, his arms hanging by his side, as I peel off my clothes. Once I'm naked, I unbutton his shirt, slide it off his shoulders and take off all his clothes. His eyes haven't strayed once. They are fixed on my face, the golden shards ignite.

"Hold me Nik," I murmur. "I've missed you."

I've missed being in my own home, in my own bedroom, with no one around. I want my husband to show me he loves me and hold me without feeling guilty. I want him to know he is still the man I love and that it doesn't matter to me who he comes from.

He takes me into his arms and skin touches skin; the sensation of belonging seeps through to my soul. He falls on his back onto the bed and pulls me on top of him, gently pushing my legs apart.

I wince as the pain of my stitches sears through my body. He lifts me down to his side and turns to gaze at me, his head raised on one elbow, his eyes full of concern. "Heavy petting?" A small smile draws across his face.

"More like heavy kissing," I tell him, pointing to the red blotches on my breast.

"I like heavy kissing," he says as his soft lips brush mine, gently at first and then his tongue searches mine with lust and longing. His hands massage my body gently in all the places that don't hurt. I stroke his body in all the places he wants me to. Once we have satisfied ourselves with the feel of our bodies, we get under the covers. I rest my head on his chest, and he begins to tell me how he feels about the news he has just received.

He is hurt that his papa didn't tell him in person. He rants about the unfairness of not having him here to quiz him on who, why, and how it happened. He recounts times when Motaba has said things that didn't make sense which do now. He feels like he doesn't know who he is, and he has lost his identity. He cries silent tears as he talks of the mother he will never know. I listen, holding his hand, squeezing it for reassurance and kissing his palm when I sense his pain.

***

"HOW WILL WE KNOW if it's my genes that have caused Amar's brain injury?" he asks me.

"The same way we don't know if it's mine. I don't know much about my mother, either," I tell him.

He raises a smile when I say that. "I love you Reena

Raja, my wife, my life." He stops and kisses my knuckles one at a time. Two off-duty nurses walk past us and giggle at the sight. We walk back from the car park to the specialist ward where our son has defied all odds and is still alive.

Dinner has been brought by Suresh; the night-time vigil crew are due to arrive soon. Rajesh and Rita take Nik aside and talk to him quietly as everyone else in the kitchen fills a paper plate. Sarladevi has provided a feast for dinner.

"You can eat most of it, Reena, except I've got juwar ni bhakri instead of rotli for you," Suresh instructs.

Anne-Marie is with Amar, and I promised her I'll go down as soon as I finish eating, so she can have dinner, too. Nik hugs his older brother and sister and sits next to me, grabbing a plate and filling it with food. I take his hand in mine, and our fingers entwine. He gives me a kiss on my lips. Everyone gawks at us and smiles. "What?" he asks, his eyebrows raised.

"Nothing, nothing. It's nice to see you two behave like your old selves," Rupa Bhabhi replies.

Vigil Dinner

Khaman Dhokla
steamed cake made with gram flour and spices

Ringda mattar nu shaak
aubergine and peas curry

Tuwar ni dall
thin pigeon pea broth

Baath
plain boiled rice

Rotli
rolled unleavened round flatbread roasted in a griddle pan

Dhana marcha ni chutnee
fresh coriander and green chilli chutney

Kachumber
salad made with lettuce, cucumber, carrots, tomatoes and onions

Chaas
natural yoghurt drink blended with water

Burfi
traditional sweet made with milk powder and sugar, cut into squares

Kaju Katli
traditional sweet made with ground almonds and sugar, cut into diamonds

Phulli Gathiya
deep fried noodles made with gram flour and black pepper

Fruit

Saturday, January 13th, lunchtime

JAISHREE AND ANIL HAVE BROUGHT us mushroom soup, brown bread, salad and some fruit yoghurt. I'd requested it as spicy food burns my throat, and I'm still struggling to keep food down. Sarladevi had succumbed and allowed Jaishree to make the soup.

"Go and eat your lunch," Jaishree had told us, shooing us away from the ward.

We are finishing our yoghurt when Nik's parents enter the kitchen. They wait at the door. Nik rushes to hug his mother; she buries her head in his chest, her arms holding onto her son. His father is holding a large brown envelope, his expression tearful as he watches his wife and son. Nik releases her, still holding onto her hands, and says, "Thank you for being my mother and never making me feel I wasn't your flesh and blood."

She gulps back a sob, hugs him again, and says, her voice almost a whisper, "But I woke up at night for your feeds; I held you when you were hurt. Flesh and blood aren't important to me, Niku. You are my son."

He smiles at her and grabs his father's shoulder, pulls him close and says, "Thank you for being the best father anyone can have. I love you both."

I watch them relax, and Nik guides them to the kitchen table. "Do you want some tea?" he asks.

I lean across the table and clasp their hands, my eyes glistening. I wasn't sure how this meeting was going to go. Nik hasn't mentioned his birth mother again; both of his parents' eyes are rimmed with red, and the dark circles that we have all developed recently are much more pronounced.

When he comes back to the table, he sits down next to me and takes my hand. We sit opposite each other; the envelope is like a burning sign of the secret between parents and child.

Nik's father taps the envelope and says, "It was given to me by Motabhai. He told me to take care of this until you were ready to find out about your origin." A tear rolls down his cheek. "I wish you never had. I wanted you to be my son forever; now you'll prefer to be Ramprakash Raja's son. My brother is a tough act to follow."

The sentence is barely audible; his wife places her hand on top of her husband's as it rests on the envelope.

"Kaka … Kaka, please look at me. I will always be your son. I just need to find out who my birth mother is. Where's my mother's family? I want to know where some of my habits are from. I'm different; I've always felt that. I want to know why the first thing I do when there's a problem is run. No one else does that in our family. That must be from my mother's family."

"I can't tell you those things, Niku. I know you have her eyes. I'm not sure you'll be able to find that in here." He taps the envelope. "Perhaps you run away because we overindulge you. All of us, including your brothers and sisters."

We drink our tea in silence as Nik builds up the courage to view the contents of the envelope.

"Can we go to the canteen? I think we'd probably get a bit more privacy," Nik asks as we hear footsteps in the corridor.

Nik's father picks up the envelope, and we make our way to the quiet canteen and settle on a table in the farthest corner.

I ease myself onto the chair that Nik has pulled out for me, his hand resting on my lower back. His father does the same for his wife. I think that if anyone saw them, they would think that father and son had the same mannerisms. Nature probably has very little over nurture when it comes to habits.

"Do you want us to tell you why we became your parents and not Motabhai and Bhabhi?" his mother asks. Nik nods, his eyes resting on the brown envelope.

"We had a little girl who was born on the seventh of September. She had to be delivered by an emergency c-section." She pauses and wipes her nose with a handkerchief. "I was in Nairobi for the delivery, and there were some complications ... she only lived for five minutes. I didn't know that then. Your kaka was with her when she ... I had to have an emergency hysterectomy. I was devastated, we both were ... "

A sob leaves her; her hands shake from the memory. Her husband lifts her up and takes her in his arms. They hold each other for comfort, and I realise they have felt what we have been feeling before and are reliving their nightmare again.

"Do you want me to carry on?" he asks her as he pulls her chair closer to his and she shakes her head.

"When Bhabhi found out about our daughter, she came to Nairobi straight away. She saw how the loss of our child took its toll on us. We couldn't function. That's why it's been difficult for us to help you. It brings back too many memories for us. We're sorry we've not been strong for you," she continues.

"That was when she found out about you. Motabhai confessed to her. She was furious; she has always hated the way we behave, our drinking, our visits to hotels, our eating of meat. We had grown up in Africa with the British; she came to Africa after her marriage from India. She was angry. She hated that her husband had betrayed her; she wanted to meet the woman who had become pregnant with his child. She berated him every day until he gave in and took her to see your mother," Nik's father adds, his eyes saddened by the memory.

"That's when they came back with you. You made me want to live again. You are my saviour, your glittering eyes, your beautiful voice. I nursed you, my milk made you strong. You are my son, Niku, and no one can take that away from me," his mother adds defiantly.

Nik reaches across the table, takes his mother's hands and kisses them. "I know that, Kaki. You are my mother; you will always be my mother."

I feel warmth for the woman, who is holding her ground, telling Nik he is her son.

"You knew my mother, didn't you, Kaka?"

"Yes, I knew her. She worked as a typist at an office we shared when we first started trading in machine parts. She was intelligent and good-humoured; she used to sing at a hotel I used to frequent with some of my friends. She had the most beautiful melodious voice. That's where you get your musicality, Niku."

I recall a conversation I had with my father at the beginning of my third year, about a friend of my mother's.

"One evening I'd wanted Motabhai to meet with new

clients at the hotel. We'd eaten at the restaurant, and they wanted to go to the bar for drinks. Alma was singing that night. She had an emerald-green dress that showed off her curves, and she had put her hair up, so Motabhai didn't recognise her. But he was mesmerised; he couldn't stop staring at her. He didn't listen to a word we'd said. He turned himself around and watched her sing like a songbird. Motabhai insisted on seeing her after she had finished. I protested, naturally. I reminded him he was married. He told me it was purely business, that she could be the next Lata Mangeshkar. When she greeted him using his name, he was shocked. She told him she needed a steady income as she was paying for her younger brother's boarding fees at Dehradun, and she was also supporting her widowed mother. She told him Hindi film playback singer was not the job she wanted. He was impressed with her reply. He promised he'd find a well-paid job for her." He paused and stroked the knuckles on his wife's hand.

"I'd secured a big deal for us and had to come back to Kampala," his lips twitched upwards as he turned to his wife. "When I went back to Nairobi three months later, she was his PA, and she had given up singing in the hotel. I warned Motabhai about his infatuation. He tried to keep his distance, but your mother fell for his natural charm, hook, line and sinker. They began spending time in our flat. She would sing to him while he unwound. She was a good listener, never judging; people were drawn to her. Everyone shared their problems with Alma. Your motaba comes from a wealthy, traditional Hindu family; the women don't sit with their husbands. They do work in the house. The men sit with men. We are very different from how she grew up. He would ask her to come to the hotel for drinks with us, but she would decline. Bhabhi's religion is her rock. She lives by it daily and going to hotels didn't, still doesn't, sit well with her. She didn't take the time to sit with him or listen to his fears."

"My Pushpa," he continues, squeezing his wife's hand, "is born and bred in Africa. She can appreciate the advantages of both cultures. I think he was lonely. He needed someone. He saw how my life was different from his and Alma gave him what he needed. It's not an excuse, but it can explain what happened."

There is a long silence as Nik absorbs the information. "You'll have to look at the documents. There's a letter from your grandmother and a few postcards, an original birth certificate. I've not read them. I've seen your birth certificate because we needed it for our adoption documents."

Nik reaches for the envelope and drops the contents on the table. There is an airmail envelope, two photo postcards, a black and white photograph and an official-looking A4 card with an embossed stamp. He picks up the card. "Her surname was Merchant?"

"Yes, she was a Parsi, born and educated in Mombasa. That's where her mother lived," Nik's father tells him.

"But I was born in Nairobi?"

"Motabhai paid for the hospital fees," he replies.

"Were you in the same hospital, Kaki?"

"Yes, I was. I had to stay there for a month after my operation. I remember the day you were born. The day is imprinted in my brain."

He holds up the photograph; it is a landscape portrait of a happy couple, looking directly at the camera and smiling. The man resembles Rajesh with slicked-back hair; he is wearing a light safari jacket, his arm around the woman's shoulders. She is younger than him. She is wearing a boat neck sleeveless dark-floral dress and a white wide-brimmed hat, and they are each holding a glass. She looks like a European woman; her irises are light and sparkly and they glare challengingly at the photographer. He reads the postcards and passes them to me.

Ram
You've turned my world upside down. I cannot sleep. I cannot eat. I cannot play my harmonium. I'm useless. Please believe me. This is love. I know it deep in my soul.
AM

Ram
When you ignore me, my heart breaks. I need to be with you. Trust in your feelings. Trust in my feelings for you. I'm a grown woman. I know what I'm doing.
It is what I want. I don't want anyone else. I want you.
AM

They are the words of a woman who has fallen in love, perhaps for the first time. They are the words of someone who knows what she wants. I wonder why he'd kept them; was it to prove he wasn't responsible for his actions? That he had no part in the birth of their child? I'm not sure that Ramprakash Raja is deserving of adoration from his family. I feel for the young woman, who had been charmed by the older married man and the new life he'd shown her.
He opens the letter and takes my hand. I glance across to his parents, who have been handed the postcards.

They read the words written by the young woman who had given them their son. He inhales deeply and rubs his forehead. I hold my breath and reach for his face.

"My grandmother got money for me." His voice is low; he is holding back the tears. He hands me the letter.

28th December 1964
Dear Ramprakash,

It is with a heavy heart and great sadness that I write to you about the death of my daughter, who didn't wake up from her sleep last Friday.

It has been difficult for me to do this, but I think you should know she never recovered from the day you took my grandson away. I understand why you did it, it was foolish of my daughter to have let herself be seduced by you. She pined for your child. I believe her heart broke the day you and your wife came to take him away. She sang one last time that day. Her beautiful voice, full of clarity and soulfulness, she sang of her lost love and the child she had given up. Did you know when she held her son, she sang to him? The nurses at the hospital told me. She had the voice of an angel, my beautiful daughter, but you already know, wasn't that what drew you to her?

You told me you loved my child, you wanted her to be happy, but she wasn't after your betrayal. She never sang again, the girl who sang all the time disappeared from my life.

I am grateful for your generosity, but what use is the money now? If I spend it, I'll feel the guilt of making her give up the child. I understand her pain better. I should not have let you do what you did. I was a foolish woman, my daughters are still angry with me for giving you my grandson. But how was I going to send school fees for my son if Alma could no longer work? No one wants to employ a woman who had seduced her married boss. Why is it always the woman who is the seducer, was it not your fault too Ramprakash? You are older, and she was naive. You should have controlled your urges. You should have observed your vows.

Her heart broke little by little as she coped with the separation. I saw the life draining out of her like a dripping tap. You have ruined my family, and now you have taken my child from me too. I will never forgive you for my loss. Remember what you have done, remember my daughter's soul. Pray for my evil deeds, only I know what I will have to bear in the afterlife. Think of my daughter when you look upon your son and remember her sacrifice for you and your family.

I send a photograph that I found in her possession. She seemed happy with you.

Banou Merchant

I read it quickly, stroking his knuckles with my thumb, telling him I understand his hurt. I stand and pull him upright, and I put my arms around his neck.

"Nik." I raise my face up to his. "None of this is your fault. Do you remember telling me the same when I told you about my mother's death?"

His eyes are staring into the distance.

"Nik. Look at me. Nik, please ... please."

I move my hand to his face. He is very still; his heart thuds, one, two, three, four. I take deep breaths; my lungs burn from the lack of oxygen. The light in the canteen darkens, and my legs turn to jelly.

Twelve

"MY LOVE, I'M SORRY. I WASN'T THINKING." Nik is sitting on the floor, my head resting on his lap.

A doctor is taking my pulse; he takes out his stethoscope and asks me to sit up. Nik lifts me in his arms and holds me up to sitting.

"Which ward is your wife in?" he asks Nik.

Nik tells him our son is in the Specialist Neonatal Unit and I had given birth six days ago. A porter brings a wheelchair to where we are. My husband lifts me onto the chair; I wince at the pain and hold my breath to stop myself from crying out loud.

"We're going to take you to the maternity ward for a full check-up," the doctor instructs. "Can someone bring all the medication your wife's on to the ward?"

Nik gives the key to our room to his parents. Their faces are ashen.

When we enter the maternity unit, a bed has already been assigned to me, and a plump grey-haired nurse introduces herself and tells us she will need to do some observations. She takes my temperature, checks my blood pressure and monitors my heartbeat. She hands me a pot and asks for a urine sample. She adds notes to my folder.

"You've been through the wars, you poor love. Rest, the doctor's over there and will come to see you soon, and we've told the desk in Neonatal Paediatrics where you are." She draws the curtains around the bed. "I'll be back to take your blood."

I'm numb with shock. I'm back where I was before, my son in one room and me in another, but in this hospital, we are in two different parts of the building.

A slight, bespectacled Chinese man in a white coat pulls back the curtains of the bed and explains that I am harbouring an infection.

"Can I examine you?" he asks and checks my stitches and then my breasts. "You have mastitis, and you have an infection. I'm going to give you a stronger antibiotic and stronger painkillers. You will need to drink lots of fluids, otherwise, you'll do more damage to your stitches from constipation. Are you breastfeeding?" I tell him I'm not. "In that case, I can put you on a drip." He begins to write in my folder.

"Please, can't you give me tablets? I want to be with my baby; he's getting better, please?"

He looks at Nik, and then at me; his eyes soften as he sees the anxiety of separation from our child in our eyes.

"Okay, but if after three days this doesn't work, you're on a drip. You will need to come up three times a day for monitoring." We thank him.

The friendly nurse comes back to take my blood and says, "You're lucky he's in a good mood. I'll get your meds as soon as possible, and I'll let your family come see you."

She opens the curtains. A teenage mother occupies the

bed on the left of me; her baby is tiny and swaddled in a pink blanket. All the beds have mothers and babies, some with visitors, others alone. I'm the only one with an empty cot. Stinging tears well up in my eyes as I lie back on my bed and close my eyes. The wet tracks run into my ears, and I cry silently. I wish this is a dream. *Someone, please wake me up from this nightmare. When will it all end?*

The sound of a baby crying wakes me up; the taste of bile catches in my throat. *Have I fallen asleep and forgotten our son?* I begin to question my sanity. *Is it a dream? Is my baby okay?* I open my eyes, and my father stands up from the chair. Then my eyes focus on the rows of beds.

"Daddy?"

"Just rest, Reena. Everything's fine."

I search to my left for the cot, but it is empty. "Where's my baby?"

My father takes my hand. "He's with his dada and dadi."

"What! Why have they taken him?" My voice rises; every cell in my body wants me to jump out of bed and run after them. I pull myself up.

"Reena." He takes both of my hands in his. "Listen to me. Amar is fine. You're in the maternity ward at Hammersmith. You can go to him as soon as they give you the go-ahead to go back."

I yank my hand away to cover my mouth; my stomach lurches and he yells for a sick bowl.

* * *

THE WHEELCHAIR SQUEAKS INCESSANTLY. I smell of sick and my heart is in my mouth as I come back to the Specialist Neonatal Unit. I want to change out of my shirt, but the need to see Amar is greater.

The sister on duty greets us. "We've moved Amar and you to a more comfortable room."

The porter wheels me to a small room that is for parents and children who stay for a few days.

It has a three-foot bed positioned by a wall and a small cot placed against a large glass window that separates it from the unit. Behind the bed, there is a wall lamp. The walls are painted mint green, and there is a stencilled border of the alphabet at coving height on the walls.

She turns to me. "You can pull the blinds down for privacy, but we ask that anytime you leave your baby alone, you open them, so the nurse on duty in the room can keep an eye on him. Obstetrics have told me you have to keep off your bottom and rest as much as you can."

I pull myself out of the wheelchair, slip my shoes off and slide into the bed. My father has gone to see Amar. I close my eyes briefly and hear the wheels rattle as my son's cot is brought into the room. I turn onto my side. His grandparents are bringing all his belongings into the room: the ducks, and his small suitcase of clothes.

"How are you feeling, Beta?" Nik's mother is sweeping the hair off my face.

"Where's Nik?" I ask her. She turns to her husband.

"He's gone for a walk," he replies.

My face drops as the anxiety returns. She continues to stroke my hair. "I'm sure he's only gone for a cigarette break."

"Do you know where he's gone, Kaka?" My voice comes out sterner than I'd expected. He shakes his head, and his shoulders drop like a child who's just been reprimanded. "I'll get Anil to check." He leaves the room.

My father and his mother sit on the armchairs, and I try not to think that my husband might have run away again.

Nik has been gone for three hours; no one knows where he is. I lie on my side facing the wall, deflated and wounded that he isn't here when I need him most. For all he knows I could be in the maternity ward alone and upset. I'm angry at his ability to be so selfish. The door to the room opens. He comes in with our holdall and a Mothercare carrier bag. I turn myself around; he swiftly kneels in front of me and says, "You needed new supplies, and I thought we'd need fresh clothes. I had to go to the laundrette to dry the clothes. Haven't ironed them … sorry."

I burst out crying from the relief that he hadn't left me. "How … did you know I was here?" I gulp through the tears.

"I asked the doctor on the ward if he'd arrange it for us to come here."

Nik's father puts his hand on his son's shoulder and says, "Shabaash, Niku, shabaash." His son gazes up at his father's face and smiles.

I pull him to me and kiss him on the lips, not caring that our parents are in the room.

They leave discreetly.

* * *

NIK IS FEEDING ME GRAPES as I recline on the bed, my body raised by my elbow. I had been told off once for sitting by one of the nurses and felt odd eating in this position. My mind takes me back to the villas we had visited on our honeymoon, the frescos on the wall of Roman parties. I smile as my husband pops another grape into my mouth.

As it is the weekend, we have a lot of visitors and our friends stay later than usual, talking about our future and telling us what they could do to help us raise our son. I am happy. Nik has reacted well to the news of his parentage; the envelope is stuffed in the side pocket of our holdall. Amar is taking steady breaths, and his blood oxygen is normal. He is still struggling to keep warm, but my husband has bought a variety of little quilted coats and thick cardigans to add to his growing wardrobe. I have kept my food down, and the feeling of nausea has eased. We listen to Holst's The Planet Suite as we talk of old times at university when we would stay up into the night. Nik is behind me, instinctively rubbing away the pain in my lower back. Even Jay has joined us and is participating in the conversations about what we'll do once Amar is home.

Monday, January 15th, 11.30 a.m.

WE ARE BACK IN THE WAITING room waiting for Professor Rossi to meet with us. Jane has come prepared with a handful of questions to ask the professor about Amar's condition and discusses them with our parents.

The professor begins, after taking a deep breath. "I am sorry, I was hoping to give you some good news, but all the tests indicate your son is profoundly disabled. The EEG has not recorded any brain activity and the scan this morning shows some calcification of the brain. You have two options: you can transfer him to a paediatric disability home, or you could take him home and have the community support team visit. In both cases, I can say his life expectancy is limited."

Silence cloaks the room at the enormity of the news. Yesterday we had been discussing trips to Disneyland and remodelling one of the stable blocks at Shakti Bhavan.

"Where is this paediatric home?" Jane asks calmly, letting the grandparents come to terms with the news. Nik and I are dumbstruck, our hands entwined. My father has taken my other hand and Nik's mother his.

"There is an excellent one in Buckinghamshire I can call up. If you can pay for private care, there are a few more."

"We have the money for private care," Nik's father informs her.

"If Reena and Nik decide they'd much rather take him home, what does that involve?" Jane questions.

"You will need the community nurse team to come and check on him, and we can give you some basic help. It depends if you want nature to take its course or you want to intervene. We have not added a feeding tube yet." She lets the last sentence sink in.

"So ... let me get this straight: we leave him to starve." Jane clarifies the information.

"Yes, but we would keep him comfortable."

"What else do you mean by nature take its course?" I ask her, unable to choke back the tears.

"No intervention, only a feeding routine, and when he gets an infection, we do not treat it. We would again keep him comfortable, but that is all."

"I can't let him starve. I just can't," I say and focus on my feet.

"I will look at managed care. We will want to feed him soon and then we can see how he copes."

"Will this increase his life expectancy?" Kaki asks the doctor. She has taken her husband's hand.

"Some children live for a considerable time. The risk of immobility causes the infection."

"How long?" she asks quietly.

"I can tell you of a case in my care. A boy who had a stroke at birth six years ago, not as severe as Amar's, but he is still alive. The problems come with puberty for most children with a disability."

"When can I take him home?" Nik's voice is authoritative.

"Friday is the earliest. We will need to train you on how to insert and replace the nasogastric tube, how to use the suction tube, and simple physiotherapy. You don't have to make the decision now; you can tell us later today or tomorrow. If you are considering a transfer to a care home, it will take longer. I will start the feeding routine today. It would be good if you are there at first insertion, and I will get the paperwork sorted for the discharge. You can change your mind anytime. You don't have to take Amar home if you don't want to. If you have any questions, please call my secretary. I am happy to come to meet you."

She stands up, and I ask, "What does calcification of the brain mean?"

She sits down again. "Sorry, I should explain. In this case, I use the word loosely. There are some lesions in the brain as a result of the stroke, and these are building up with calcium deposits. That is why we ordered a genetic test for both of you. Some genetic conditions can lead to this. I do not have the results yet, but when I do, I will let you know." She nods at us and bids us goodbye.

We are being shown how to record times and amount of milk after the feeding tube is inserted into Amar's stomach, and the door opens.

"We'll come back later," Rajesh apologises.

"No, no worries, come and sit. This is how Amar is going to have his food."

Su is on duty and has told us about her experience of looking after premature and disabled children when she was in New Zealand, and our spirits have lifted. The news that our son hasn't long to live left us bereft and she senses it and lightens the mood with her chirpy chatter.

I'm confident we will be able to manage this at home, and both Nik and Su agree that I am a natural at inserting the feeding tube.

"Okay, I'll leave you to it. Don't forget to burp him once he's finished."

Nik smiles at me. He is sitting on the bed holding our son in one arm, and in the other, he is lifting a syringe filled with baby formula. I watch as the milk slips into our son's stomach.

I've already given him his first feed of ten millilitres of milk, which has stayed down, and we are hoping this next ten millilitres will stay down, too. I put the ready-prepared carton of baby formula back in the small fridge in the room.

"Is this how you're going to feed him from now on?" Rajesh asks Nik as he bends down to stroke Amar's face. Nik nods at his older brother. "Do you have to take the tube out every time?"

"No, Bhai, it stays in for a week," I tell him.

While this conversation is going on, Sarladevi is sitting upright in the chair, her arms crossed, staring at Nik and Amar.

This is her first visit since Nik was told he is the child of her husband's indiscretions. I take our son off him and walk with him, his body held upright, gently massaging his back. This feels normal to me. We are beginning to do what most new parents do in the first days of their baby's life: feed, change, wash, sleep.

"Can I hold him, Reena?" Rajesh asks once I'm confident I've heard the slow release of air from Amar's stomach. I wrap Amar in a blanket, hand him over, and slide back into bed. Nik has moved to the end of the bed, watching Motaba. The air is thick with apprehension. I know he will have to bring the subject up, and so far, he has been good at making the people he cares for feel at ease, but this relationship is different. He leans towards her and takes her hand in his. My heart is in my mouth; she is not making it easy for him. I sense the resistance in her body.

"Motaba, I want to thank you for finding me and fetching me to live with you. I ... I don't know how I'll ever be able to make it up to you. I'm sorry I brought you pain. I can't begin to understand what you must have gone through."

I'm desperate to pull myself up and hold my husband. His shoulders slump when she doesn't respond. Her head is bent, as she stares at his hands on hers.

"I forgave my husband a long time ago. We have a bond witnessed by Agni Dev, and it was my burden to bear. Beta, Beta, Beta, even if your mother is someone else, you are still a Raja. Hai Bhagwan, thank you for bringing you into our lives. Poor Pushpa and

Anantbhai were suffering. I can't argue with God. How can I?" She raises a thin smile.

Nik slides off the bed and rests his head on Motaba's lap. His body shakes from the silent sobs. She strokes his hair off his face, rhythmically, until he quietens down. I smile up at Rajesh, and he nods and smiles back, rocking our son as I've seen him rock his own children.

"How often do you have to feed him like this?"

"Every hour," Nik informs her.

"And you've decided you'll do this at home? You'll be worn out by this. Send him to a care home, Nikesh. You and Reena will at least have a life."

"I'm not sending him to a home, Motaba," I tell her. "We'll be fine."

She stands and turns to Nik. "Na, na, you won't. How are you going to do the household chores, wash, bathe, eat? You've moved out of Shakti Bhavan." She snaps at me. "He's not going to be with us for long, it's in his janam kundli." She points to Amar by my side. "This child you're holding onto has come to live his last breaths. It's his karma, not yours." She points her index finger at me. "As for you, you don't listen to anything. So full of your modern ways. I told you when you decided to get married that you would bring pain to my son, and look what you've done." She spits out the words like stones. Tears burn in my eyes.

"Motaba! You are the elder here, show some restraint." Rajesh stands up, his eyes dark and angry. My vision blurs because of my tears, and Nik's shoulders are slumped in defeat.

"I am telling the truth. Even the doctors have told you. He will not live for long. This playing at mummy and

daddy is just that. Better to put him in a care home."
She picks up her coat and bags. "I'll be in the waiting
room. Persuade them to do what is right, Rajesh," she
says as she walks out of the room.

Nik's older brother didn't persuade us; instead, he
pulled Nik up for a hug and said, "Bring him home. If
you want, we can clear the rooms above the garages
and set them up for you."

"I want him at our home, Bhai. Our home," I croak.

"Okay, then let's get the house set up. I'll speak with
the sister in charge and find out what we need to get.
Do you want a night nurse?"

I hadn't even thought about how we would take care
of him.

"Can we tell you that later, Bhai. We're still learning
what we need to do," Nik mutters softly as he strokes
our son's cheek.

Rajesh's words give us strength, and I remember what
had happened to him and Rupa when Anousha was
born and the pain and rituals they had to endure.

Thirteen

Sunday, October 23rd, 1983

AFTER THE SUMMER OF 1983, I had been invited to many functions at Shakti Bhavan, and I had politely declined. However, Nik had insisted I attend the Sunderkand Paath after Navratri. The ceremony was held on a Sunday, and we had come down on the Saturday afternoon from Warwick.

When Nik came to drop us off, he'd asked Umi's father who declined, saying, "No, thanks, Nikesh. It's not my thing, you know. Take my daughter though; her mother was the one who did the religious rituals. I fear I have neglected to educate her in our customs."

Nik came to pick us up at seven in the morning; both Umi and I felt a bit jaded from the night before. Umi's father had gone out with some friends, and she had complained she felt left out. To cheer her up, we had gone to Blockbuster and the off-licence, hired An Affair to Remember, and drank vodka and Coke, crying at the insensitivity of men. I had a feeling Umi was not just upset at her father's new lifestyle, but she had fallen for someone at university but wasn't willing to tell me who it was yet.

On the drive up to the house, Nik told us his faiba was visiting with them, but his fua had stayed in India. We had met them at Suresh and Ashveena's wedding reception. I remembered her easy nature and how similar Vijaya was to her brothers. Nik had told me how she had quizzed him about me when he had gone to India in the summer break. I was happy she wanted to know about us but was still unsure about our relationship.

Going to Shakti Bhavan filled me with anxiety. All the residents were aware I was Nik's girlfriend. Even if they had had any doubts, the events of the summer had clarified my position. But the place was too grand for me and made me feel inadequate. Umi, however, felt right at home and, when we arrived for breakfast, she rushed into the family room, waving at the younger members of the family, pressing her palms together to the elders. I had walked hesitantly behind her. Nik's motaba and faiba were sitting on the sofa next to the empty armchair that was usually occupied by his papa, and tears pricked at my eyes.

She had seen my eyes glisten. "Jai Shri Krishna, Reena. Back again. It seems Nikesh can't come home without you," his motaba retorted. His faiba smiled, her eyes filled with an apology, and I remembered how Nik's papa had done the same thing. I'd turned away quickly, my eyes stinging. I knew the reason why she didn't like me, but Nik and I loved each other. I'd made a promise to myself that whenever he needed me, I would be there for him.

Nik's mother approached the sitting area and had heard the comment, wrapped her arms around me and kissed my cheeks. "Lovely to have you here, Reena.

My Niku has made an excellent decision to bring you to the paath." She said it slightly louder than her usual tone. Nik turned his head, said something to Anil and approached us.

"You need to eat something." He kissed his mother on her cheek, and took my hand. "Come on." He pulled me to the breakfast bar and said, "Ignore her. She's in a particularly bad mood today." He had smiled his beautiful smile and said, "Idli or plain dosa?"

FOR THE PAATH, UMI AND I had decided to wear chaniya cholis for the ceremony. Mine was made from pale-pink Georgette with dark-blue and gold appliqué flowers, and Umi wore a magenta and green silk brocade one. I had lost the discomfort of holding hands with Nik in the summer. But, in Shakti Bhavan, under the scrutinising eyes of Motaba, I had to resist the urge to pull away as I walked with him to the space saved for us by his family in the temple. I had heard the whispers from the members of the mela mandir and kitty parties that Sarladevi presided over. I felt the need to distance myself from him and took my hand out of his, feigning I needed both hands to lift my skirt. I sat down next to Jaishree, and she smiled at me, waving at Umi to join us too.

Rupa and Rajesh sat in front of the shrines, the Guru was performing the Ganesh Prathna. Anousha, dressed in a bright-orange silk outfit, was placed in a baby bouncer by their side. She was a contented baby, and, at three months, she had filled out. No one could tell she had arrived early.

A trio composed of a man, woman and a young boy sat against the wall, each with their instruments: tabla, tambourine and harmonium. They were getting ready for the singing, the norm when performing the ceremony. We had been given sheets to recite from; the script was in English and Gujarati.

"So, what's this?" Umi had whispered, and I'd told her we would need to recite the words in song accompanied by the musicians. "Oh, I'll try to keep up. Do you know this one by heart too?" she'd asked.

"No, I don't know this one."

She pulled a fake look of shock. "Good God. Something that Reena Solanki doesn't know." Nik and Jaish chortled. "I've found a flaw, Nik," she whispered, leaning towards him.

He took my hand and squeezed it. "She's wrong, you know. You're perfect," he whispered.

Lunch was served in a marquee attached to a mobile kitchen in the grounds. The tables were arranged in long rows facing the Guru, who was seated at a table with his disciples, the elderly Raja family members and their in-laws. The Raja children had lined up next to the women in orange sarees and served the lunch to the elders, before sitting down at the long tables near the front.

Nik had sat opposite me as we ate the prasad, his long legs either side of mine under the table, his need to touch me overwhelming me.

After lunch, most of the guests left to go back to their own homes. Anil and Sunil's parents bade the family farewell and headed back to the Midlands and beyond.

Ashveena's brother Bhupesh and his wife Mona went home to Edgware with their young son. Those that remained went back into the house, heading to the drawing room to relax.

Our change of clothes had been left in the stable block in Rajesh and Rupa's new cottage. Their house was on one side, and work was underway to create another. Nik pointed to the perpendicular block, explaining that it was going to be Suresh and Ashveena's new home. He guided me towards it. As we entered the development, he picked up two hard hats; the walls had been plastered, and loose electric wiring was hanging everywhere. I told him it would be a lovely home once it was completed. He took me in his arms and said, "That's not why I brought you here, my love. I need your soft kisses."

I wrapped my arms around his neck and offered my lips to him; he bowed down and our hats bumped. He turned our hats around. His eyes were golden; his soft lips sent an electric charge through my body. I hadn't expected to feel this yearning from spending only one day apart. I told myself to slow down. I knew what the books and the films show, but in real life, no one could be this much in love.

When we entered the cottage, we saw that Rupa Bhabhi had changed out of her clothes into a pale-green churidar kameez and Umi was dressed in jeans and a boxy purple jumper.

"Your bags there?" Umi pointed to the hallway.

When I came back downstairs, Nik was lounging in the armchair by the fireplace, and Umi was sitting on the floral country-cottage-style sofa, asking Rupa Bhabhi what the paath was for. Rajesh walked in from the kitchen with a tea tray.

"It's because Motaba listens to a man who thinks he is

a God." His disapproving tone showed his annoyance. He sat down next to his wife, took her hand and kissed her on the cheek. She raised a tight smile, and we listened to them explain how they had endured Motaba's superstitious outbursts. I recalled the conversation I'd overheard, gave them a sympathetic smile and walked to the armchair opposite Nik's.

"So, when does Anousha wake up again, Bhabhi?" Nik asked.

"She's just gone down, Niku. She'll be up when she's hungry or needs a nappy change."

"What time is that?"

"Probably at five," Rajesh explained. "Darling, do you want to go and have a nap too? Anousha's kaka is here to keep her occupied and change her nappy when she wakes up." He laughed.

"Nappy! I haven't been taught that yet," Nik exclaimed, his jaw open. "Ben won't allow me near Sammy when it's nappy changing time."

"Ritu doesn't trust you, but we do. Besides you're going to have to learn sooner or later." Rajesh raised an eyebrow at him.

"Sure, Bhai, you can teach me today." While this exchange was going on, Umi and I had both been watching them. Finally Nik raised a smile that filled his face from ear to ear. "Thought I'd disappear like a shot? But that's not happening today, Bhai."

"I can see you've changed, and I like the new you." He looked in my direction and smiled.

When Rupa Bhabhi and Anousha woke up, we were all summoned to the nursery to watch Nik learn how to change a nappy. The room was painted pale pink, and there was a comfortable nursing chair covered in dusky-pink velvet. There was a changing mat placed on an antique pine dresser. Anousha's cot had been placed against the wall, and by the window there was a white daybed scattered with comfortable cushions.

"It can't be difficult. If Bhai can do it, so can I," he told us for reassurance.

"Ah, but I don't change nappies," Rajesh replied as he led the way up the stairs.

"Why not?" Nik questioned, slightly shocked.

"You'll find out soon enough."

Nik pulled a face when Anousha was handed to him.

"Now you know," Rajesh laughed.

Rupa was clinging to Rajesh's arm, anxiety on her face, as their daughter was taken to the changing table.

Anousha was as good as gold as soon as she heard Nik cooing and praising her. He started to undo the poppers on her shoulder.

"You don't need to take the whole thing off, Niku," Rupa instructed. "Only the poppers on her legs." She showed them to him. As he opened them, Anousha raised her legs up, assisting her kaka. Umi and I stood as far away as was polite; the smell was unbearable.

Once he had changed the nappy, he handed her to her mother, wiggled his fingers and said, "Shame on you, Bhai. If I can do it, so can you." He came towards Umi and me, and we stepped backwards. He laughed and turned to the door on the right to wash his hands in the bathroom.

"I can't believe she did that. With me, she's constantly trying to turn around." Rupa's voice was full of astonishment and we headed downstairs.

"Hello, where are you all?" Suresh was standing at the sitting room door; he had changed out of his jabo pyjamas and was wearing jeans and a cream jumper. "Let me have Anousha, Bhabhi. Haven't had a cuddle all day."

Rupa handed her to him, and I watched the three brothers, smiling and cooing at her with love in their eyes. I was glad they had found a way to be with the beautiful girl, despite Sarladevi's attempts to keep her away from the Raja men.

After a simple supper of thepla, chana nu shaak and chaas, everyone gathered in the family sitting room. Sammy was asleep in his playpen, and Anousha was being lulled to sleep by Jaishree. Motaba and Ashveena's mother had gone to the temple to tidy up.

Anil glanced at his watch and said, "You should head back to university, the traffic will have died down, Niku."

"I'll go get my laundry bag," Nik said. "Do you want to come to help me, Ree?" He raised his left eyebrow; it wasn't a question, more an instruction.

"Sure," I said quietly, and we walked out into the ornate hallway to take the stairs down to the laundry room.

We heard voices as we climbed back up from the basement. Nik stopped short on the stairs.

"Poor you. First you have a girl as your first grandchild, and then your husband passes. It has been a tough summer. The child must be very unlucky."

Nik and I both recognised the shrill voice of Savita, Ashveena's mother.

"Haan, haan, Savita. You are so lucky your son and his wife have given you a grandson. I will have to wait and pray that Jaishree or Suresh give me mine soon."

"I'm sure Guruji's prayers will lessen the weight on

your sons and Anantbhai's health. Such a shame she was born with so much bad karma," Savita condescended.

Nik's grip tightened; he moved to continue climbing. I held him back and shook my head. I had been here before; he needed to listen to how this woman's superstitions affected every decision the family took. I was certain it would determine whether we would have a future together or not.

"Bhabhi, you will never say anything like this about my children again. The child is innocent." Nik's father must have overheard them. His voice was raised and full of anger. "I know you are grief-stricken and unhappy at the loss of Motabhai, we all are … I have tolerated the nasty comments about the baby, but no more. I will remind you of what Motabhai said when Anousha came home. Our house has been blessed with the goddess, Laxmi. You believe in Laxmi, don't you? As for your grandson, Savita Ben, neither your son nor his wife could determine his sex. Unless they've done something unforgivable. Bhagwan is the one who decides. You do believe that your God is all-powerful?"

"Anantbhai, I didn't mean to offend you. Of course, Anousha is innocent, but Guruji has told us she has some weakness in her janam kundli. We're doing all we can to strengthen them, that's all," Ashveena's mother replied, justifying her narrow-minded views.

"I'm only doing what I need to do to uphold our traditions and to protect the family, Anantbhai." We heard the grief in Sarladevi's voice as she choked back a sob.

"Come with me, Sarla," Savita said, as we heard them

leave the entrance hall.

We climbed up the stairs slowly, hoping his father had left too. Nik saw him first, let go of my hand and scrambled up the stairs to be by his side.

His shoulders were slumped; he turned to his son and tried to raise a smile. Nik put his arm around his father's shoulders and drew him closer.

"It was my fault, Niku. He wasn't well from our trip to Kenya. If anyone needs to be blamed for his death, it is I."

"No, you're not to blame for his death, Kaka," he told his father, both men remembering the man they loved so much.

Nik's father pushed his son to arm's length and said, "You've grown into an admirable young man, Niku."

He held his hand out to me, and we walked together into the sitting room.

Fourteen

January 16th, 1990

"COME AND FIND ME, MUMMY."

I'm in an old house; the lights are dim and cast shadows on the wall.

"Wait! Wait! Don't run too fast. We don't know this house."

My legs are leaden as I climb up the stairs. I glimpse her white ankle socks, and the red shoes disappear up another flight of stairs. I take a breath at the landing, my legs aching from the effort of climbing the stairs.

"Mummy, Mummy, come find me." Laughter is in her voice.

"Coming, coming, where are you?"

I'm at the top of the house on a long landing. There are closed doors on both sides. "Where are you?" I begin to feel the panic build up.

"Oh, look at this, Mummy," she says again and turns around to the open door and stairs. I struggle to climb up the steep stairs and stand in an empty, dusty attic; something catches my hair, and I brush it away.

"Come out now! This isn't a game. Mummy's very

worried."

"I'm here," a faint distant voice calls.

My heart is pounding in my chest. The attic is empty. I run around it, trying to find where she could be hiding. Then I notice the alcove and a small cupboard covered with a dustsheet.

"I'm coming to get you, you naughty girl," I laugh with relief.

I pull off the dustsheet. There is a doll's house on a table, and I crouch down to search under the table. No one is there.

"That's enough, come out. You win. Come out of hiding now!" I raise my voice, swivelling frantically around the attic.

"You've found me," she says. "Look again, Mummy."

That's when I notice that the doll's house is a replica of the house I'm in. The decor, the furniture, all of it in miniature; it even has a doll's house in the attic.

I hear faint laughter and my eyes are drawn to the basement kitchen. Sitting at a large oak kitchen table is a lady in a red saree. She is rolling out puris and putting them on some brown paper. Opposite her, standing on the chair, is a little boy, playing with the dough, making worms and showing them off. The little girl sitting next to her takes a dough ball, starts to roll out a puri and shows it to the woman, who smiles up at her and says something.

"Mummy?" I shout into the house, and the woman smiles at me.

I wake up with a start, gasping for water. My body is burning. I search for Nik. He is sitting in the armchair feeding Amar.

"Did you have a bad dream again, my love?" he asks

with concern in his eyes.

I lift myself up on one elbow, reach for a glass of water and quench my thirst.

"I dreamt of my mother," I tell him. I don't want to tell him that our children were with her too. My subconscious is telling me that I am powerless, no matter how hard I fight for my son, he will be lost to me, just like my mother and the child whose life I'd cut short. Burning tears roll down my cheek; this has been entirely of my making. My karma has ruined my son's and my husband's lives.

* * *

TEN DAYS AFTER THE BIRTH of our son, we wait for our discharge papers. The doctors have been to see Amar, and I've been up to the maternity ward for a final check-up. My stitches are beginning to heal and my last dose of antibiotics has kept the infection under control.

Our parents took our belongings this morning. Rupa Bhabhi bought us a baby-changing bag as a gift, and I have filled it with nappies, spare clothes, and all the other accessories parents of newborn babies carry around with them. She also brought a car seat to transport our son safely to our home. We've asked our family and friends not to come to visit us; we want to spend our first day at home alone, just the three of us. Nik and I have worked out a routine which is relatively straightforward and easy. Amar is not like other babies; he doesn't demand to be attended to, he doesn't cry when he is in discomfort. I've seen our family struggling to take care of a baby who cries. I long to hear him cry. Her words resurface in my mind again, 'This playing at mummy and daddy, is just that.'

Nik brushes his lips on the back of my hand. "It will be all right," he reassures me, as he sits down on the bed with our son on his shoulder.

"Hello, I have all you need in this bag." The duty sister who had been in charge when we first arrived is holding up a large white plastic carrier bag. "If at any time you run out of anything, call us, and we'll get someone to drop it off, or you can come and visit us. Your next appointment with Professor Rossi is in two weeks, and someone from the community care team will come tomorrow morning."

Nik takes the bag from her. "Thank you for all your help." He shakes her hand. I put a quilted pram suit with a hood and gloves on Amar. We will need to be careful about keeping him warm. I wrap him up in a blanket, too. As we prepare to leave, the nurses and parents who are in the unit come to say goodbye.

This is the first time in days I have stepped out for fresh air, and the cold, dank fog takes my breath away. Although it is lunchtime, it feels like the night, the lampposts struggling to throw their light. The yellow ellipses like floating UFOs in the eerie mist. The thickness is so dense that we can hardly see what is in front of us as we walk towards the car park.

Nik opens the car door, and I strap our son into the baby seat. The large seat engulfs him. The sight of seeing him, so vulnerable and tiny, brings a lump to my throat. When I pull up from leaning over him, Nik takes me in his arms and touches his forehead to mine. "Do you want to sit next to him in the back?" he murmurs in my ear.

"No, I want to sit with you," I tell him, although every part of me wants to be in the back seat with Amar.

He turns the radio on and switches through the channels until he finds Sunrise Radio. The presenter is hosting in Hindi, and as we pull out onto Du Cane Road, Lata Mangeshkar's voice reverberates through the car's speakers. "Yeh kahan aa gaye hum?" Where have we come?

I wonder if the lyrics are a sign of how far we have come together and if this is the journey we were meant to take.

* * *

THE HOUSE IS LOVELY AND WARM as I walk into the lobby. I open the door to the sitting room as I take off my coat. Nik has lifted the car seat out completely and brings Amar home and places him on the sofa.

"He's home, Ree. We're finally home."

He smiles at me. We both admire our son wrapped up against the cold. The only bit of him visible is his face, his eyes closed, a white cloth tape strip on his left cheek to keep the small tube inserted in his left nostril in place.

Amar is comfortable; I've taken off his pram suit and he is strapped back in the seat. His next feed isn't due for another thirty minutes, and I am in the kitchen putting on the coffee percolator and the kettle.

"It feels strange," he says as he holds me, my back resting against his chest as I wait for the infused liquid to pass into the coffee pot. "Strange being home, just the three of us."

I lean back into him, acknowledging the strangeness of finally coming home. The house is tranquil. Small knots form in my stomach, and I feel the panic rising and try to push it away. The lack of the cacophony of noise we were accustomed to adds to my anxiety. How will we cope? Perhaps Motaba was right: we should have taken him to a care home?

Nik pulls me to the soft sofa and wraps his arm around me. He has turned on the TV, not to watch anything, but just for the comfort of hearing some noise, and we sip our hot drinks.

The incessant sound is like a mosquito in my ear, and I try to bat it away, only to feel a hand. The noise moves away. I open my eyes. Nik is up and switching off the alarm on his wristwatch. He starts rummaging through the baby-changing bag and he pulls out a round plastic syringe.

"Time for his feed." He waves the pack at me, his lopsided grin filling his chiselled face, even his eyes are smiling.

"Lie down, Ree, I'll do this."

I lie down on the sofa and close my eyes.

"Wake up my darling, time to eat something." He is sitting in front of me on his haunches.

"What time is it?"

"6 o'clock." He kisses me softly on my lips.

"Why did you let me sleep that long?" I ask him even though I can't stay awake. I am exhausted; the relief of coming home has sapped all the energy from my body. He laughs, "Because you needed it. Let's eat and then a hot bath for you, my love."

Amar has been taken out of his car seat and is in the Silver Cross pram that is parked between the dining area and sofa bed of our long narrow open-plan living area. I pick him up and sit down on a chair that has the rubber ring on it. Although my stitches have healed, it is still painful to sit on any hard surface.

Nik has taken out some Tupperware containers and put them on our round dining table. There is a note from his mother.

Welcome home, children. There's a variety of food for you to eat today. Sleep, eat and relax as much as you can. Call me at any time you want us to help. We'll come to see you tomorrow morning. Love you, Kaki.

He opens them up: vegetable pasta bake, cauliflower cheese, green salad, baked potatoes, fresh fruit salad, apple pie, vegetable pilau, mattar paneer, udad ni dall, rotli, raita.

"Oh good, something different. I was getting a bit fed up with the rotla and bhaji." He smiles at me playfully. He doesn't mind the food. I've been complaining about not being allowed to eat baked potato and pasta. Once we have eaten, Nik fills the bathtub, and we both walk upstairs to our bedroom. The little crib that was by our bed has been moved into the other room. The furniture has been rearranged. The spare bed is against the wall, the changing table placed at its feet and the crib is placed next to it. On the changing table, there is a changing mat, a pile of nappies and the suction machine. All the other equipment we need is arranged on a stainless-steel trolley next to it. The white cot is by the window, and the ducks are inside. Amar's little suitcase is on top of the white wardrobe we'd bought for him.

My eyes water, my husband's face darkens, and his eyes glint with a suppressed anger. He takes a deep breath and begins to move his bedside table and the bed towards the window; he picks up the crib and places it by my side of the bed and moves my bedside table to the wall.

"We'll keep this in here." He points to the changing table and trolley.

I am on the small landing, unable to do anything, recalling the numerous conversations I have had about not wanting a night nurse, a stranger to take care of our child. I'd insisted we didn't need paid help for this task. Nik had tried to persuade me but had eventually conceded that as Amar may not be with us for long, we would work around it.

He pulls me into our bedroom, taking my clothes off slowly and deliberately. We stand naked facing each other. He pulls me to him, and we hold each other, skin touching skin. "I've wanted to do this for so long," he whispers longingly in my ear. I understand what he means; although we've been together, the intimacy of our marital home is something we've both missed.

* * *

"GET INTO THE BATH," he tells me as he walks back out to bring Amar in his baby seat into the bathroom. He slips his dressing gown off and slides in behind me, and I lie back, my head resting on his shoulders. Our stereo is playing Nat King Cole, telling us never before in our life has there been someone more "Unforgettable" than Amar.

The nurses at SCBU have suggested a four-hourly feeding schedule as the first couple of days of feeding Amar had been successful. We'd managed to get in a routine. Nik did the midnight feed, I did the early morning feed and slept until eight o'clock when we fed Amar and had breakfast together.

The routine of the last two days in the hospital had made it easier for us. I liked that at 10 a.m. we bathed him and gave him his massage, we played music to him until lunchtime, and we both had a nap until his next feed and our tea break. We ate dinner at 6 o'clock, held our son until it was time for his feed, and managed to go for a walk around the hospital when it was less busy after our visitors left. The rhythm of the day had calmed us down, and we had been reassured we would be able to do this on our own.

After our bath, we feed Amar at eight and take him upstairs into his nursery where we change him into a sleepsuit. The small electric blanket that keeps his temperature under control is plugged in and ready in his crib, and we watch his chest as we lie in our bed. Sleep comes quickly for us, a deep, exhausted sleep, dreamless and dark.

***

THE TIME ON THE BEDSIDE CLOCK reads seven-thirty.

I check at the crib and notice the empty baby milk carton on the bedside table. Nik must have woken up for both the feeds that I'd slept through. I pull his arm off my waist, and he opens his eyes.

"Go back to sleep. I'll wake you up when Kaka and Kaki come." I give him a quick kiss.

I take Amar downstairs and put him in the pram while I get the carton of formula milk from the fridge.

The phone rings. I rush to pick it up. Nik is still sleeping, and I don't want him to be disturbed.

"Is that Reena?" An unfamiliar voice speaks to me in Gujarati. "I asked for your number from Sarlaben. Listen, Reena Beti, I had a dream last night. There's something wrong with your son. She tells me he hasn't opened his eyes yet. The Mataji who came to me says you have wronged her. For the curse to be lifted from your son, you must not wear red and fast on Friday. Fridays are special days for women and mothers. You can only eat once, but it has to be without salt. Are you still there, Reena?"

I say yes quietly, trying to understand why this woman has rung me.

"Start the fast on Friday and don't wear red: that means socks, underwear, anything that has red in it, even flowers. I can tell you that everything will be fine. I've seen other children recover after only five Fridays of fasting. He'll open his eyes and be normal. I can guarantee it. Jai Mataji."

I hold onto the phone until it switches to the dial tone and put it down. I walk to the pram, lift Amar out and slump on the sofa. I know our son will never open his eyes. I know he'll never be normal. *Why would anyone believe it? Why would Motaba give our phone number to the woman? Didn't she tell us he hasn't got long to live?* I let the tears I had been holding back come out and I begin to cry, long silent gulps. I feel like wailing and screaming, but I want Nik to rest. Then I start to whimper. I can't help it. I have Amar in my arms; his milk slips slowly into his stomach, and I rock backwards and forwards to ease the pain. I wish I could do something as simple as not eating on a Friday: *I would stop eating for months if he would open his eyes and be like any other newborn baby.*

"What happened, Ree? Who was on the phone?"
Nik is sitting next to me, holding me to him. I continue to cry. I don't want to tell him what I've just been told.

* * *

"JAI SHRI KRISHNA, REENA. Why are you wearing red?" Motaba says as she sees me in my floral print shirt and dark-green leggings. Nik's mother's head turns. She is standing at the stove warming up our lunch. I have Amar in my arms. "Did you get a phone call from Devkurben this morning?"
"Yes, I did," I tell her.
"So why aren't you doing what she told you to do?"
"Why would you give a stranger our phone number, Motaba?" Nik steps out of the bathroom lobby.
"She isn't a stranger. She is a powerful lady who has visions from Mataji."
Nik's mother continues to warm up the food, her head bowed.
"What did she tell you, Motaba?" he asks quietly through gritted teeth. The golden shards in his eyes are like flaming arrows.
"Reena has to stop wearing red and fast on Fridays."
"And then our son will be normal, he'll open his eyes, and everything will be fine," I interrupt. I glare at Nik and his motaba.
"Nikesh, you must understand me. We didn't expect him to live. But he is alive. I'm trying to find ways to make his life better for him." She holds his upper arm.
"He'll never be normal, Motaba. He is disabled, he cannot see, he cannot swallow. This is what our son is going to be like for the rest of his life." He takes Amar's hand. "I don't want anyone else to call my wife and

Fifteen

WE WENT TO THE HOSPITAL for Amar's two-week check-up yesterday and have some good news. He can digest his food, and the record we'd been keeping of his urine output indicates his kidney is functioning properly. Even the nurses commented on how he has grown. We have both noticed the newborn baby clothes fit him better. His face is rounder, and he even has a double chin on top of his double chin.

"Oh, let me see." His beautiful eyes are lit up. He has walked in on me dressing after my bath.

"Where's Amar?"

"He's in the pram, Ree." My expression is full of concern. "He'll be fine for a few minutes. I love this," he says as he strokes my huge belly.

"Don't be silly, you're only saying that to be nice," I tell him. My body still looks like I'm three months pregnant and I'm annoyed my jogging hasn't helped reduce the weight I'd gained.

"I love you, Ree." His voice is gravelly.

"If you say it too much it doesn't have the same meaning," I reply. A glimmer of hurt dances in his eyes.

Every muscle in my whole body tightens. We have kissed and cuddled, but that is all I can cope with at the moment; the thought of anything more fills me with dread. Nik has tried to be gentle, but as soon as he touches me intimately, I feel pain. I don't want this moment to turn into that again.

"Please, Nik, I don't want to … "

"I just want to hold you. I miss it … we don't even have a bath together anymore," he murmurs.

I relent and let him kiss my neck, the tops of my breasts, my flabby stomach; he gently sits me down on the bed and pulls off his T-shirt and tracksuit bottoms. I can see that he is aroused.

"Oh God, Ree, help me." He pushes me down on the bed and begins to kiss me softly at first, and then the kisses become persistent, incessant; he opens his eyes, and the creases appear around the edges. He lifts himself off and turns towards me, his head resting on one elbow.

"What's the matter? When I hold your hand, you find an excuse to take it away. You don't want to kiss me anymore. What have I done, Ree?"

"I'm just tired, Nik. These pills don't help." I point to the painkillers and the sleeping pills, using them as an excuse. If he isn't aroused, then he won't want anything from me. My life is centred on the care of my son; his wellbeing is all I can concentrate on. I can feel the small knots in my stomach. He has been left alone, no one watching him for five minutes. *Anything can happen in that short time. He could stop breathing, and we'd be none the wiser.* I pull myself out of bed, put on my clothes hurriedly and run down the stairs. I search in the pram. Amar is breathing, his chest rising up and down, and the relief that he is alive floods my body.

**

WE HARDLY HAVE ANY VISITORS during the week now, except for the food deliveries on the days Nik fasts for our son's health. He had begged me to fast with him, but I'd told him I wouldn't pander to Motaba's beliefs. We argue about the trips I've arranged to see the alternative therapists: the cranial osteopaths who help with trauma to the head at Harley Street; the homoeopaths who prescribe tiny pills I grind and give to Amar in his milk to prevent nappy rash and ease his pain; the acupuncturist, who uses pressure points to activate his muscle memory. I've seen him jitter and stretch and believe that it's helping. Nik says that it's reflexive and the same as his fasting. These disagreements and differing opinions have created a wedge in our marriage. I no longer sit with him and talk, too tired and busy, washing, ironing, and cleaning, all my spare time used to keep the house running.

The days merge together; the cold, dark, short days are slowly replaced with some brighter ones. We go to Walpole Park every day. I sit with Amar by the duck pond and stare at the black water to calm me down. Sometimes Nik will go for a walk around the pond, sometimes he'll sit with me, his hands in his pockets, his eyes locked on the water.

At weekends our life is very different. We are very different; the children come to play with Amar, and we become the bubbly, happy couple they expect us to be. Nik fools around with them. We always go to the park; the older ones run around playing tag while the younger ones go to the play area to ride on the swings and the animal-shaped spring riders. They all climb on the slides, shouting encouragement as they stand at the bottom. Nik takes Amar in the baby sling as he runs and plays with the children. Before we leave, we have to go to the petting zoo to see the baby animals, the rabbits, the ducklings, the chicks and the hamsters. The children want Nik's attention all the time, and he smiles and laughs as they shout Neenukaka, Neenumama, can I have this, can we do that, can we go here. The name that Anousha first called him has stuck.

This has become a ritual since the first weekend Amar came home when they all visited and brought gifts, excited to meet the newest member of their family. That weekend Nik was excited to be home and had bought sweets and chocolates for everyone, telling them it was a gift for the birth of our son.

At times like this, I think there is nothing wrong with Amar and we will continue to go to the park and spend time with our son for years to come until he's too big to want to go to see the animals.

***

WE HAVE JUST FINISHED OUR DAILY massage and are getting ready to put Amar on the crunchy sensory mat Jessica and the children had made for him and the doorbell rings. It isn't one of Nik's fast days, so it's unusual. Nik goes to open the door.

"Hello, Bhai?"

Rajesh walks in from the hallway straight into the room. He hands his coat to Nik who takes it and hangs it up.

"Hello, Reena. How's Amar?" He kneels in front of him and lifts him up. "He's put on weight." He smiles.

"Yes, almost ten grams," I tell him.

"Can I get you a coffee or tea, Bhai?" Nik asks as he walks towards the kitchen.

"Can I have a coffee, please?"

Nik brings in three mugs on a tray and puts it on the coffee table, which is placed by the wall.

Amar is on the mat on his back, and I continue to jingle bells, use the wooden maraca and blow soft whistles to help stimulate his mind. I take his hands and brush them against the different types of cloth on the mat.

"How often do you do this?" Rajesh asks.

"Three times a day," I reply.

He strokes his bare foot, and Amar moves it away. "Did he feel that?" His expression is full of surprise.

"Yes," I nod as Nik tells his brother that Amar is responding more to touch. We'd noticed the changes in the last few days. It has been four weeks since he came home.

He takes a sip from his coffee mug. Nik sits on the sofa, facing his elder brother.

"I need you to review a new contract we're drawing up, Niku."

"Do you have it with you, Bhai?"

"Can you come into the office for a couple of hours?"

He turns to me. "He can only come if it's okay with you, Reena? I'll understand if he can't."

I ask Nik, "Do you want to go?"

"Only if you don't mind, Ree. It's only for a couple of hours, right Bhai?"

"Yes, and I can ask Kaki to come and keep you company."

"No, Bhai, we go to the park in the afternoon, and I've already prepared dinner," I reply. "I'll be fine."

Nik kisses me on my cheek and his brother smiles.

For the first time in weeks, my husband is wearing smart trousers, a shirt and a jacket. Even his walk has changed back to the confident man I used to know. He takes Amar from me, hugs him and whispers something in his ear. I wonder what he's said to him as he gives him back to me. Rajesh is waiting in the hallway. Nik takes my face in his hands and rests his forehead on mine.

"Thank you, Ree. Thank you for letting me do this." I raise a smile. "Call me if you want me to come home." He squeezes my hand.

It feels strange on my own with Amar, but I find peace in the fact that I'm responsible for him. I feed him and eat a sandwich, and then I put on his pram coat, buckle the baby sling and lift him into it. I wrap a weatherproof cover on the sling, and I step out for a walk in the park.

As I watch the ducks at the pond, an elderly woman in a camel coat and a red beret sits next to me. We've met several times before, nodding a greeting as people who frequent the same place at the same time do.

"How old is your baby?"

She has kind eyes.

"He's six weeks old," I reply.

"He's quite big … " she says as she peers into my chest. " … Oh, is he having difficulty swallowing?" she asks me.

I'm surprised she knows what the feeding tube is.

"Yes, he is." I raise a thin smile.

"He'll learn soon enough. My grandson couldn't feed

for a while."

My eyes water and the tears start to roll down my face. "I'm so sorry," she says and takes my hand.

Once I'm calm, I explain he probably won't recover and this week he has been most active, stretching and lifting his arms and moving his legs. I also admit for the first time that I'm scared of losing him. The thought has been gnawing at me for weeks and today is the first time I've voiced it. She listens to me and waits for me to compose myself and then she searches in her handbag and takes out a small blue address book. She opens her purse and finds a receipt and writes something and then hands it to me. "That's a phone number for the support group for parents with sick children."

When I get home, I phone the support group and arrange to go to one of their meetings. The lady I speak to also gives me numbers of families whose children are as profoundly disabled as Amar.

"How was the park without me?" His face is strained, the creases in the corners of his eyes deepen.

"It was good. I spoke with that old lady we usually meet, and she gave me contact numbers of local parents who have sick and disabled children."

He strokes my cheek. "You seem tired, my love. I'll feed Amar. Go and have a rest." He can see the reluctance in my eyes. "I've missed him, Ree."

He picks him up from the pram and kisses his cheek.

"Lie down on the sofa, you don't have to go up."

After dinner, we sit curled up on the sofa. I rest my head on his shoulder, and he tells me about being away from Amar. He talks of how he enjoyed looking through the paperwork, but also about the guilt of leaving us. His voice lifts when he speaks of the clauses he amended and added. I see the man who thrives in making deals and negotiating. I lift myself up and gaze into his golden eyes.

"Do you want to go in again?"

"Would you mind if I did?"

"We have to get into a routine. You can't stay at home all the time."

"But, what about you, Ree? You can't do this on your own."

I wonder about the other families who do and think about the additional support we get. We can get food prepared and delivered, and, if it becomes too difficult, Nik can come home quickly. His eyes are drawing an arc on my face, searching for any sign of what I'm thinking.

"Let's start with a few hours."

He kisses me softly. "Thank you, my love."

I kiss him back with longing and tell him how much I missed him. I want him to be happy and I could tell his work gives him some normality.

He pushes me to arm's length and says, "Are you sure?"

"Yes, but only heavy kissing and a bit of petting."

He laughs softly when I say that, and he returns the kisses.

* * *

WE HAVE SETTLED INTO A ROUTINE. Every morning Nik gets up at six for Amar's first feed, and I have a lie-in until seven-thirty. When I wake up, I usually have a quick cup of tea and go for a jog. Nik has breakfast out and ready on my return, and we eat together. We check Amar, his feeding tube, the weight of fluid loss and make a record on his card for the community nurse, who usually arrives while we are bathing him. Nik and I take it in turns to massage Amar. He reacts to our touch a lot more, and sometimes I imagine him smiling, even though I know babies don't smile until they are much older.

Nik goes into work just before twelve and returns at four. Recently he's gone to Shakti Bhavan to use the gym, and I can see the difference in his body shape, the muscles returning to their former tautness. I've joined the support group. As most of the sessions are in the afternoon, it fits in well with our daily routine.

***

WHEN I OPEN THE BLINDS there is a thick, dense fog that has come down overnight; the flats opposite our small workman's cottage are hardly visible.

I am in two minds about taking Amar to the park today, worried the damp air won't be good for him. Jenny, the community nurse, reassures me that it won't be a problem.

"We'll have to get used to it, Ree. We can't keep him indoors every time the weather changes." Nik kisses me as he places Amar on the mat for his exercise.

I decide on taking Amar around the park in his pram today. I sit at our usual spot by the pond. I can hear the ducks, but the visibility is so poor I don't know where they are until one comes and pecks at my foot. The shock of it makes me gasp, and my heart races in my chest.

A memory bursts into my mind. I feel the panic; a duck has just nipped at my ankle, and I'm running towards a shadow lit from the top by lamplight. I can't see. There is a mist that obscures my view. "Mummy!" I shout.

"Come here, Reena." Her soft, reassuring voice is calling to me. When I come close to her, she pulls me onto her lap, and I tell her what has happened. She rubs her hand over my ankle.

"I don't like ducks."

"It's confused from the fog, baby. Come on, give me a hug."

"No, I don't like you," I say through sobs, and she sings the words that used to make me smile.

"Little Doll … Look at the beam of light … here comes the smile."

I smile when I think of my mother singing the song from *Dosti*, and her nickname for me, Gudiyaa. I make a promise to myself that I will sing to Amar, even though my voice isn't as beautiful and melodious as his father's.

I am playing '60s Hindi film songs when Nik comes home.

"We haven't listened to these for a while?" He reads the back of the CD, cuddling Amar in his arms. I bring our afternoon tea to the table.

"Do you like the songs, Diku?" he asks him. Amar stretches his left arm over his head and we both laugh at our son. It's moments like these that make my heart sing.

Sixteen

ONE FRIDAY, UMI AND ANNE-MARIE arrive in the morning with shopping bags.

"So, what's all this?" Nik asks as he takes the bags off them and places them on the dining table.

"You two are going on a date tonight," Umi explains as she turns to me.

I'm putting Amar back in the pram after his massage. I look across at them. They are both grinning.

"I ... we don't need to go on a date." I try to keep my voice calm. Inside my stomach, heavy stones are piling up, and my throat has constricted.

Nik has his arm around my waist, and whispers, "Breathe," in my ear. I allow my lungs to inhale. "That's very kind of you, but I don't think we need to go on a date," he says to them.

"No arguing," Anne-Marie points her index finger at us, her green eyes glinting with determination. "You've read the leaflets, you need to get away even if it's for an hour."

"We're not asking you to go far, and it's only to the pub," Umi adds. She takes my hand, and frown lines appear on her forehead. "Ree, you need to do this.

Amar is getting stronger. Let us take care of him."

Nik pulls me closer to him. "What do you think?" he says, his eyes questioning.

I take a deep breath in and say, "These two aren't going to give up." I ask Umi, "So, what's for dinner?"

"I'm making methi chicken and all my favourite Punjabi side dishes." She is waving a pale-blue hard-backed book with illustrations of herbs and spices

I had given Umi the personalised recipe book for her twenty-first birthday and think about the times we'd spent in our first year at university, she watching and learning how to cook. She uses it often and has begun to write her own adapted versions as footnotes in it.

"I haven't had Reena's methi chicken for a long time. My mouth is already watering," Anne-Marie says.

We argue after lunch about who could carry Amar in the sling during our daily walk in the park. I'd insisted only Nik and I carried him and they could push the pram.

"Why just you two? What's wrong with us carrying him and you coming with us?" Anne-Marie quizzes. I was taken aback by her question. I'd spoken with other people in the support group, who did let family and friends take their child to the park. They'd all agreed the stress of twenty-four hour care had no respite. Any help given should be embraced. I reluctantly agree to allow his masis to carry him in the baby sling.

When we walk in the park with Amar on Anne-Marie's front and Umi holding on to his hand, I think about our future. I should let our family and friends help us, instead of insisting Nik and I are the only ones who can care for Amar. Most of them had fed Amar through his nose tube in the hospital. It is easier than feeding a healthy baby in some ways. When the twins were small, they would be exhausted after suckling for a short time, and we had to coax them awake, Smita Bhabhi crying that they needed their milk in a bottle as they found it easier. Even bathing him was easy. He didn't cry in protest at the water or flail his arms. Perhaps I have been overprotective? As the thought enters my mind, a weight lifts off my shoulders.

Nik is already at home when we come back from our walk. He lifts Amar out of the baby sling and cuddles him, his eyes glistening.

"What's wrong?" I sit down next to him.

"Nothing, just missed him today … couldn't concentrate." His eyes are fixed on Amar's face. I wrap my arm around his waist and rest my head on his shoulder.

"Come on, you two, snap out of it."

Umi brings in some hot drinks, "Besides, it's my turn to hold him."

Nik reluctantly hands Amar over to Umi and raises a thin smile. "Sorry, can't help it, Umi, he is the other half of my heart."

"For a bloke, you're so soppy, Nik." She laughs and squeezes his upper arm.

Umi insists on feeding and changing Amar and suggests we should rest in our room while they prepare dinner. Nik begins to object until I take his hand and say, "Thank you, we'd like that," and walk him upstairs to our room.

I wrap my arms around his neck. "What's wrong? Did something happen at the office?" I stare into his eyes.

He brushes his lips on mine and his soft kisses are full of pain and anguish.

"Just hold me, Ree," he murmurs and pulls me to him tightly.

I feel his warm breath on my face and open my eyes. Our legs are entwined, the cover discarded, our bodies hot from our afternoon of intimacy.

"I love watching you sleep," he says as his mouth comes into contact with mine.

"Did you sleep?" I frown at him.

"Oh yes, one of your body twitches woke me up."

I have been getting quite a lot of them recently; it's something that happens to me when I'm stressed.

I lift my hand and caress his cheek, "Do you remember our Saturday afternoons?"

"Our afternoon delight," he sings; his eyes twinkle, the golden shards dance and he kisses me fervently. I let him work his mouth down my body.

Umi's Punjabi Meal

Methi Murg
chicken and fenugreek curry

Aloo Gobi
potato and cauliflower curry

Dal Makhani
*matpe beans slow cooked stew with cream speciality
of Punjabi cuisine*

Jeera Chawal
pilau made with rice and cumin seeds

Keera ka Riata
cucumber and yoghurt

Quick Naan
*unleavened flatbread made with baking powder and
plain flour cooked under a grill*

Kachumber
*salad made with cabbage, cucumber, carrots, tomatoes
and onions*

Lassi
thick natural yoghurt drink blended with water and spices

After dinner, Anne-Marie instructs us to go and change. We both object and say in unison, "This is fine."

"Oh no, you don't, you're not going out in those. Go and get dressed to impress," she insists. "Pretend it's your first date."

I search through my wardrobe, viewing the little dresses and the pencil pants, not sure what to wear. I've been wearing leggings and big baggy tops since I began to show at seven months into my pregnancy. My stomach has shrunk back since I've started running, and I know I can fit into my pre-pregnancy clothes. Nik has put on a cream shirt and a pair of dark-grey trousers and pulled out a navy blazer.

"I'll wait for you downstairs." He kisses the top of my head. "Surprise me." He raises his left eyebrow.

I find the cardigan jacket first and search for the trousers that match, hoping I can still fit into them. I stare at myself in the mirror; apart from the dark circles under my eyes, and the prominent cheekbones, I look exactly the same as I did when we first started dating.

I pull on my boots and walk down the stairs; he lifts himself up from the sofa and stands at the bottom. It reminds me of all the scenes in romantic films when the boy is waiting to take the girl out on their first date, parents watching. Anne-Marie and Umi stand, one holding Amar and the other with her hands on her hips.

He reaches his hand out to me, and I take it as I climb down the bottom step. His eyes are smouldering; he lingers a little too long with his lips on the back of my hand. The butterflies crash against the wall of my stomach. My breath catches.

"God, Ree, you are beautiful," he groans. "Isn't that the outfit you wore when we went for our first date?"

"You have a great memory, Mr Raja." I smile up at him.

* * *

WE ARE SITTING AT A SMALL TABLE by the fireplace, our legs entwined under it. Nik is holding my left hand, caressing the top of my knuckles with his thumb. My anxiety about leaving Amar created little knots in my stomach as we walked the short distance from our house to the pub.

"Better?" he asks after I've taken a couple of sips. The alcohol burns my stomach. I nod, still afraid that Amar isn't close by.

"The masis will be fine. It's two minutes away, and Umi can run that in thirty seconds if she has to."

I take another sip and the knots release as the warmth of the white wine eases my nerves.

"Do you mind?" Nik asks as he takes out his cigarette case. He lights his cigarillo. "I've cut down." He sees the anguish in my eyes. "It's harder when I have a drink."

"You know I don't like it." I squeeze his hand. "But I understand," I add.

We sit in quiet contemplation, holding hands, remembering our life before Amar and the many evenings we'd spent in the Queen Victoria.

"So, did you sign the contract?" I ask him, remembering the times we'd discussed our work here in the same spot.

He smiles, flicking the ash into the glass ashtray on our table. "Yes, all the i's dotted, and t's crossed. Do you remember I went to that Foreign Office do just before Christmas? The one organised with the Africa Development Group? Well, Kaka has been negotiating an expansion into Zambia and Zimbabwe."

I wonder how Nik's father had managed to do that and be at the hospital with us when we needed it, and I admire the man's ability to handle things calmly and quietly.

"It will be great. Papa would have been so excited; he had wanted to go into Zambia for too long." His eyes cloud over, and he concentrates on his drink, turning it anticlockwise on the polished wooden table.

"He would be very proud of you, Nik." I reach for his face and caress his cheek.

He fixes his gaze on mine and clears his throat. "I want to tell you something, Ree."

My stomach drops. What can make his eyes so pained? "Jay has found an address for one of my mother's sisters."

"I didn't know you were looking?"

"I wasn't … I'm not sure if I want to find them, but he was in Zanzibar for a couple of weeks and made some enquiries."

Why would Jay be searching for Nik's family? I wonder what are his reasons for doing this?

"It's good, right?" he asks, and I frown back at him. "When we decide to have a brother or sister for Amar, we'll know a bit more of my family history," he continues. "I'm not even sure if it's the right person and she might not want to know me or speak to me."

"I didn't think it was that easy to find relatives in Africa?"

"Apparently it is. Most people know of each other, and

the Parsi community is tight-knit."

I'm concerned this new piece of information will add to Nik's stress. I take both of his hands in mine and say, "Don't get your hopes up."

He nods, "Just wanted to tell you what else is going on."

"Is that why you were upset this afternoon?"

"Yes, I was shocked Jay's been searching. I would love to find out more, but I'm not ready yet. When Amar gets older, and we decide to have another child … " He pauses. "You do want more children, Ree?"

"I … I'm not sure, Nik. It depends … I can't think about it yet." My eyes betray me, and doubts form in my mind. Could we cope with Amar and another child? Would it mean moving back to Shakti Bhavan? What would happen to my job? I don't voice my concerns. His eyes show signs of hurt at my response. "But I do want more than one child, Nik."

We nurse our drinks thinking of the implications of having another child. We know of families who do have other healthy children, and the gynaecologist has ruled out any genetic conditions that have led to Amar's disability.

There's raucous laughter from the bar, and we both stare at a group of friends; a sandy-haired man in a dark suit is wearing a L-plate on his back.

"It's nice to be at the pub with you, Ree. We should go on dates more often." He smiles at me.

The alcohol helps me relax, and I've enjoyed being with Nik. When I'm at home, I'm always glancing at the clock, my routines set in stone. One deviation and the adrenaline increases sending me into a state of panic.

He lifts his watch arm, "Time we head home."

His glass is empty, and I take one last sip from my half-full glass.

He takes my coat and holds it up to me, leaving his hands on my lapel. He takes a deep breath and whispers, "Can we do more kissing when we get home, Mrs Raja?"

I turn around, lean my body into his and kiss him. Someone at the bar shouts, "Oi, get a room."

Faint music can be heard as we turn into our road, and as we get closer to our house, it becomes louder. The lights are off in the hallway. Nik turns to me and smiles, "Anne-Marie's brought her CDs."

Rick Astley is warbling at full volume, "Never gonna give you up." We take off our coats and walk into Umi, Peter, Dick and Anne-Marie. Dick has Amar in his sling and is dancing the only way he knows how, sliding and jiggling rhythmically to the music. The lights are dimmed, the music is loud. We used to have these nights before Amar arrived, using my silk scarves to cover the lamps.

They stop like teenagers caught in the act when parents return unexpectedly.

"Oh ... sorry, is it eleven o'clock already?" Umi grips Peter's hand, looking shamefaced. Anne-Marie and Dick are like musical statues in mid-dance pose. I sneak a peek at Nik; his face is like a stern parent. The sudden urge to giggle overwhelms me, and I stifle it by covering my mouth.

His grip tightens. "You are a traitor, Mrs Raja. I'm trying to be an adult here." His golden eyes dart at me.

I can't stop my grin spreading from ear to ear. The sight of our friends dancing with our son makes me happy; it's one thing we hadn't even thought about. I begin to laugh and take my husband's hand and dance, joyfully, enjoying the moment, vowing that I'll use more of our time in the joy of living instead of the sadness we've been carrying.

Our little disco finishes at midnight. The exhilaration of dancing has helped ease our burden. We are on the sofas drinking tea and coffee.

Peter clears his throat, "We have something to tell you all."

"You're back together again!" We shout in unison.

"How did you know?" His eyes are big.

"How could we not know?" Dick mutters. "You can't keep your hands off each other."

Umi rests her head on his shoulder. "We're serious this time, my dad knows, and Peter has asked to marry me."

"What? How could you have kept that a secret from me?" Nik asks.

"I just thought with all your problems, I didn't want to … " his voice trails off.

"Oh, a wedding, what will it be, Nigerian or Indian?" Anne-Marie asks.

"Haven't thought that far ahead yet," Umi replies. "All suggestions greatly received." She smiles at us.

Later, Nik says, "They're lucky to have a family who doesn't mind." He pulls me to him. "I'm sorry Motaba makes things difficult for you, Ree."

My eyes fill with tears as I think about what she'd said about me and to me.

"Why doesn't she like me, Nik?"

"I don't know, but I know this, Ree: I love you, always have, always will. My heart is empty without you." He begins to plant small kisses on my wet cheeks, and we continue with the kissing we'd started in the pub.

Seventeen

OUR LIFE AT HOME HAS BEEN A STRAIN recently. One day I'm upbeat and buoyant, and the next, I'm drowning in pain and sorrow.

No one can really explain the stress and anxiety of taking care of a sick child. It has been difficult. We've argued about the slightest things. I can't help being overprotective of Amar, and Nik feels inadequate as my possessiveness increases. I've researched every diagnosis possible, gone to groups, taken our son to doctors, and he has resorted to fasting and giving up foods, asking Motaba for guidance. I'm not sure if it's the guilt that he is the child of her husband's deceit or that the rituals and customs are so ingrained in his life. She had come to see us at the beginning of this week, and I'd overheard the conversation between them.

"Your wife is too stubborn to understand these rituals, Nikesh. You have to tell Reena to at least follow some of the instructions Guruji has given her to do," she scolded him.

"Can't I do them instead of Reena? She needs to recover from the birth and the infections," he pleaded.

"No, your son's planets are weak. It has to be both of you. Convince her. If she wants Amar to live, you will need to perform the havan, as soon as possible."

I didn't walk away, this time. I lashed out, saying I was not wasting my time, sitting in a havan when my son had days to live.

"My son, my son." She'd spat the words out like bullets. "You forget he's also my son's son, and if Nikesh wants to perform the havan, you are duty-bound as his wife to sit with him."

I had picked up Amar, put him in a pram coat and walked out of the house, leaving mother and son to deal with each other.

At our routine appointment with Professor Rossi last week, we had received the news that Amar's tests did not show any improvement, even though he is moving more than he has ever done before. Professor Rossi explained as the brain stem is beginning to deteriorate, the muscles are stimulated, and his movements are reflexes and nothing more. We had asked how long he would live, and she had said that the blood results showed it would be days, maybe weeks, until complete organ failure. We cried when we heard the news, and Professor Rossi had been very kind, telling us we had been exceptional parents and were very courageous to take care of him at home. She had explained what the signs would be. I argued with Nik that I wanted to keep the news to ourselves and eventually he agreed not to tell anyone. But he had broken his promise and told his motaba. *Why else would she be discussing more fast days and rituals?* He tried to comfort me after she had left, kissing and caressing and I pushed him away, unable to forgive him for telling her of all people about our son's diagnosis.

* * *

NIK HAD TRIED NOT TO go to the office the day after the news, holding Amar in his arms, changing him, feeding him, telling me to sleep, but his need to run away from the things that hurt him overwhelms him. It's what he does. He would go out for a few hours at night, returning smelling of smoke and drink and cry, his body shaking. Not wanting to talk about how he felt. Not wanting to confide in me. The grief of losing our son has become a chasm between us. Neither of us wants to express our feelings. Last night was one of those nights, one of his nights of being anywhere else but at home with me.

I pick up the phone in the bedroom to call Divya Ba. Nik is talking on the phone. I hadn't heard him come home and look at the alarm clock.

It's two-thirty in the afternoon; he's probably tired and wants a nap before he goes out again, I think resentfully. Jay has started to come in the evenings, tempting him to go to the pub or for a walk. I must have been in deep sleep when he came back last night. I cannot recall the time. As I am preparing to put the receiver back, I hear her name.

"We had a good time last night at Jules's. She called me earlier, you dirty boy. What time did you get home? Do you want to go clubbing again, tonight?" Jay asks.

"No, I think I'll stay home tonight," Nik replies.

"Come on, Nik. Last night with Jules means something, right? You can't really love Reena as much as you say. You wouldn't have slept with Jules if you did."

"You don't understand, Jay." He sighs.

"You've told me, Nik, how she's always tired, how she's besotted with Amar and doesn't give you the time of day."

"She is my wife. I love her. I've told you how she makes me feel. When she left me last time … " He pauses. "I nearly … I couldn't cope if she did that again."

"I thought that was all about getting rid of the baby, that you'd felt betrayed. Leave her. Pay her off, you've got the money. Think of the possibilities. You can go anywhere, anytime, no guilt, no responsibility, no wife. It would be like old times. I'll make you happy. I love you, Nik. You must know how much I love you. These one-night stands are just that, nothing but sex," Jay implored

"I don't love you the way you love me. I love you like my brothers. I thought you'd realise when I started seeing Jules. I'm not like you. What we did was sexual exploration. It made you who you are, Jay, but it isn't who I am. You'll never understand. I've tried to tell you so many times; I can't leave them, they are my heart. I've been stupid. I've forgotten they are my responsibility. The news of finding my mother's family has made me lose my way. It upset me, and I forgot about my love, my life. I'm going to be with my wife and son as much as I can. I've told Kaka I'm not going into the office anymore." He pauses. "If you were a true friend, you'd support me." Nik put the phone down.

I hear the fizz from the can and the glug as it pours in the glass. An agonising pain sears through my body.

Nik slept with Julie and the words, 'You can't really love Reena as much as you say,' resound in my head. I fall back on the bed, my bones unable to support me.

I replay all the times we accidentally bumped into her when he went away and how Jay had mentioned meeting her when they were away on business trips. All the short breaks and holidays when she had turned up.

I pick through every conversation for evidence of his infidelity, gnawing at the boil that is our faithless marriage. I thought Nik was okay with the news that his birth was a result of his father's cheating. "Like father like son," I say quietly to the air.

He's probably done this many times before. He was caught off guard last night and Jay saw. Jay, the friend, who facilitates all the outings, the man who has never liked me and has said many times he is the only one who understands him. The man who is in love with my husband and has finally admitted it to him. I thought I understood Nik, but I was wrong. I believed him when he said he loved me, and he even said the fake lines back to Jay. 'They are my heart.' What a fool I've been; it has always been about Julie.

I suddenly understand why he was so upset about the pregnancy, why it would put a damper on his life. He would have to spend more time with us, be part of a family. I know his father would have changed his schedule. Turning the long business trips into shorter ones. It must have taken all his willpower and charm to pretend he was happy when Amar was on his way, the way he would smile and sing to my belly. His excitement at the scans, and how he had a copy in his wallet. I'm in admiration at his ability to lie so convincingly. Jay is right: only he understands him.

He sulks and complains to Jay that I don't spend any time with him. *How can I?* I'm exhausted from always being positive, still fighting to keep Amar alive. When all I want to do is curl up and sleep and forget what has happened to him. To sleep, to drown out the pain and sorrow my bad luck has brought to our son. *Why doesn't he understand that every time we are intimate, I feel pain?* I had read that the first few months change you, these things happen in a marriage. Sex isn't my priority. The agonising pain of the stitches and the fact they have not healed add to my reluctance to be intimate with him. I'm not a machine who can turn my feelings on and off to satisfy his needs. *How could he tell Jay, Jay of all people, the only other person who wishes Nik had never met me?*

I hear his footsteps on the stairs, and I pretend to be asleep. He picks up Amar and whispers, "Come, Diku, let's take you downstairs. Your Mummy needs to rest."

He closes the door of our bedroom, and I cry sad, silent tears, my life shattered. The only man I've ever loved has torn my fragile heart apart. No matter what happens to our son, I always believed Nik would still love me. He promised he would never hurt me. He would protect me. *How wrong have I been?* I cry until my tears of hurt and betrayal run dry.

I'll wait and bide my time. I won't allow Nik or his mistress to ruin the last few days of our son's life. I'll let him play happy families, but when the time comes, I will not let Nikesh Raja or his family hurt me ever again. I won't make the same mistake twice. I repeat the words over and over in my mind until I can no longer hold onto my anger and fall asleep.

His beautiful voice is singing the lullaby from *Aradhana*, "Chanda Hai Tu." He smiles up at me, and I rub my eyes, trying to wipe the hatred from them. He's singing the song I always sing to Amar, the song that reminds me of my time with my mother. The song I sing to tell our son that I only live to be with him.

"What's the matter, Ree?" He frowns.

"Nothing," I mutter. He has taken away the only precious memory I have of my son and made it his own. The words, that mean so much, of my feelings for Amar.

"You're my moon, you're my sun, you're the star of my eyes. I only live by looking at you. You support my broken heart."

Eighteen

Friday

NIK HAS TOLD EVERYONE about the conversation we had with Professor Rossi. Amar has not been passing urine for three days, and every time we test before a feed to see if his meal has been absorbed, we get undigested milk.

At ten o'clock, the community nurse confirms he is no longer digesting milk and his kidneys have stopped working. Our GP comes for a home visit and confirms the diagnosis.

Amar seems healthier than he has ever done before; his cheeks are fatter, his arms and legs chubbier, his face is brighter, and I keep asking the doctor if he is sure. It is difficult for me to accept he won't survive the weekend. I cried hysterical convulsive tears, my ribs aching from the effort, when he told me he was ready to leave us. I cried for the loss of my life: I would no longer be a mother or a wife. I ache at the thought of Nik leaving me. *When will he think a decent amount of time has passed before he tells me he wants to be with Julie?* The loss of my husband tears a hole through my debilitated heart. *Is this what happened to his mother? Did her heartbreak feel the same?*

My daddy arrives at lunchtime. I stare at him, my eyes unable to focus, and see an old man, his shoulders slumped, his familiar black eyes looking back at me.

"I look like a proper nana," he says as he runs his hand through his hair. His hair has turned white in the last two weeks. He puts his arm around my shoulder, and I say, "Yes, you do." I look at the baby that is in my arms, who'll never know his grandfather. Nik comes to take Amar off me, and I yell, "Take your hands off my son!" unable to keep the contempt out of my voice.

Daddy's face is full of sympathy and apology for my behaviour, and I think if only you knew, Daddy, what this man has done to me. *You would protect me, you wouldn't believe he was that great.* Nikesh Raja, the son-in-law you've begun to look upon as a son.

My father holds Amar, whispering in his ears, barely making eye contact with anyone but Amar. I dread seeing him like that; it is too much like the times he remembered my mother. Staring at her photographs, talking to her image, listening to her favourite songs, watching her favourite films. *He will reach for the whisky and drown his sorrow this evening.* When Nik takes Amar from him, I hardly give him time to hold him, pleading with him to give him back to me; sorrow fills his eyes as he reluctantly hands our son back to me. *Why do you care? I think. Isn't this what you want?* Once he's gone, he'll be free to leave and be with Julie.

At four o'clock, Sunil and Nik's parents arrive, bringing food in the black holdall that became a familiar sight at the hospital.

"How are you, Beta?" His mother sits down next to me

as I hold on to Amar. "Would you allow me to hold him for a little while?"

I nod and give my son to the woman who I have begun to regard as my mother. She gently takes him and walks with him to her husband and son.

"Hello, Reena, how are you?" Sunil asks.

I want to say I'm angry that Amar doesn't have long to live and want to scream and shout at the injustice of losing my baby; tell him about the outrage of being used as a pawn in some game that the man who I had given my heart to was playing. Instead, I say I'm fine, and I clasp my hands together to stop him from seeing that my whole body is shaking from fury.

"Can I check you out?"

I nod. He takes my pulse and examines my eyes.

"Have you been sleeping?" I shake my head. He turns to Nik and asks, "Did your doctor prescribe sleeping pills for Reena?"

"Yes, Jijaji, I'll bring them to you."

Nik comes out of the kitchen, his eyes drifting to Amar as he walks back to us.

Sunil hands a glass of water to me and holds out a pill. "You're going to take this and go for a rest," he instructs. "Niku, I want you to take Reena upstairs and wait with her until she is asleep."

He tries to take my hand, but I clasp them together; he puts his hand on my elbow, and we walk side by side up the narrow stairs.

"Lie down, my love," he instructs as he slips off my slippers.

I see the empty crib, and flop to sitting on the bed and start to cry into my hands. He gazes at me for an eternity, knowing I don't want him to comfort me.

"Please let me help you, Ree," he pleads.

I dare not look at him, because I know my resolve to keep him at a distance will dissolve, and I'll melt into his arms.

I lie down, turn my back to him, pull my legs up to my chest, and close my eyes. I feel him sit on the edge of the bed, and count his breaths, one, two, three, four, five, six, seven, eight, nine, ten.

Darkness surrounds me, and I feel nothing.

* * *

MY HEART IS RACING. My lungs are pleading for oxygen. I gasp for breath. A bitter taste of bile fills my mouth, and the contents of my stomach rise up. I reach for the bin and throw up. My eyes are watering; the sting of the acid burns the lining of my nose. I retch again until there is nothing left to expel from my body. The bedroom door opens and Umi frowns at me. She switches on the lamp and sits on the bed, pouring a glass of water from the jug. I hold it in both hands and take a sip. "Where's my baby?" I can feel the panic rise up again. She takes me in her arms.

"He's still with us, Ree. Let's get you cleaned up and go downstairs."

The house is full of family and friends; every seat is occupied, and some people are sitting on the carpeted floor of the lounge.

Nik's mother and his sisters are in the kitchen, taking out pans. My son is being held by Anil. I wonder how long I have been sleeping. The lights are on, and the living room curtain has been drawn.

"Sit down, Reena."

He hands my son to me. I search Amar and check he

isn't in pain. His face is serene, his eyes are closed, and I can feel him breathing through my hand as it rests on his back.

My eyes search the room for his father, and I wonder, *where is he?* There is a discreet knock on the window. Peter stands up from the floor to open the front door.

One of the three people who are missing enters the house. Motaba is carrying a couple of carrier bags. She hands them to Suresh, who has stood up to take them off her. Peter follows with a holdall in each hand.

The kitchen worktop is laid with dinner, and everyone is instructed to eat. I ignore the call and I concentrate on putting to memory all the tiny differences in my son's face. His left ear is slightly lower than his right. His lips naturally curl upwards into a smile. His nose is just like Nik's, long and thin. His forehead is more like my father's. His eyebrows are faint and arched.

A plate of food is presented to me. I stare at it and then look up to see who has brought it.

"I know you don't want to, Reena." She raises a small smile, and the dimples do not appear on her cheeks, "But you have to eat." Rita's eyes glisten. "May I have Amar for a little while?" she asks me, as she places the plate on the small coffee table that has been put in front of me.

***

"DO YOU KNOW WHERE THEY'VE GONE?" Nik's father asks Peter.

"No, sir. I thought they were going for a walk. Didn't expect them to be gone so long."

"Can you go check in the pub for me?" he directs.

It is ten minutes to nine o'clock, and neither Nik nor

Jay have come back home. I expected him to run but hadn't expected him to run off today of all days. The last couple of days have been a strain. I've tried to pretend everything is fine, but the phone call replays and replays in my sleeping and my waking hours, and he has begun to realise that something is wrong.

He could have waited. Our world is falling apart, and all he can think about is running to his mistress. He is so selfish. *How could I have misread him?* I thought he was so thoughtful and kind. I think about all the sweet things I had seen him do. The way he told his parents he loved them after he had found out about his birth. The way he spent time with my father when we first got engaged. The small acts of kindness to my brother and Smita when the twins were born. The knife that has lodged into my heart slides in a little bit deeper as it dawns on me that it is all an act, a selfish act to get people on his side.

Everyone is wondering where Nik and Jay have gone, but no one is voicing their concerns. The elders are sitting around the dining table, murmuring. Amar is being passed around so that everyone can say their last goodbyes. The Bhagavad-Gita is being chanted on the music player. I let my mind concentrate on the shlokas to ease the betrayal and anguish caused by my husband. As the late hour approaches, people begin to say their goodbyes.

"Can we bring the children tomorrow?" Rupa Bhabhi asks me, as she hands Amar back to me.

"Won't it upset them?" I ask her, worried the memories will haunt them. My thoughts drift to the time of my mother's death and how the nightmares affect me.

"They know he's not well. I want Anousha and Tarun to come, and I'm sure Ben and Jaish feel the same. Rishi and Rakhee are coming tomorrow, aren't they? They will have company."

He stumbles through the door. Jay is holding him up and smiling adoringly at his face.

"What time do you call this, Nikesh?"

His father's voice is filled with suppressed anger. That's the first time I've heard him call him by his full name. He must be furious. His mother rushes next to her husband and touches his arm.

"Sorry, sorry." Nik puts his palms together in submission, his head is bowed, and his words are slurred. He puts both of his hands in his pockets and sways towards me, his bloodshot eyes locked on mine. "So, you have him all to yourself, Ree. But you forget he's my son, too. I have every right to hold him and take care of him. He doesn't just belong to you. He belongs to me, too. Give him to me." He pulls Amar out of my arms. "I won't allow you to keep him to yourself."

He is hurting him with the force of his hands. I let go of Amar, unable to endure the pain.

"Hello, Diku. Don't go … stay with me." He sits down on the sofa next to me, a big fat tear plopping on Amar's chest. I cover my face with my hands and the sobs escape from my mouth. He pulls my hand down and caresses my cheek. "I'm sorry, Ree. Please forgive me. I didn't mean to hurt you."

It's always the same. I'm sorry, please forgive me, didn't mean to hurt you. *How many times have I listened to those words and believed him?* "Not this time," I say to myself. I know it's his guilt that makes him say the words. It has nothing to do with love. I have deluded myself for far too long. I get up and go to the bathroom, without saying a word. Not yet, I tell myself. I want him to be in real pain when I tell him I know.

Nineteen

Saturday

A SMALL CURLY-HAIRED CHILD is running away from me. Suddenly a white mist obliterates my view. "Wait, wait, you're running too fast." My legs are as heavy as tree stumps, and no matter how hard I try, he seems to be going further away from me. I run through the mist and find myself in a clearing in a forest. I run around in a circle until I glimpse a view through the trees. He is running towards a tree, encircled by a white picket fence. My stomach clenches. I won't be able to stop him before he gets to the gate. The feeling that the gate is dangerous overwhelms me. "Amar, Amar, STOP, STOP. Please, you don't want to go inside," I shout as loud as I can.

He turns around and smiles, "But, I want to go, Mummy." He opens the gate and runs towards a girl on the white swing. She is wearing a white dress, her dark-brown hair in two pigtails. He stops in front of the swing. I'm frightened it will hit him. He lifts his arms up to her. She halts the swing with her feet and pulls him up onto her lap. I'm at the fence and searching for the gate that is no longer there. I run around it to find a way in. My lungs are bursting, and I cannot breathe. I'm bent double, holding my stomach, gasping for air. "Please don't take him, please," I ask the girl.

She smiles at me and says, "But it's time."

"No, it can't be. It's too soon. Amar, come back, don't go. Please don't go."

"I have you, Ree. It's only a dream." I'm choking. I can't breathe. He's suffocating me; I hold my hands against his chest to push him away.

My eyes fix on the empty crib. "Where's Amar? Amar! Amar!"

He is holding my shoulders. "Look at me, Ree. He's okay, he's with Daddy."

My hands fist and I pound his chest. "Let me go, Nik. I don't want you here. Leave me alone. Please." My throat hurts.

I take my son in my arms, a sense of relief floods through my veins. He is alive and breathing. I see the pain in my father's face. He must have heard my screams and shouts.

* * *

THE TWINS BURST INTO THE SITTING room, holding a sheet of paper each.

"Papa, look what we've drawn," Rishi shouts.

I sit at the dining table, nursing a cup of tea. Rakhee comes up to me and shows me her drawing, "Mummy says I'm as good a drawer as you, Fi." I take the sheet off her and examine it.

"Your mummy's right, Rakhee," I say. "I think you'll be even better than me." The noise of the twins brings a smile to everyone's faces.

"What about me, look at mine, Fi." Rishi thrusts his drawing at me.

"You're good, too," I tell him and he grabs hold of my face and plants a wet kiss on my cheek.

The door to the bathroom opens, and Nik steps out. They both run at him, each grabbing a leg. "Neenufua, it took ages to get here. We did a drawing." Rakhee looks up at him and smiles.

"Fi has it, come and see." Rishi pulls at him.

"I can see you need a run around, munchkins." Nik pulls one on his front and then squats down as the other climbs his back. "Shall we play in the garden?" He heads for the kitchen door. They are clinging to him like limpets, and he steps into our little courtyard garden and closes the door.

"Hey, Sis." Amit is on his haunches gazing at Amar who is being held by my father. I kneel down next to him, and he wraps his arm around my shoulders and pulls me closer.

"What am I going to do, Bro?" I utter.

He gives me a kiss on the cheek. "You've done so much. He's lucky to have a mummy like you. Daddy, can I hold him?"

Amit sits beside him. My father hands Amar to him. Smita lifts me up to standing and hugs me, her eyes wet from the tears she shed quietly as she stood watching us. Amit pulls at her hand and gestures for her to sit down next to him.

I walk away, unable to watch my family, saddened by the prospect that Amar doesn't have long with them. I can hear excited squeals from the garden, and I watch as the children chase Nik around the tiny courtyard, trying to catch him as he dodges them. His eyes lock with mine, and he smiles a thin, sad smile. His eyes are sad, the golds are ochre, the eyes that caught my breath no longer visible; a brown mist has coated them.

By lunchtime, the house is full of children, chattering and sitting on the stairs. They all want to give Amar a hug, the older ones knowing they may not see him again, the younger ones copying the older ones. I'm sorrowful that today will probably be the last time I'll see Nik's nephews and nieces. I know once I leave Nik, the bond we have will be broken. The children will be discouraged from coming to see me, especially if Motaba has her way. Once Nik brings Julie home, they'll soon forget their aunt who did the strange drawings of them. *Another part of my life that has brought me happiness will be torn from me by my husband's deception.*

The children had wanted to take Amar to the park, as usual, but Rupa Bhabhi had told them it wasn't possible. In the end, we agreed to play in the nursery, and they laughed and whooped. I've placed Amar in the cot, while the children fan the foil and paper butterfly mobile they've made for him. I watch over them from the Victorian nursing chair and try not to cry, clenching my jaw tight, smiling at the energy and vitality of life that surrounds my son. Thoughts of their lucky parents tug at my mind, crying babies, the tantrums with food, the sleepless nights, and the time spent nursing them back to health when they become ill. Jealousy fills my core: they have it all, and I will have nothing once he leaves me.

Samir is guarding the cot against the younger ones. Ram is trying to climb into it. I get up and pick him up on my hip; he pulls at my face and points, "Baby sleep."

I nod, "Yes, baby sleeping," and my eyes fill with tears. Anousha rushes to the top of the stairs and shouts, "Ashikaki, can you take Ram? He's making Reekaki cry."

I wipe my face with my sleeves. "No, it's okay, Anoo, just a bit tired today, that's all." Nik enters the nursery and takes Ram off me.

"My turn to babysit you lot." He smiles at them. I walk across the small landing and lie on my bed, burying my head in the pillows so the children don't hear my sobs.

By the evening, the house is quiet again, the children and their parents have gone. Only our parents remain, sitting around the dining table, while Nik and I change Amar into his sleepsuit on a changing mat on the floor. I lift him up and hand him to Nik's mother. The urge to keep him with me still gnaws at me. Amar convulsed at nine o'clock. We had been told this would happen and the only thing we can do is to try to keep him comfortable. Everyone remaining in the house is devastated, knowing that he won't be with us for long.

Twenty

Sunday

WHEN I WENT TO BED LAST NIGHT, I had Amar in bed with me, enveloped in my arms. I turned my back to Nik and held our son. Nik had put his arm around me, too, and I'd been too sad to push him away. I pretended he had never cheated on me and imagined he loved me as much as I loved him. I stayed awake to watch Amar, scared I might miss his last breath.

I hear a baby crying in the distance and wonder where the noise is coming from. I pick up the pillow and cover my head, trying to drown out the sound. It's too soon to get up; the street is hushed, and the room is in darkness. The cry is persistent and doesn't go away. I take the pillow off my head and try to focus on where it's coming from. I open my eyes and Amar is no longer by my side. I search for him. He is back in the crib. He is crying, real loud cries. I rub my eyes, unable to comprehend what I'm seeing. How can he be actually crying? He's never cried before. My heart leaps. Nik is stirring next to me. I pick up Amar, and my tears fall on his cheeks.

"Shush, shush," I say to him softly, "Mummy's here,

you're safe," and he stops. Our son has cried for the first time in his life, and I was the only one to witness it, even his father slept through it. I glance at the clock: it reads 2.15 a.m., exactly eight weeks after his birth. I hear Amar. I finally hear his voice. I rock him in my arms, hot fat tears continuing to fall on his blanket. All this time I wished to hear him and I had shushed him. "Please cry again, please cry," I whisper in his ear.

I place him by my side and watch him in the dim light. His breath is no longer steady. Sometimes he holds on to his breath for far too long, and his exhalations are too short. The rhythmic beat of his heart has changed; he is at the end of his life. No parent should witness the death of a child. No parent dreams that it would happen to them. Just like that my heart tears in two; one half slides into Amar's chest. I hold him tight and will my life to end and my son's life to begin. I want him to live, to stay, and to live forever, even if I'm not with him. I beseech God to take my life in exchange for his. I let my salty tears soak through his night suit, hoping the tears will carry my life force to sustain him. A man whose face I cannot see is pulling me through a long corridor.

"Please, I can't leave my children! Why are you doing this?" I'm talking to his back; his grip is hurting my hand. I'm trying to pry my fingers from his. We slow down as the people in front slow down. I kick him in the shin, and his grip loosens. I run back through the winding corridor, pushing against the stream of people walking towards the plane. I can see the children sitting in a huddle in the airport lounge, one holding a blonde-haired doll, the other a wooden aeroplane. Relief floods over me. They haven't noticed

I left them; I can still get back to them. Suddenly I'm grabbed by my waist and lifted off the ground. My legs suspend in mid-air, unable to go any further.

A woman in a red saree approaches and crouches down. They smile at her, they stand, and she takes their hands. She turns her face to me and says, "Don't worry, I'll look after them, you need to go away." The children smile up at her.

"No, no, you can't have them. Please, Mummy, don't take them from me. Please don't take him from me, please. PLEASE!"

"Ree, Ree, wake up. I have you." I'm in Nik's arms. "You're safe."

Beads of sweat trickle down my neck, and I gasp for air. My lungs are bursting from the lack of oxygen. "She's … taken … him … Nik … She's taken him." I croak the words out in between deep breaths.

He turns me around. "Look, my love. He's still here."

I see Amar sleeping on the bed. I put my hand on his chest and feel it rise and fall.

The bedroom door opens. *Who is this old man with stooped shoulders is?*

"Reena, you have to be brave," he tells me as he comes to sit on the edge of the bed. His expression is full of sadness; the voice is familiar.

***

"HELLO, SARLA BEN. NAREN SPEAKING. You should come … he hasn't got long now. Oh … they should be here soon. Can you tell everyone else? Jai Shri Krishna."

As soon as he puts the phone down, the doorbell rings. He answers the door. I hear a whispered exchange.

Nik's parents enter the lounge.

His mother comes to where I am holding onto Amar, afraid that if I let him go, he will stop breathing.

She turns my face to hers and strokes my damp hair away from my forehead. My body is hot, hot from the panic that he is dying, and I cannot do anything. Nik has his arm around my shoulders, his eyes fixed on Amar's chest, watching the intermittent rise and fall as he gasps for breath.

"Niku, Reena, we're here now. Don't worry, everything will be all right." Her comforting soft voice is hushed.

The Bhagavad-Gita is chanting on the music player; the low incantations, for the first time, do not comfort me. What is the point of listening to words? It means nothing. It is all a sham. *If there was a God, how could he take Amar away from me? How could he watch us suffer?*

The community nurse comes at her usual time of ten thirty. She is taken to the kitchen, and someone speaks with her in a hushed voice.

"Oh, I see," she says. She sits down next to me and asks, "Reena, can I check Amar?" Her features are softened, and she smiles at me. "I'll look after him. Why don't you go and get changed?" I'm reluctant to leave him.

She holds my hand. "Just a quick check."

Nik's mother takes my elbow and leads me to the bathroom. "I've brought your clothes down for you." She is holding a pile of clothes and hands them to me. "Have a shower, Reena, it will make you feel better."

Why would I want to feel better? I want to hold onto the pain and sadness. I don't want to let it go; I'm afraid that if I do, I won't feel anything.

Nik is sitting with Amar in his arms on the sofa that has become my preferred place to sit. He moves to one side; he turns to me, his eyes dark and muddy. A lump forms in my throat.

"I'm sorry, Ree." He hands him to me.

"Is he … has he gone?" My question is barely audible.

"No … no … my love."

As soon as I wrap my arms around our son, he sighs a soft, slow sigh.

I release a loud, gut-wrenching sob and Nik holds onto me, his arm around my shoulders, his head resting on my head. This is it. Our son, who came into the world unable to breathe, leaves this world with one last breath. A river of tears washes over my face, and I feel the wet tears that Nik is shedding on my head.

**

AMAR'S GRANDPARENTS ARE HUDDLED together on the other sofa. The door opens from the hallway. Jane walks in. My father gets up and she hugs him.

"How are you, Naren?" she asks, kindly.

Nik's parents stand up and embrace her.

"Anant, Pushpa, I'm so sorry." She stands back, her arms hanging down by her sides.

She turns to where we are sitting, and she sits on her knees in front of us. She strokes Amar's face. He is at peace. Her grey eyes water and a single tear runs from the edge of the creases. It is the first time I've seen Jane cry. Her professional face shows very little sign of emotion, but just in that brief moment, I see vulnerability. The moment washes sadness over me, and I sob.

"I tried, Jane, I really did try to keep him here. I've failed. I'm useless."

"No, you're not, Reena. You're a strong, courageous woman. You're both the strongest people I've met. You did a brilliant job looking after him. Sometimes we can't fight what's meant to be."

* * *

A MAN IN A THICK WOOLLEN COAT with a grey goatee beard stands over me.

"Can I check him?"

He has a thick Mancunian accent. I let go of Amar while he takes him off me and puts him on the sofa we've vacated. He kneels and takes out a stethoscope from a small black leather bag. He takes out a leather-bound notebook, examines his watch and writes.

"Can I use your phone?" he asks.

Nik nods his head, and the man picks up the telephone, dials and speaks into it, requesting an ambulance, providing our address and telephone number. He quietly adds, "I want to report a death." At those words, Nik's head bows and he shields his face.

Although he is gone, I do not want anyone else to hold him. He is mine, he grew inside me. People are filling up the room. Their bodies make the room unbearably hot. I cannot breathe. My stomach lurches. A sense of panic overcomes me as the house becomes crowded.

"Daddy, can you tell all these people to go home?" I say to my father who is sitting next to me, trying to keep the panic from showing in my voice.

"No, Reena, they've come to see you."

"Why? I don't need them. I'm fine," I tell him, and

that's when I taste the bile in my mouth and gulp back the tears. He takes my hand.

"Let's step outside for a minute. Can I have Amar?" he asks me. He sees the reluctance in me to let go. "He'll get cold, Reena. I'll give him to Pushpa Bhabhi."

We step outside the front door, and I see her climb out of the car.

"Jai Shri Krishna, Naren Bhai, Reena, where is he?"

"He's gone Sarla Ben, you're too late," my father says, his expression full of sadness.

She gasps, "I … I thought I had time, I … I brought some gangajal."

She fumbles through her handbag and pulls out a small bulbous copper pot. She wipes a tear as it appears from under the gold frame of her glasses.

"It's Nikesh's papa's birthday today. He's taken Amar from me. He didn't wait for me, for me to say my goodbye."

The pot slips out of her hand and clatters on the pavement. Manu Kaka opens the driver's door, rushes to hold her up straight, and escorts her into the house.

* * *

TWO YOUNG POLICEMEN ARRIVE. They shake hands with my father and say something. I hear nothing but the rush of blood in my ears and the thudding of my heart. Nothing is important to me. He is gone. The child who was the centre of my life and who took up all my time and was the reason for me to live has gone. They stand guard outside our front door; the man with the goatee beard talks to them and they wait.

The ambulance crew arrives, and I hold my son tightly.

"Reena, you need to let him go." Jane's hand is on my arm. "Can I take him from you?" I nod. "Give him a kiss goodbye."

And I do. *His face has always been cold,* I think, as my lips brush his cheek. I run my fingers over his nose, his mouth, his eyebrows, his forehead. I etch to memory the contour of his chin, the feel of his tiny body.

She stands up and hands Amar to Nik; he holds him tightly to his chest, his head bowed. His face is ashen. He walks with him to the hallway. I watch him, his broad shoulders stooped, his strong gait halting. My heart breaks at seeing him walking alone, and I stand up and walk to him, placing my arm around his waist. Even though he has hurt me, his pain is my pain, too. *I'm probably the only one who understands what he's feeling.* He turns his head, his voice hoarse.

"He's left us, Ree. Why did you leave us, Diku?" he asks our son.

A single tear falls onto our son's face and we step outside.

"Please, may I take him?" the paramedic asks.

"No! I won't let you take him." His face has darkened. "I … I can't let him go."

The man waits, his face filled with sympathy.

The doctor and the policeman step closer to us.

"Please, sir. They need to take him," says the dark-haired policeman with an Irish accent.

"Niku, let him go. You've done all you can." Nik's father touches his arm.

Nik hands our son to the paramedic, and he grabs me closer to him. The ambulance crew close the door and it pulls away. We watch it leave the road, flashing its blue light as it turns left and disappears.

He turns to me, and I bury my head in his chest. I feel his body spasm, as he gasps for air in between waves of sorrow. I hold onto my husband, feeling his muscular back as I allow my body to take comfort in the warmth of his body in my anguish. I savour the warmth of him, and my mind takes me back to the time when I was innocent and unaware of his deception and how safe I felt in his arms. He promised to protect me. I wish I hadn't heard the phone call, the one that sent my world out of orbit. The one that means after the funeral, I will no longer be his wife. I should have listened to my father: men like Nikesh Raja cannot change. Their lives are very different, their morals are very different. *How could I have forgotten about Indian men?* The stories I'd heard at the mandir; an Indian wife at home and English girlfriend on the side. I pull away, unable to forgive him, unable to forget the words as they play over and over in my mind.

'You can't really love Reena as much as you say. You wouldn't have slept with Jules if you did.'

He holds onto my hand as I step back into the hallway. I turn to him.

"Let me go in, Nik."

He releases my hand reluctantly, puts his hand in his pocket and pulls out his cigarette case and lighter.

The hallway door opens and Nik walks in; his eyes are swollen from crying.

"Where have you been, Nik?" Umi asks him quietly.

"Had to go for a walk, sorry," he says.

"Go and eat. Kaka and Kaki are waiting for you," she says.

He had probably gone to the phone box to speak with

Julie. He needed to tell her he cannot see her for a while. He needed to hear her voice. The thought invades my mind, and a huge boulder rests on my chest. *Even today, the day we've lost our son, he couldn't keep away.*

* * *

THE ROOM IS STILL FILLED with warm bodies. Smita's brother has taken the twins to her parents'. It was nice to have them running up and down the stairs, lining up Amar's soft toys, discussing which one is the leader and should be at the top, asking me which one I thought was most important.

I observe the people remaining without any emotion. I wonder why I don't feel anything; my heart is empty, my eyes dry, my vision dull. The noise of soft whispers reverberates in my ears.

She is standing up, her back to the television, Blankety Blank is on, the sound muted. Les Dawson's rotund frame is holding up a cue card and a ridiculously small mic and he is reading to a bank of celebrities sitting in two rows. I wonder what he's reading out as the stars write on their whiteboards. Nik comes out of the bathroom and sits down next to me.

I listen to Sarladevi's authoritative voice talking about flowers, the rituals we will have to observe on the day of the funeral, the lunch, the fasting.

"Rajesh, when you go to the funeral director's tomorrow, find out where they take the babies?"

"What do you mean, Motaba?" Rajesh speaks, his voice low.

"Well, in India and Africa, we used to take the babies to the cemeteries, and they would bury them for us, no need for a coffin."

Nik's grip tightens on my hand.

"We can't cremate him. He needs to be buried," Kaka tells Rajesh.

"Why can't we bury him in a coffin, Kaka? He needs a coffin."

The father and son are the only ones talking. Everyone else is sitting silently, fearful of what she is implying.

"That's what you need to ask tomorrow," she says. "These things happen; we knew he wasn't long for this world. His janam kundli told us this."

I straighten up as she says this, every cell in my body filling with anger.

"An unmarked grave is the best. You will soon forget and have more babies." Her words are callous.

I think of the mini shrines at Shakti Bhavan the children have created for their lost pets, the goldfishes and hamsters, and hate the idea that our son doesn't deserve the same.

I am numb with rage. My heart no longer aches from this pernicious woman's words: it is an organ that is keeping me alive, telling me that I'm still here and my son, my beautiful son, is dead. His heart no longer beats. I have nothing to do with my time. I am no longer a mother. The woman who has bullied and berated me since the first day I met her is telling everyone that our precious child should be buried in a mass unmarked grave. Forgotten forever.

"Tell me what you want, Ree." Nik murmurs softly, turning to me.

I look up and reply, "I want you to promise me, one last thing, Nik." He nods. "Our son will not be put in a hole and forgotten. I want a grave with a white headstone in the cemetery. I want his name and his date of birth and death engraved on it. I don't care about the rituals or rites we have to do. I want to be able to go to his grave and remember him. I want people who visit to see his name and how old he was when he died and reflect on his short life," I tell him flatly.

I stand up and walk up the stairs and close my bedroom door, get under the covers to dull the conversation. To sleep, to forget or even drown in pain, but neither happens.

The house stills as the people leave. He comes to bed later; I am awake. He gets in fully clothed. Neither of us has the energy to change out of our clothes. He turns me to face him; he knows I am awake. He kisses me on my forehead, on my eyes, on my cheeks and kisses me slowly on my lips, pushing his tongue against my teeth. I can taste the tobacco and alcohol. I resist and do not respond. I don't need him to pretend to want me, to continue the charade. He can go back to his old life, no responsibility, no wife. He is free to meet with Julie whenever, wherever he wants. His face is so close, I can feel his warm breath.

"Ree, I love you, please."

I open my eyes; he gasps. I do not have the energy to disguise the hate and loathing I feel for him. He turns on his back, his arm wrapped around my shoulders, holding me close to him, and his breathing slows. I want the warmth of his body to comfort me and to stay where I am. My heart is a traitor: it will insist on loving him, wanting him.

Twenty One

THE CLOCK ON THE BEDSIDE TABLE says seven-thirty; the room is dark. I was supposed to feed Amar at six. He must be starving. I reproach myself for being an inept mother and sleeping through the alarm. I swing my legs out of bed and turn to his cot. It is empty. Bile builds in my stomach. I look at the bed: perhaps Nik has taken him? The vague outline of my husband's sleeping body is next to me.

"Oh, God! Oh, God! Oh, God! Wake up! Wake up! Nik! Nik! Someone's stolen our baby." I shake Nik, but he won't wake up. I stand and shout, "AMAR! AMAR!"

He holds me in his arms. "Ree, Ree, I have you. You're safe."

I gulp and sob into his chest. The deluge of tears drowns me. "Is he here?" I ask him. I search his face and see watery tracks on his cheeks. I push him away and turn to the empty cot. I pull myself out of bed and walk downstairs to the glass door that looks out into our small courtyard garden. A miserable, misty drizzle is falling, making the light grey slabs glisten in the dull light.

I hear footfall on the stairs and the quiet slap of his

bare feet on the kitchen floor tiles. He wraps his arms around my waist. I lean back into him for comfort; my treacherous body yearns for him.

'We had a good time last night at Jules's. She called me earlier, you dirty boy.'

The words echo in my mind, the telephone conversation from three days ago.

My skin crawls from his touch, but I make myself stand still and let him rest his chin on my head.

* * *

"YOU HAVE TO EAT, REE." His eyes are full of concern.

I stare at the soggy cereal in my bowl and lift the spoon to my mouth. The warm milk and the gloopy texture make me retch and I rush into the bathroom and throw up, holding on to the toilet bowl, tears burning my eyes, and stinging bile filling my nostrils. My stomach convulses until nothing but dry spasms cause pain in my rib cage. He is kneeling behind me, rubbing my back, his warm hands easing the ache. I'm seated on my haunches, unable to lift myself, no energy left in my being to survive. He lifts me up, carries me upstairs to our bedroom and sits me down on the bed. He hands me a glass of water. "Small sips only," he instructs. The water tastes of metal and I try to swallow it. He lifts the covers and says, "Lie down." I do as he tells me. He tucks me into bed, kisses my forehead and sits on the bed, his hand stroking my hair, and I fall asleep aided by the rhythmic caresses.

***

"WHAT ARE YOU DOING, REE?" Nik is leaning on the doorframe, his arms folded across his chest.

"Just sorting through these things." I lift up a Babygro. All that remains of Amar are his clothes and this room. The neat pile of vests, Babygros, cardigans, socks, hats, gloves and pram suits. The room we'd painted and decorated before he was born. The room we shouldn't have decorated until he was born.

'It's bad luck to do this … Why won't you listen to me … You and your modern ways.'

He walks in and sits down beside me. "We don't need to do this yet, Ree." He takes my hand. I pull it away from him.

"Yes, we do. Amar doesn't need them anymore. He won't need them again."

"But … " He sighs. "What do you want to do with them?" he asks me, resignation in his voice.

"Take them to the Oxfam shop. Someone else can use them."

"Let's go and eat breakfast, and we'll put them in bags later."

"I'm nearly finished," I say to him. "I'll come down in a minute."

He lifts himself up and walks down the stairs.

I sort through the clothes, some with the labels still attached. Our friends and family had been generous; he has an outfit for each day of his short life. I count them slowly, one, two, three, four, five, six … fifty-six. Our son has fifty-six different outfits.

I pick up a mint-green quilted coat bought by Amit, and a white with mint-green trim velour Babygro that Rita had given us. White cloth boots and gloves given by Umi and Anne-Marie; a pair of green socks from Jane; a white hat Divya Ba had knitted for Amar. A crochet blanket that Nik's parents had bought to wrap him in when he was taken off the ventilator. These will be the clothes our son will be wearing when he is laid to rest on Thursday.

***

THE DOORBELL RINGS.

I hear voices in the hallway as I walk out onto the landing.

"Morning, Ree." Anne-Marie glances up at me as I walk down.

"Hello." I frown at her. "Aren't you working today?"

"Swapped my shift days. I'm taking you out for lunch today."

"I ... I don't want to go for lunch," I reply, suppressing my anger.

"Okay then, we'll go for a walk," she says.

Why would she do this, come and insist that I go out; *what is wrong with everyone?* All I want to do is stay in this house with my memories. I know he's gone. I know I'm alone. Even Nik has someone to go to after all this is over. Why won't they just leave me alone? I'll have to get used to my own company, and I'd rather start now than later.

I'm dressed and sitting on the sofa. Nik has gone shopping to Safeway for food. He disappears periodically, using some excuse or another. It must be difficult for him, keeping up the show of being my husband and not being able to see her. He's probably in the phone box at the end of the road speaking with Julie. He's learned from his past mistakes; he heard the anger in his father's voice when he disappeared on Friday. He is only gone for a short time now, as long as a short walk. A trip to the shops to get milk; not long enough to arouse suspicion.

The doorbell rings again.

Anne-Marie walks to the small hallway to open the door, and two young police officers walk in with a bunch of flowers.

"These gentlemen have come to see you, Ree," she tells me. They stand awkwardly near the door of the open-plan living room. "Can I get you some tea, coffee?" she asks them as she steps into the kitchen.

"Yes, please, tea would be good."

I stare at the policeman who spoke; he has kind dark eyes and has taken off his helmet. His complexion is fair, and his jet-black hair makes him paler. The other one is shorter and stockier with light-brown hair, younger, his face showing signs of a recent breakout of acne.

The younger one approaches and hands me the flower. "Thank you," I say as I take them off him.

"The people at the station wanted to say they are sorry." The soft, lilting Irish voice is calming.

"But … you don't even know us," I reply.

"But we do, we do. We've seen you in the park with your baby."

My eyes burn with tears, and I dab at them with the tissue. A faint memory of meeting them floods back, the good afternoons and the nods.

"Didn't mean to upset you, miss," the younger one says.

"No, no, it's all right," I say, blowing my nose on a tissue.

Anne-Marie walks in with some mugs of tea, and a plate full of biscuits, and the two men sit to share in our grief. Carl, the one with the Irish accent, stands up first after they've eaten all the biscuits. "Thank you for the tea and biscuits. If you need anything, anything at all, let us know." He hands me a card with his name and the number for the police station.

"We'll need parking restrictions to be lifted on Thursday," Anne-Marie tells them as she sees them to the door.

"What part of Northern Ireland do you come from?" Carl asks Anne-Marie, and she steps out. I hear their voices but can't make out their conversation.

My eyes drift to the various bouquets that have arrived in the past two days. We have run out of vases, and some of them are in tall beer glasses and jugs.

"Why were they here?" I can hear Nik asking her, the shock audible.

Anne-Marie answers, "They came to pay their respects and brought some flowers."

"We don't know them," he says.

"Nice of them to come, don't you think?" she says as she comes in with one of the shopping bags.

* * *

AMAR IS RUNNING through the field on the other side of the stream. I am on the bridge running after him. "Amar! Stop, wait for me," I shout.

"Come on, Mummy, it's not far."

I'm breathless. I'm running as fast as I can, but he is too far ahead of me. My legs are heavy; the long grass feels like a mat of fibre that is knitted too tightly around me.

He jumps on the rope swing.

"Push me, push me." The young girl begins to push the swing.

I stop, panting for breath, then I see her. She stops the swing, lifts him onto her hip and takes the little girl's hands. I can feel the bile rise in my mouth; the bitter taste overwhelms me. I gulp it down.

"STOP!"

She continues to walk to the other side of the tree. I lose sight of her and run to the top of the hill. I turn around in a panic. Where could she be taking Amar? She is walking down the hill.

"He's my son, stop! Please give him back to me. I haven't done anything wrong, please why are you taking him?"

She turns around. "Stop worrying, Reena. I'll look after them."

"But … Mummy, I want to take care of them." I am facing her.

"You can't. You have to go back."

"I don't want to … I want to be with you."

"No, go back, Reena … Go back."

I wake up smelling of sick. Loathing fills my mind: no one would miss me, no one would care. I have not really made anyone happy. Everything that has happened so far has been because of me. My father drinks to obliterate what I'd done to his wife. My brother, my wise brother, who should be living a happy life with his wife and children, will have to endure the news of my unfaithful marriage. Nik, the man who wants his first love, is with me due to the obligation of a piece of paper. Even my friends' lives have been disrupted by all the things I've done. Dick and Umi, who are always there when I need them, drop everything to come to my aid. Everyone would be better off without me. I'm useless; even the simple job of taking an overdose has been unsuccessful. My body has expelled the extra sleeping tablets I'd swallowed. Hot, angry tears prick at my eyes, and I cry. When I am done, I take off my stained nightclothes and the bed sheet and walk down the stairs. The house is quiet and empty. I load the washing machine and glance into the courtyard garden. I see the red glow of his cigarillo as he puts it to his mouth. I wonder how long he's been sitting in the cold, dank air; my heart aches for him. He is dealing with the loss alone, in the only way he knows how, by drinking and retreating, fighting the urge to run away into the arms of his first love. I stand rooted to the spot as he stares at the high fence that shields us from our neighbours. My deceitful heart yearns for him. I have never loved anyone nor will I love anyone as much as I love this man. I want him to hold me and tell me everything will be fine. That we will be fine; that he will stay with me, help me cope with the pain. Instead, he is biding his time until it will be respectable to leave me. Leave me for his English girlfriend. I wish I had never met him. If all he wanted was an Indian wife, he should have asked his motaba, I know she would have found him one; one who didn't bring him pain and suffering, too.

He turns his face, and locks eyes with mine and raises

a small smile. He stands up and opens the kitchen door.

"What happened? Why are you washing the sheets?"

"I was sick in my sleep," I tell him and move away before he can put his arms around me. His hands are already raised to reach for me.

He lowers his hands and lets them hang by his sides, letting the cold air into our warm house.

Twenty Two

I KNOW I WON'T BE ABLE to stay in this house beyond the day of the funeral. There is nothing left for me here. So last night, I spoke with my two dearest friends about my plan to leave the house and Nik. Umi and Dick had been furious with Nik, and I'd made them promise not to act differently towards him. I want to savour the moment, see the look on his face when I tell him I know all about his duplicitous life.

The last few days have been intolerable; the waves of grief and anger have left me empty. Every evening the house is full of people who sing bhajans to calm our souls. My father came back to stay with us on Wednesday. I can tell he finds it difficult to see my mood swings; one minute I'm sobbing and the next angry. I'm surprised he hasn't once taken the drink that Nik offers him after everyone has left. "I don't drink anymore," he had informed him, sorrow in his eyes, as Nik filled his glass to take comfort from it.

Every night since Amar's death Nik hasn't come up to bed until the early hours, his breath smelling of alcohol and tobacco. When I woke up this morning, I had somehow crept under his arms and was hugging him, the warmth of his body comforting me. I quickly moved away, and he had opened his eyes briefly, smiling. If I stay, this will happen again and again, and my treacherous heart will forgive him, and I will give myself to him. I tell myself to be stronger. It is only one more day. I climb out of bed and walk downstairs.

My father and Nik's parents are sitting at the dining table, drinking tea. The Bhagavad-Gita is playing quietly in the background. As soon as I see them in their white clothes, my throat constricts and the full realisation of what is happening today dawns on me. I halt at the bottom step and slump down. Nik's mother is by my side in seconds; she sits on the step and takes my hand.

"Reena, Beta, you'll have to be brave today."

Hot rivers of tears stream down my face and run along my jawline. Sarladevi stands above me and says, "You must stop crying. His soul won't be able to rest."

I nod my head and wipe the tears from my face with the back of my hands.

The dread of the ticking clock makes my stomach fill with bile and the contents of the toast and tea I'd eaten an hour ago begin to churn. The acrid smell of bile and half-digested food hits my mouth. I swallow the taste down, gasping for air to help ease the sickness. The house is full, and the warm bodies add to my anxiety. Every cell in my body is telling me to run away, get away from the place. The house that I've called home; a house full of memories. I twist the handkerchief I'm holding in my hand. There is a quiet knock on the door and a tall man in a black morning suit enters. He has wooden folding table legs in his hand, and he opens them in the centre of the room.

A square white cloth has been placed on top of the carpet, and Nik's mother takes some flower petals and puts a divo on the floor.

My lungs stop as I watch the door. A slightly shorter man in the same attire as his colleagues enters holding a small white casket. All the pain I'd held onto escapes. I let out a yell and the sobs cannot be stopped. My body folds from the pain as I am led to the sofa. I want to leave the room, go somewhere far, far away, away from the Guru and the chanting of the mantra, away from the woman who has just given me a disparaging stare. A little voice in my head tells me to look away, but I can't take my eyes off the casket. A dark shape is lifting the white lid. Everything is blurred. The white of everyone's clothes hurts my eyes.

"Come."

Nik is taking me to the casket. I don't want to say goodbye. *If I do this he will be gone forever*; I tell him all this in that one look. He must understand how I feel; he must feel something for our child. My eyes implore him to stop. He nods and tears roll down his cheeks. We are instructed to place a sandalwood tilak on his forehead. We give him a teaspoon of gangajal and are told to walk around our son's body. He seems peaceful, exactly as he has all his short life; nothing has changed in his expression. We step back as everyone else picks up some flower petals and walks around the tiny coffin. I lean into my husband's arm. My legs do not have the strength to hold me up; I am using all my willpower to stop the scream that is building up inside me.

"Nikesh," the Guru calls out, and Nik hands me to my brother.

I watch him place the dough balls in the casket and put a small silver coin on Amar's mouth. He is handed a lit joss stick, and the Guru takes off Amar's shoe, and sock.

I shout, "Stop! Why are you hurting him? You're his daddy. You promised me to keep him safe." I pull away from my brother and grab Nik's arm. "Please, Nik, please don't do this," I say quietly.

He turns his face to mine; his eyes are flooded with tears. "We have to do this, Ree." He touches the burning ember to our son's toe.

"I'll never forgive you, never, do you hear me, Nikesh Raja!" I shout at him and fling myself into my daddy's arms, sobbing uncontrollably.

"You have to watch him leave, Reena." My father turns me, and I watch our son's casket being carried out by Nik. The memory burns into my eyes. The image is etched into my corneas.

We reach the cemetery, the clouds shield the sun again, and we stand and greet the people who have not come to the house. I shake hands, embrace those I know well, and my heart betrays me again. My eyes search for her in amongst the people. I try to search the faces for Julie. She must be here. *How could she not be here for Nik?* She should be supporting him today, even from a distance. *Why are you so concerned about his wellbeing?* He doesn't deserve your kindness. He's betrayed you, I tell myself.

My thoughts wander to a time when I didn't want to be pregnant, and the guilt of my first reaction to the conception gnaws at my soul. You did this, I tell myself, you wished him to be gone. What did you expect, a happy ending? Your selfishness has led to his illness and death. My child, the baby I had grown inside me and taken care of, has gone. I'm no longer his mummy; I don't have a purpose in life. I don't deserve to live.

Nik guides me to a wooden pew; he has held me close to him since we stepped out of the car. The speakers chant, "Om Namo Shiva, Om Namo Shiva." The Guru is standing at the lectern. He instructs everyone to chant after him. I follow the chanting, but it has no meaning for me; my mind cannot cope with the words. The funeral director lifts the casket, and we walk out of the chapel behind him in pairs, down to the children's cemetery. It has begun to rain, a misty miserable thin rain that soaks into your pores. A hole, one metre by half a metre and one and a half metres deep, has been dug, the burnt-sienna soil left in a mound alongside it. My son's coffin is lowered into the vast muddy hole. The small white casket disappears under soft earth as people throw handfuls in. My fingers ache from holding on too tightly to the stem of the yellow rose.

"Let go of the flower," Nik whispers in my ear. As I throw the flower into the cavernous hole, the clouds separate and a shaft of sunlight falls on the rose, revealing it as a golden offering to Bhoomi Devi. I whisper a prayer to her to guide my son onwards to his next life. In that moment time briefly stops, the birds stop singing, the trees stop rustling, the noise from the road disappears, and I feel at peace. My heart sighs; he is safe and back from where he came.

"We have to go, Ree."

I lift my gaze to Nik. "You go, I'm staying," I tell him. He stands by me, no longer holding me, our bodies separated by the chasm of our grief. The grave digger fills up the hole with heavy wet soil.

"Sis, come on, we have to go." Amit has placed his arm around my shoulders.

"No, I'm staying … you can go." The thought of leaving him in the cemetery fills me with dread. "I can't leave him alone tonight in this place," I implore.

"He isn't here anymore, Ree. He's gone," Nik says.

"Yes, he is. He's in there." I cannot pull my eyes away from the mound of earth.

"No, that's just his body. Do you remember what the Gita says?" I frown up at him.

"The body is like a costume we wear. His soul has left it. He isn't in there, Ree."

"You promised me he would be fine, but he's left me, he's left you." I stab at his chest with my finger. He encloses me in his arms, and I cry into his chest. "You promised me. You said we'd be happy. You said you'd protect me," I croak into his chest.

***

WE ARE TOLD TO HAVE a shower and change into fresh clothes. Someone has placed a set of my clothes in the bathroom, and I take a shower, the tears from my eyes mixing with the water as I wail and sob, not caring that the people in our small house can hear me. When I open the door, my daddy is waiting for me. He pulls me into his arms.

"There, there, Reena," he says as he strokes my damp hair. "Come and sit with me."

He guides me to the sofa, and I let all the tears that I've been holding onto since the birth of my son come out. The tears of pain, the tears of indignity, the tears of resentment, the tears of jealousy, the tears of inadequacy, the tears of injury, the tears of hatred, the tears of sorrow, the deep, deep tears of sadness.

The house falls silent. The conversation turns to gestures and unheard whispers.

There is a tap at the window, the front door is opened, and the men bring in large pans of food.

***

I HAVE BEEN SENT UPSTAIRS to rest. I had tried to eat something, but even the small morsels I ate to placate Divya Ba have come out in a violent expulsion from my mouth. The marital bed digs into my body. It no longer feels like a place of refuge; it is telling me I do not belong here anymore. My stomach is heavy at the thought of leaving this house, this home, this life, the nerves in my body on edge. The people I will be leaving behind, the new family and friendships I've developed. My mind wanders to the tennis matches with Rita, the days at museums with Jaishree, the days spent with the children, the cliquish conversations with Rupa and Ashveena about our husbands. The times I've spent with Anu Masi and Manu Kaka in their small flat above the garage, the only people who I felt I belonged with at Shakti Bhavan.

My ears prick up as the sound of Motaba's voice travels through the open window. "Haan, haan, I know, I know Savita, we don't do this. But, Nikesh and Reena insisted, what could I do?"

I will not miss the woman, her false smiles and her acts of righteousness.

When I come down to say goodbye to my family, Sarladevi has placed herself by the door to the hallway as people begin to leave.

"Do you know what happened to Reena's mother, Divya Masi? I've heard that sometimes if the soul is tormented, it haunts their children."

"Do you know Sarla, I used to believe in all this nonsense? When poor Usha became ill, I thought she'd been possessed. That's not the case. Even in India, the doctors recognise postnatal depression. It is the superstitious and the manipulative who whisper about bad spirits and karma. If you really want to know what happened, Usha died from a heart attack in her sleep. Naren cannot talk about it."

I am glad Divya Ba has told her a lie.

"Oh, I thought she might have … " Sarladevi's voice trails off.

"I think we'll be going now, goodbye. Jai Shri Krishna, Sarla, Pushpa. Mayur are we ready?" She takes me in her arms. "Reena, be brave Dikri, come home. I'll take care of you." She kisses me on my cheek.

I'm waiting in trepidation outside our house, watching my family leave; my stomach churns, but I'm not going to run away this time. Nik is standing behind me in the hallway. Last night we had discussed why I wanted to stay a little longer in London. Even Nik asked me if I was sure and had said he'd come with me. I was worried about my father's health; he had developed a chesty cough. I wanted him to rest. I know that he would be unable to cope with another hospital stay.

I tell myself to be strong. I can do this on my own, do it today, *why wait when there will be no reason to stay?* I know Motaba will be the first person to mention my poor family and my inadequate upbringing, regardless of when I go.

I'm in my bedroom upstairs after saying goodbye, the thought of telling Nik I am leaving vibrates in my body like a quake; the fear has filled my cells.

The whispered conversation downstairs is like a marching band playing in my ears. My eyes hurt, my ears hurt, my skin hurts. I try to keep my stomach from clenching and throwing out its contents, taking big gulps to fill my lungs with air. Deep breaths to quieten my heart. I rest my head and tell myself to sleep, but it deserts me. I stare at the ceiling, count the tiny cracks that appear outwards from the ceiling rose. I toss and turn, I need to rest my body to build up my strength. The dread of telling Nik that I know about his deception tenses my body like a coiled spring.

'We had a good time last night at Jules's. She called me earlier, you dirty boy.'

The pain comes in waves as I recall the conversation. The man who has been at the centre of my life has forsaken me. He has used me for a means to an end. He has found a suitable Indian wife to marry like so many others in my community. A wife at home and English girlfriend they could not give up. A double life that has left all concerned unhappy and bereft.

I open the door to the landing in the late evening. Someone puts on the tape of bhajans that we have been listening to for the past week.

"Didn't you hear what Guruji said, Nikesh? We don't need to have a prathna anymore."

"But, I thought we'd do the prathna like we did for Papa for thirteen days." His voice is shaky.

"It was at the insistence of your wife that we've had all this. Babies do not have funerals."

I halt in the middle of the stairs, every cell in my body

electrified, anger for this interfering, soulless woman bubbling to the surface. I take a deep breath, continue climbing down, and I walk into the bathroom.

"Don't cry, don't cry, don't cry," I tell my reflection in the mirror. "Stay strong, stay strong." I gulp back the lump in my throat.

Sarladevi's words fuel my anger, and I'm ready to leave this family once and for all. They can deal with Nikesh Raja's new life. She thought I was bad, not listening to her drivel, but wait until he brings Julie home. *What will her mela mandir and kitty party friends say then?* I hope she chokes on the words she'll have to tell them. "My Nikesh's new wife is a tthoydi."

Nik is sitting on the sofa, his head bowed. On one side is his father with his arm around his shoulders and on the other is Jay. I'm taken aback he is still here. Suddenly a thought surfaces in my mind. He's here to take him out tonight. They'll wait for Nik's parents to leave and then he'll give me some excuse about going for a walk and go and meet Julie. How stupid of me to think that Nik might at least pretend we are a family one last time. He must hate me so much that he'd want to leave me alone on the day of our son's funeral. I'm heartbroken that the man I loved doesn't feel anything for me, not even sympathy. *How could I have been so wrong?* I try to think of what I have done to create his loathing, what was it I did that made him want to hurt me?

'I thought that was all about getting rid of the baby, that you'd felt betrayed.'

Of course that was it. I had made the choice of terminating the pregnancy; that's why he tried to get back from India, to stop me. Everything has led to this moment, the revenge, the urge to pay me back for what I did to him. He's been playing a game with my emotions. *How else would he hurt me as I hurt him?*

I sit next to Nik's mother, on the edge of the sofa, unable to sit back. She takes my hand. The silence grows like an empty void that engulfs us, the music from the bhajan no longer there to ease the tension.

"Enough of the sadness. You'll soon have another child." Sarladevi stands. "You're not staying here tonight; let's go to Shakti Bhavan. Nikesh, go and get your clothes packed."

His eyes focus on Motaba. "We won't be coming to Shakti Bhavan."

"Oh … are you sure you want to be alone?" she asks.

"I'll stay with them tonight, Bhabhi. Only if you want me to?" Nik's mother turns her head to mine.

"Reena, I know it's difficult, but you'll get over it. You'll have another child and forget. I'll help you," his motaba continues.

I glare at the sharp-tongued woman as she towers over me, my fury rising.

"How will you help? Will you get me a baby to look after too, Motaba? Is Julie pregnant, Nik?" I spit the words out like pebbles, aiming them at the two people who have made my life unbearable.

The shock ripples on everyone's faces and there is a fleeting hint of hurt in Nik's mother's eyes. I didn't mean to cause her pain, but my adrenaline has built up. *I am ready for a fight.* It's about time someone told this righteous woman what she did to her husband's mistress was not right. It had killed Nik's birth mother from a broken heart.

"Yes, Nikesh Raja is following in his father's footsteps.

He has a mistress." He is frowning at me. "I know Nik, I know about you and Julie. Will you give her up for me?" My words are sharp. "Will she give her child to me? Just like your poor mother."

His expression is full of confusion.

"Don't act the innocent, Nik. I heard you and Jay talk about your night with her. Jayesh!"

The name comes out of my mouth like a dagger. He is startled I'm addressing him. I am on my feet, unable to stay seated and stand towering over him. He is trying to make himself small. "Why don't you tell Motaba where Nik was on Friday? I'm sure she would love to know what you two do when you disappear for days."

"Ree, please, I … nothing happened." Nik has stood up. I can feel his breath on my neck. I tilt my head and lock eyes with his.

"I'm leaving you, Nik." I take off my rings and hold them up to him. "I made excuses for you. I tried to forgive you. You said you'd never hurt me. You promised me, a long time ago, when I had to get rid of our child that you would protect me, but you've broken my heart. I can't forgive you for this."

"What does she mean 'get rid of our child'?" Sarladevi interrupts. "I told you she was bad luck; she carries a bad karma. I knew Guruji could see the sins she's committed." She throws a triumphant stare at his father.

"My bad luck, my bad karma, maybe it's his?" I point my finger at Nik and turn to her. "Since Nikesh came into my life, I've suffered. I have had to endure pain. Did you ever look at his bad karma, his sins?"

"Reena, Beta," Nik's father says. "Please sit down and let's talk about this."

I stare at him. "Sorry, Kaka. Sorry, Kaki." I turn to his mother; her shoulders are slumped, her gaze fixed on her clenched hands.

"I can't bear the pain anymore of always being blamed for what has happened. It wasn't my fault. It wasn't my fault! Tell her, Nik!"

Nik's eyes cast down to his feet, and there it is, no one is here to defend me. No one believes I'm not at fault for our son's life and death.

"I won't let her say this to me and watch as none of you defend me. No one is on my side. Amar was alive; he brought us joy and sadness. He was meant to come into our lives, and I want to remember him for the rest of my life. I can't forget him. I won't." I take a deep breath and gulp down the tears.

"I can't forget or forgive Nik for what he's done."

I put my rings on the coffee table and walk upstairs to get my bag. I sit on the bed and see the large black and white portrait taken on the day we took our wedding vows. Every muscle in my body lets go, and I cannot hold my body upright anymore. I flop on the bed and begin to sob, using my pillow to muffle the noise. I do not want them to hear me cry for the loss of the marriage, the marriage I fought so hard for. She was right, it would have been better if I had walked away when she asked me to. I would not be feeling the all-encompassing pain that is beginning to expand. My heart is shattered into tiny pieces and can no longer be fixed.

Twenty Three

WHEN I EVENTUALLY COME DOWNSTAIRS, Dick and Umi are waiting for me.

Nik's eyes rest on the bag. "You can't leave me, Ree. Please, nothing happened. Tell her, Jay."

His friend is silent, his eyes focused on the grey carpet. In the silence, Nik's shoulders slump.

Dick meets me at the bottom of the stairs and holds his hand out to take my bag.

As I walk to the hallway, Nik grabs my arm. "You're my wife. You have to stay!"

Dick pulls Nik's hand away. "Let go of her, Nik. I gave you a warning; she will not be hurt by you again." His voice is low and controlled. Umi touches Dick's arm, his head nodding slightly, acknowledging her.

When I step into the hallway, Nik grabs my shoulder and forces me to turn. Dick throws a punch and Nik's head reels back.

"Dick!" I shout, "Please don't!"

My eyes water as a bead of red builds and trickles on his upper lip.

Umi puts her hand on Nik's arm. "Let her go, Nik. You've blown it this time. We know what you've been doing."

Nik is barefoot on the pavement outside the front door, and comes to the passenger door of the car, tapping at the window. "Please, Ree, I love you. Please, don't go!" he shouts and then his motaba steps out of the house, pulling at his shoulder with a wet handkerchief in her hand. Her sharp words sting into my ears as I lower the window.

"Let her go, Nikesh. Some people are unlucky, and Reena is one of them. You had all the warnings. God was telling you not to do this."

"Why are you saying these things, Motaba?" he says with anguish.

She continues to give him examples of my bad luck. "Look at how well her family is doing since she married you. They have bought a lovely big house; the children are much healthier, even Naren Bhai is looking better. Now you can get on with your life. She was never good for you."

Dick pulls the car away. Her words are just audible as we drive down our short road.

Dick turns on the radio, and Briana Corrigan is singing about broken promises and wedding bells that turn to rust.

When we get to Dick's flat, we sit in silence at the enormity of what I've done. I have finally left Nik; all those times when I should have walked away flood back. If only I had the strength then, I would not be feeling the heavy shroud of pain in my chest now.

The intercom rings.

"Come up," Dick tells whoever it is.

Peter walks into the sitting room, sits down next to me and asks, "What's happened?" I tell him about the phone conversation I'd overhead ten days ago and

Nik's recent late nights out with Jay.

"I don't believe it, Ree." He turns to me with sadness in his eyes. "I know Nik, he loves you and only you. There must be a mistake?"

"No mistake, even Jay couldn't deny it. Nik has been seeing Julie. I've seen them together, Peter. She's turned up at lots of places we've gone. How many times has he disappeared to hotels, hotels that she works for?"

"Think about it, Peter. Jay has been his accomplice," Dick adds. "We've just thought they've gone on a drinking binge, but it's not been that at all. It's been an excuse to meet up with Julie."

He falls silent, and Umi takes his hand. "I know he's your friend. He can't deny it, even Jay didn't support him. We need to stay strong. Ree needs our help. Nik will survive like he always does." He nods.

The adrenaline that was keeping me upright is depleted; my body becomes leaden. I lie down on the sofa, and my eyes close. The buzzer wakes me briefly. I open my eyes and remember I'm at Dick's. A gut-wrenching ache fills my heart. I have lost everything. My child and the man I love. I would have done anything to have them in my life. I have neither now. *How can I live without them?*

I hear voices and peer at the unfamiliar room. I am lying on the bed in Dick's spare bedroom. I cannot remember how I got here. I swing my legs off the bed and open the door ajar and stop. I'm stuck, unable to make my body move forward.

"I don't believe he could do that to Reena. I lived with him: he's besotted with her, checking on her, surprising her, always looking after her. I don't believe

Nik is capable of that kind of deception. Reena must be mistaken. They've been under a lot of stress," Anne-Marie says with disbelief in every word.

"You're so gullible, Anne-Marie. Have you forgotten the time when he disappeared and we didn't know where he was?"

"He was upset about the setback, that's all. He hasn't done that since, Umi."

"Yes, he has. Do you remember Gino at the hospital?"

"I … " Anne-Marie's voice breaks off, and she sighs.

"I'm sorry, I didn't mean to upset you, but there are times when Nik can be self-centred. Maybe it isn't a full-blown affair; maybe he slept with her just once, but he didn't deny it," Umi continues. I make myself step out of the room.

"Good morning, Ree." Dick rushes to my side. "Tea's brewed. Come and sit down."

I sit next to Anne-Marie, and she takes my hand. Her usually twinkly green eyes are dull.

The betrayal gnaws at my soul. I have to tell someone of all the times I've seen them together or heard of them being together. It can't be a one-off. He has been doing this throughout our relationship, but I don't understand why he needed to hurt me. Since I found out, I have wracked my brain for anything I may have done to hurt him. What was it about me that made him want to hurt me with his dual life? My mind keeps going back to that day in August.

"More tea?" Dick leans across the round glass table and takes my hand.

I shake my head. "Thank you for being with me today," I say to them.

I begin to recount the times Julie Ramsbottom has

turned up to the places that Nik and I had gone. The scenes have been tormenting me while I waited for our son to leave this world.

"You all remember his Papa's funeral when she kissed him in front of everyone. I should have understood then that he hadn't really given her up, that it was all a lie. I saw Nik and Julie again in our second year, at the dinner we went to at the Leofric Hotel. I'd gone to the ladies, and when I came out, Nik was hugging a blonde in the hotel foyer. She had her hair up, and it was only later I recognised her. I asked him if it was her and he told me she was working there. He told me it was a coincidence and nothing more. You know what it's like with Nik: so many women can't resist that charm. I was jealous, but he always insisted I was the only one he loved." I pause to push back the lump that has formed in my throat. Dick stands up to fetch me a glass of water. "When Nik asked me to marry me, she was in Brighton."

"What the fuck! Why didn't you tell me, Ree?" Umi interrupts.

"We went for a meal at a French bistro in Hove. She saw us. She said she had come for drinks with some friends. I was very upset that night, but he reassured me it was another chance meeting. I was so happy, I guess I didn't think much about that meeting," I continue, my mind wondering if he'd asked her to be there to comfort him if I had said no. A sob escapes as I realise that is precisely what he had done. Silence engulfs us.

Peter takes Umi's hand. Her jaw is clenched; her anger barely controlled. I take a deep breath and tell them about our honeymoon and the cafe at the Spanish Steps.

"I'd gone to the toilet and was heading back to the table where Nik was waiting for me. I saw a woman in a white linen dress with loose blonde hair approaching him from behind. I watched by the door, she covered his eyes with her hands and whispered something in his ears. I saw his face light up and he grabbed her hand and kissed it." I gulp back another sob and pause to regain my composure. "He pulled up a chair from a nearby table and called the waiter. I waited as long as I could, hoping not to speak with her, but he came looking for me. We had coffee together. She told me she was on a hoteliers' conference, and thought she should at least take in some of the tourist sites. She was surprised to see Nik at the cafe table and thought she'd come and say hello."

Dick has become very quiet, and his breathing has slowed. I know what that means: he will not let this matter go without retribution. I grab his hand, imploring him with my eyes not to do anything he may regret.

"On your honeymoon! When did he get the time to see her?" Anne-Marie's voice is raised.

"It can still be innocent, just coincidence. She does work in the hotel trade," Peter adds.

I can't deny his loyalty to Nik; he has been at his side often. It must be hard for him to realise his friend isn't who he thought he was.

"I'm sorry, Peter, I know you are a good friend, but … tell me the truth. How many times did you bump into her on your boys' nights out?" Umi asks.

"Yes, okay, but it's not what you think. She goes to the same pubs and bars we go to, that's all." His eyes betray him for a split second. He, too, has developed doubts about Nik's love for me and me alone.

"I've been stupid. I let my love for him ignore all the signs. He mentioned he had dinner with her when he went to the export exhibitions. Jay has told me they met up in bars. I trusted him; I believed him when he said he loved me." I cannot hold the tears back anymore and let them run down my face. Dick hands me the tissue box.

"Come on, Ree." Umi pulls me up from the chair. "Let's lie down. You need to rest."

I lie down on the bed; Umi is lying next to me, holding me.

"I have to tell you one more thing."

"No, you can tell me later." She pushes the hair that is clinging to my forehead away.

"No, I must. I want it all out; I won't be able to rest until I tell you."

"Okay, I'm listening," she says.

"When we went to Miami at Easter, she was at the airport lounge waiting to get on a plane back to the UK. She came up to us and said, mockingly, 'we can't go on meeting like this, Nikesh Raja'. Nik was quite angry and asked her if she was stalking him. She seemed flustered and sat as far away from us as possible. I think she wanted me to know about them and he was angry she'd done that."

"Oh, Ree, why didn't you say something? If this has been going on for so long, why would you let him do this to you?"

"I don't know. I love him so much, so much that it hurts. I thought it was my jealousy, that I over-analysed everything. I really did believe he loved me. Always have, always will. My heart is empty without you. I dream about him saying those words when I close my eyes. I can see him saying those words. Was it all an act? Was I so taken in by the charm?"

"No, this is not your fault. You have nothing to blame yourself for, and … " she tells me angrily, " … the likes of Nikesh Raja use their wealth and their privileges to enjoy themselves, not caring who they hurt. As for Julie Ramsbottom, she is a stupid woman to let a man have her at his beck and call. He won't marry her. His family won't let him. He's the type who likes to straddle both worlds: his traditional, 'I'm a good Hindu, abiding by the rules,' and, 'I'm a playboy, with my fast cars, mistress and expensive hotel stays.' It's in his blood. You were right all along; he is one of those rich Indians. If it's anyone's fault it's mine. I shouldn't have insisted on us being friends with them." She strokes my hair until the numbing darkness engulfs me, and I fall asleep.

* * *

BY FRIDAY EVENING I'M TRAVELLING up to Leicester. My brother has come to pick me up from Dick's flat. I tell him what has happened between bouts of crying as we drive home. He listens when I speak and holds my hand when the words fail me. My father is waiting for me as I enter the hallway, his eyes glistening and red. I don't want him to know I've left Nik and hope that the news hasn't travelled to his ears, but when he envelopes me in his arms, stroking my back, telling me that he would support me in any decision I make, I realise that Nik's father must have called him.

There is a rapping at the door. It opens and my bhabhi

enters with a tray of biscuits and two mugs of tea. I'm lying on the bed in the guest bedroom of the tall Georgian house my brother has bought recently. The house is not familiar to me. It's Amit and Smita's home.

"I know you're not hungry, but you will need to eat," her singsong voice cajoles.

I sit up, pick up the cup of tea, and take a sip; it's sweeter than usual. She waits for me to finish my tea, then takes my hand and says, "We've kept the old house furnished, so if you can't sleep here and want to stay in your old room, you can. Daddy can come to stay with you and Divya Ba can help."

I hug her and thank the gods for bringing Smita into our lives.

* * *

THE FAMILIARITY OF MY CHILDHOOD home and the dull routine of having to cook and clean helps ease my pain, although I don't want the pain to go away, as it is the only emotion I feel. I spend the first week in my room barely eating, barely sleeping. A distant voice shouts to end this life. The gnawing voice of Sarladevi tells me my birth and my life are to blame for what happened.

'I told you she was bad luck. She will bring you pain. You will ruin my son's happiness. You bring a burden of unhappiness and bad luck with you, Reena. The road you'll travel is full of hardship and sorrow.'

The doctor has prescribed me pills to sleep, pills to wake, pills to help me function. My mind is a fog; every memory is muted. It feels like the saturation button has been turned down on the television and all

I can see are dirty browns. My world has turned sepia. Even the sketches I draw to come to terms with what has happened are in black and brown pastels. The vibrant colours that I used previously sit tall and unused in the box. I can't draw anything that reminds me of Amar, or Nik.

The waves of grief take my breath away; one minute I'm sad about the loss of my son, the next I'm sad about the loss of my love. I wonder how long it takes to recover from losing both. Maybe I don't deserve to recover. Perhaps this is what my new life will be like, full of heartache.

I see Nik's face in every conversation or every piece of music I hear. My treacherous heart yearns for him: my mind wonders what is he eating, what is he listening to, where is he now. The minutes turn to hours and the hours into days. Time slows to a snail's pace; everyday tasks take longer than usual.

Night-time is the worst. I punish myself, imagining him with Julie at the pubs and bars we frequented, in the nightclubs he liked to go to, dancing the waltz, their bodies perfectly attuned, unlike my clumsy attempts, his wicked eyebrow rising as he leans in to whisper something in her ear. The raucous laugh and the way she places her hand on his heart when she leans in for a kiss. Their bodies entwined in the bed I thought was my own. My eyes burn from the sight of them. I stop going to the park by the river, as all I can see is Nik waiting under the tree, leaning against the trunk. I avoid all the places we used to go to in Leicester before our wedding when he came and stayed. I cry until I no longer feel any hurt at the memory of him.

I can't think of Amar; his memory hurts the place between my chest. It is too sharp a pain; it takes my breath away. I push my memory of him deep, deep inside me. It surfaces when I'm caught unaware, and I push the ache down, down deep into the recesses of my mind.

I think about leaving the world many times; the tablets I have would make it easy. But the guilt I feel for the pain I would cause my father if he found his daughter as he did his wife stops me. I could not subject him to seeing me in the morning, in the same house; another woman who could not cope with the world.

***

EVENTUALLY, THE PAIN TURNS TO ANGER. After two weeks of punishing myself with visions of Nik enjoying his new life and me avoiding the places that give me peace, I tell myself enough is enough, Nikesh Raja will not prevent me from living my life. I don't need him or anyone else. I promise myself I will never allow any man to hurt me again. I will devote my time to my career. I will be so successful he'll see my name on the television, read about me in the newspapers and regret what he did to me. Reena Solanki will be the successful film producer she always aspired to be.

"Good morning, Daddy."

"Good morning, Reena. Are you going anywhere special?"

Instead of my baggy tracksuit bottoms and sweat tops, I have put on a pair of black trousers, a black and white striped T-shirt and my pale-blue cashmere cardigan.

"No, just thought I'd go see Rohini Bhabhi and Mayur Bhai at Roop Lila. Will you give me a lift on your way to work?"

He raises a smile as he puts down his newspaper and says, "Good, it's a nice day, and Roop Lila will be busy today. Perhaps you can help them with the customers."

"Sure, I'd like that," I reply, not confident I could talk to the customers.

For the rest of the week, I go to Roop Lila every day. The smell of the silks and joss sticks brings back memories of a time when I didn't have a care in the world.

***

ONE MORNING AS I AM GETTING ready to go to Belgrave Road, the phone rings.

"Hello, Reena. How are you feeling?"

"I'm good, Tony."

"Listen, it might be a bit too soon, but I have a load of footage that needs to be looked through and logged for the documentary on manufacturing. Would you be interested in coming to work for a couple of days a week?"

I let what he is saying sink in. Can I go back to London and go back to work again? What if I bumped into Nik? How would I cope?

"You don't have to say yes. Maybe it's too soon, but the cameraman was a bit too enthusiastic with the shots, and I need someone like you to sort the good from the bad. It … might be just the right sort of work for you to … " his voice trails off apologetically.

"No … I mean yes … I wouldn't mind coming back. Thank you, Tony. Thank you for thinking about me."

"Don't be silly, I need someone to do the job and just

thought you probably don't want to stay away until …
" He stops. "Sorry, Reena, I'm making a fool of myself
here. Think about it. Call me when you're ready to
start. I'll get the new girl to begin some of it, and you
can supervise her when you get here."

The phone rings almost immediately after Tony's call,
and it is Jane. I had a feeling she was sitting in his office
listening to his conversation. She asks if I am ready to
get back to work and if I can cope. She assures me that
if at any time I can't deal with it, I should tell them. She
asks if I've been taking care of myself. I tell her I am
ready and need the routine of work.

So that is it: Tony calling me and the lure of looking
through footage and telling the story of the decline in
manufacturing in the north brings me back to living
my life again.

My father takes a lot more time to convince. He tells
me he isn't happy. He is worried I won't eat properly
away from home. He is concerned about where I will
stay; he is scared about how I will cope with the life of
London. His eyes are full of sadness; for a fleeting
moment I think he knows. He knows that the only
person stopping me from ending it all is him. He
knows that as soon as I'm away from my childhood
home, nothing will stop me.

When Umi and Dick come up to visit, I explain to them
that I want to come back. They both offer a room for
me to stay in. They promise my father and brother they
will make sure I eat regular meals and come back up to
see them often.

* * *

"ARE YOU SURE YOU WANT TO GO?" Amit is

hugging me outside our childhood home, his eyebrows knotted.

"Yes, Bro. I have to live my life," I reply, reassuring him with a kiss on his cheek.

The day has turned out to be bright and warm. Jane came up on Saturday and we'd gone for a walk by the river after our huge Sunday lunch. The twins had run up to the tree as soon as we'd emerged from the bridge. I concentrated hard and the ghostly image of Nik loitering there turned to wisps.

It had become a place of peace for me once again, the ripple of gentle waves and the noise of the ducks calming my fearful heart. It was by the river that I drew my first colourful sketch again, mostly drawings of the vivid dreams I had before Amar died, none of them featuring him. All landscapes of the places, empty of any life, devoid of any emotions, but full of vibrant colours.

On Sunday April 1st at four-thirty in the afternoon, Jane drives me down the M1. She knew that my father needed to be reassured and had eased his anxiety of letting me go. I decided to stay with Dick, remembering what I'd subjected Shashi Kaka to in the summer of 1984. I can't think of Amar, it's too painful, but I know I can cope with the heartache that has been caused by my husband if I keep myself occupied. I am going back to my life, at least the life I lived before I was married to Nikesh Raja and before Amar.

Twenty Four

Six months later

IT'S AN UNUSUALLY WET AND COLD September evening, and I've finished a long stint in the edit suite at Suite 25, a production house in Turnham Green. Brendon has insisted on going for a drink, and we've ended up on Chiswick High Road. There is a buzz about the street; it is full of people hustling to trendy bars and restaurants.

The wine bar has a neon sign above its double doors: Gino's Wine Bar. I've been to Gino's plenty of times; I love the log-fired warmth of its lounge. The intimate seating booths that run along the wall, the small round tables with chairs placed against the large window. I've sat on the two dark-brown leather Chesterfield sofas by the fire with Nik and my friends. The décor is sophisticated chic; on the walls are black and white photographs of Italian piazza, taken in the 50s, the men in sharp suits, the beautifully-coiffed women draped or posed riding Vespas. Gino's is a respected and fashionable wine bar; their range of wine is extensive, and the cellar is full of top quality wines from around the world. The atmosphere is calm, and the acoustics help to keep conversations private. Luciano Pavarotti is singing softly in Italian in the background.

I sit at a table by the large window and Brendon steps up to the bar to fetch a bottle of wine and glasses. I look around, surprised I'm not anxious that I might bump into Nik. I've avoided this part of London for the past six months, just in case I did. But I came to the conclusion that the segregated areas I've created aren't going to work if I intend to live and work in London. I watch the people on the streets: groups in party clothes, smart designer labels suitable for the Loadsamoney generation living a carefree life. My mind wanders to a time when I was one of these people. When Nik and I didn't have a care in the world. When we'd led an idyllic life.

The blue neon lights bounce on the black taxi which has pulled up outside. Three girls clamber out, already slightly intoxicated from happy hour.

"Is a Shiraz good for you, Reena?" Brendon, my editor, asks as he sits down with the uncorked bottle. For the last two weeks, Brendon and I have worked on the final edit of the documentary on the decline of manufacturing in the UK. He's a six-foot-two sandy-haired New Zealander who is wearing ripped jeans and a faded black T-shirt with a peace sign, and a pair of old Adidas trainers. His arms are full of beaded bracelets and tattoos. The double doors swing open, and a swift cold breeze ripples through the bar. Three girls wearing identical clothes, short white skirts, low-cut blouses and short leather jackets, stumble through the door and Brendon's olive eyes twinkle. I pour the wine into our glasses as he points and says,

"Someone's going to get lucky tonight." I like Brendon, but he tends to say the most inappropriate things, and I seethe.

At the bar on high wooden stools sit four young men, talking loudly, gesticulating with their hands, all in their late twenties. They are dressed in the uniform of all their peers, Ralph Lauren shirts, Armani jeans, Oxford brogues, and expensive leather jackets.

"Hiya, Jules, come and sit with us," shouts a man with straight short-cropped platinum-blond hair. He gives a furtive look to his friend who shrugs his shoulders and carries on staring at his drink. The women bunch, whisper something to each other, and head for the men. I fix my gaze on the tall man sitting with his back to them. His dark hair is cut longer than most; he has not turned to them once. Then I recognise her. She deliberately brushes up against his thigh as she finds a gap between the stools. It's Julie Ramsbottom, Nik's mistress: the woman he always wanted to be with. I hold back a gasp. *What if that's Nik?* I don't want to be here if he is. *How could I have been stupid enough to come to Gino's?* I hold my breath. He turns to say something to her and his profile is very different; his nose is long and hooked, his skin is slightly pitted with acne marks, his complexion tanned. I take a deep breath and gulp down my wine.

"Whoa, slow down, Reena," Brendon chides.

"Great work today, Brendon." I pour myself another glass, hold it up, clink it with his and say "Saluti."

Brendon has been working as a freelance editor while he is on his travels around the world. He is mid-flow in his travelogue and is telling me about his plans to move to America in the new year. He has managed to see more European countries in the last six months than I ever have in my entire life and I live in Europe.

"You should go backpacking, Reena. Nothing stopping you, right?"

"No, nothing stopping me," I reply. I'm living rent-free in Dick's flat until he comes back from South America. I have built up a good savings pot, and Tony has told me he would keep my job open if I needed to get away.

"I have some mates who'll put you up."

I shrug my shoulders at Brendon.

"I'm okay at the moment, Brendon."

He doesn't know about Nik or the baby. It's all too soon for me. I'm okay with the routine of work, but the thought of going away from the familiarity of work and home paralyses me with panic. I am just getting used to living in London and not seeing Nik on every corner. The spectre of the love that wasn't true.

My thoughts wander to a time when my body could cope with living again. By the end of March, I'd decided I was not going to abandon my career and wallow in self-pity anymore. I am staying alone at Dick's; he left in June to film a documentary on the children of the favelas in South America, a passion project he had finally secured funding for from Channel Four.

I'm brought back from my reverie by a raucous laugh from the bar and suddenly I feel angry. If that's not Nik then she's cheating on him. *How could she do that to him?* I reprimand myself: she didn't care about cheating on you, so why would it bother her to cheat on him and why do you care? They deserve each other. Brendon is pulling on his sheepskin-lined denim jacket. "Sorry, got a steaming-hot date tonight. See you on Monday."

The bottle is empty, and I walk up to the bar, as far away from Julie as I can. I order another Shiraz, sit back at my table and proceed to drink while observing the people on the street, couples kissing, friends teasing, everyone having a good time.

"Reena! How are you?" Gino is standing at the table. "Thought it was you. Drinking alone?" He frowns.

"No, no, Gino." I stand up and give him a kiss on both his cheeks. "I was working near here … my editor's just left." He sits down opposite me.

"So, how are you?" he asks. His eyebrows meet.

I tell him I'm good and ask him how his life has been.

"Business is booming. I've met a lovely girl, think she might be the one, so, I'm good, thanks. Can I get you something to eat?"

"Not hungry, I had a big lunch." I think about the half-eaten sandwich I had earlier. He gestures to the bar, and the waitress brings a glass.

"Mind if I join you?" He pours wine for himself. He picks up the glass and takes a languid sip of the red wine.

The people at the bar whoop and I turn; one of the girls has draped her arms around the platinum blond and is kissing him without inhibition. Gino's eyes follow my gaze. "Jules is in her element tonight," he says. "She's celebrating her engagement."

My heart skips a beat. I pour myself another glass of wine and gulp it down. "Can I have another?" I wave my empty bottle at Gino.

"Are you sure, Reena?"

"Yes, Gino. I can always go somewhere else," I challenge him.

"Okay, okay, I'll get it for you." He stands up.

I want the pain to go away and the only way I know of numbing it is with alcohol. We aren't even divorced, and he's got engaged. I thought I knew Nikesh Raja, but I was wrong. He didn't really love me; he didn't have any feelings for me. It was all an act. I raise my glass to him silently. He has missed his calling; *he should have become a Bollywood heart-throb.*

I must have dozed off. I wake up to Gino's words, "Reena, Reena, time to go home."

"Oh, is it closing time already? One more for the road, Gino? Go on, just a glass," I plead.

"How about a nice cup of coffee instead, Reena?" he replies.

I hold my head up on one elbow. "Sure a coffee will be great." As he leaves, I rest my head on the table again.

"Hello."

I recognise the voice and think I must be dreaming. I don't want to open my eyes. That beautiful voice. It hadn't occurred to me that I missed it so much, but now I've heard it, I want it to say something else. Please say something else, I ask silently.

"How are you, Ree?"

It is him. *What do I do?* I know if I look up, I'll see the chiselled face, the magnificent eyes, the top lip with an indent. I keep my eyes closed. If I keep my head down then he'll go away and I won't have to see him. The scraping sound of the chair legs against the wooden floor echo through the empty bar.

"Ree, look at me." His dark chocolate voice is hushed.

"No … I don't want to." *Why do I sound like a drunk?*

"Come on, my love. Gino needs to lock up."

He is lifting me up. I rest against his warm body. My

wretched body betrays me and a shiver runs down my spine. I cling to him, the heat of his body comforting me.

I nuzzle his neck and inhale: the smell of citrus, tobacco, musk and sandalwood fill my lungs. The urge to kiss his neck overwhelms me and I kiss him just under his ear brushing the tip of my tongue on his skin. I've missed the taste of him, slightly salty with a hint of lemon.

"Let's get you home." He pulls me away and guides me out of the wine bar to the parked car. I wave goodbye to Gino. He is at the door, his arms folded in front of him, a smile on his face.

***

MY HEAD IS THROBBING, my throat is parched, and I turn to my left to reach for the glass of water that I usually have by my bed. I feel a mattress. The bedside table has moved. I sit up. Facing me is a woman in a man's T-shirt; her dark hair is loose, she has dark circles under her eyes, her cheekbones are prominent with hollowed cheeks, two frown lines appear in between her eyebrows. The room is familiar. My eyes drift to a large black and white photograph of a couple on the wall by the sash window.

The door opens, and a shard of light enters the room. I wince at the intensity and close my eyes.

"Good morning. Thought I'd bring you coffee in bed." It's that voice again.

I force myself to open my eyes into tiny slits. He is sitting on the bed holding up a small tray, a small coffee cup for him, a larger one for me and a glass of water.

I feel for sensations on my body. I'm not wearing a bra; I check lower down. I have knickers on, but that doesn't mean nothing happened. I stare at his face. I miss the face, the sculpted chin, the long nose, the chiselled cheekbones, the broad forehead covered by the slightly long hair, the way he lifts his wicked eyebrow to mock. Those beautiful eyes with the golden shards. But they are not the same anymore, *where are the shards?* I miss everything about him. The way he used to bring me coffee when I had too much to drink the night before. The little kisses he planted on my cheek, whenever he walked by. His soft lips on my wrist, and the feel of them on my lips. *How can I miss him so much after what he's done to me?*

Tears burn at the back of my eyes. I take a deep breath and will myself to push them away. I reach for the glass of water and gulp it down, and then I take the coffee cup.

"Does your fiancée know that you've brought me here?"

The creases in the corner of his eye deepen. "My fiancée?"

"Yes, don't deny it Nikesh. Is this one last fling before you settle down? I hope I fulfilled all your wishes."

His eyes glisten, and a mist of brown dulls them.

"Nothing happened last night, Ree. You … didn't think you would be comfortable in your clothes."

"So, you took them off for me, like old times."

I see the hurt in his eyes as I say it.

"I don't understand, Ree, I … " He takes a deep breath and sips his coffee.

That's when I see the wall. The wall of photographs. The pictures of our beautiful son with all the people who loved him. A timeline of his short life. A miserable sob escapes from my mouth, and my tears cannot be stopped. I'd forgotten how beautiful he was. I see his face vividly in my dreams, but during the day when I'm awake, I find it difficult. I have plenty of sketches to remember him, but no photographs, no true likeness.

He takes my cup off me and pulls me into his arms; his warm embrace pulls at my heart. I want to stay here and feel safe, be with this man who was my first and only love. I doubt I will ever find anyone who makes me feel so safe and happy again.

"Please, forgive me. Please, come back to me. I love you, Ree. Always have, always will. My heart is empty without you."

His words feel like a whiplash on my heart.

"Why do you do this to me, Nik? What have I done to you … for you to deliberately hurt me? I wasn't the one who pursued you. You did that, your songs and your charm. Why me? All this to prove what? That an Indian girl doesn't understand you? I know your parents love you. They wouldn't have objected if you'd told them you wanted to marry Julie. All you had to do was ask them. I'm sorry about what I did that August. I had no choice, I had to. Why did you do all this afterwards? Why play with my heart? You must really hate me."

I push him away and take a deep breath, wipe my face with the back of my hand and continue, "I know about your engagement to Julie. She was there last night, did you drop her home? Then make some excuse to come back and get me?"

I slide myself out on his side of the bed, walk

downstairs to the bathroom and lock myself in. I sit and cry loud, bitter wails, not caring if he can hear me. I feel the pain of the loss of my child and let it flood all over my body, relishing the sharpness and the excruciating pain that has escaped me for so long. I face the sorrow and grief I have denied myself. I see him vividly and know I'll never hold him again. Our son, Amar. His name is apt; he is immortal to me, and he will stay with me for an eternity. The child of my first and only love.

He is sitting at the round dining table watching as I open the door, silvery tracks on his cheek. His T-shirt is looser than usual; I can see his collarbone sticking out. He has lost weight. My mind wanders to the last time he was so thin, and my heart betrays me again, and I feel his pain. I understand that losing Amar has taken its toll on him, too.

He rushes to comfort me.

"Don't!" I put my hand on his chest. He wraps his arms tightly around me.

"Listen to me, Ree. Nothing happened between Julie and me. I love you too much. I could never do that after the truth of my birth. You can ask her yourself if you don't believe me. I can get her to call you. I should have been with you and Amar. I know I've let people manipulate me, use my insecurities to keep me from you. Jay has tried to separate us; he used the excuse of finding my mother's family to keep me near him. He has a misguided idea that I love him and I was too scared to tell him or anyone else. Motaba's ignorance and betrayal drive her to behave the way she does. My guilt of giving her pain allowed her to get away with it. I'm married to you. I'll always be married to you.

No matter what happens, you are my wife. I didn't even know Julie was at Gino's. He called me to come to get you. He was worried about you."

He takes my face in his hands and kisses my eyes, my cheeks, my jaw, and then finally his soft lips kiss mine, and I kiss him back softly at first and then with fervour. I want him to touch me, hold me, and possess me. I need him to show me he loves me and only me. I need to be with someone who understands my pain, who knows who I am. Who feels the loss as much as I do. I want him so badly my heart aches.

We didn't even get up the stairs; our fevered bodies could not wait. I am in Nik's arms on the sofa, listening to his breath as it releases from his mouth.

"I've loved you since the first time I met you, Reena." I nod as he's told me this before.

"No, the first time I saw you." I frown. "You were at the top of a slide, the sun framed your face like a halo. I had to protect my eyes; your beauty blinded me. I said something stupid about your legs and I saw the hurt in your eyes, the eyes that reveal your soul. I felt that just here." He points to his heart.

I gasp. "Woburn Safari Park. You remembered!" He nods.

"That was the first time. The second time, I saw you stand up when it was lunchtime. You had an orange saree on, and I felt my heart swell. I was frantic to find you and when I walked into the dining room to eat with Bapu you were there. I wanted to talk to you. I just had to hear your voice and gaze into those eyes, to be close to you."

I lift myself on top of him and scan his face, remembering the Ram Katha.

"Why are you telling me this now, Nik?"

"So you know we are meant to be together." He kisses me. "Please forgive me, Ree. Please, please." He pauses. "I should have told you a long time ago about how I knew we were meant to be together."

My thoughts take me to our early encounters. I've always felt that kismet had a significant role in our life and my husband has told me that he thought the same. "When I saw you that morning, the morning you dropped your tray, I knew it, I knew the universe had brought you back to me. You are my soulmate."

He holds me to him and waits for me. The familiarity of his arms, the security of being with him, gives me peace. I begin to cry again for the loss of our life together. The life that had engulfed ours for the eight weeks of our son's. The life I was told would bring me pain, and I remember Sarladevi's words.

'Let her go, Nikesh. Some people are unlucky, and Reena is one of them … You had all the warnings. Look at how well her family is doing since she married you. They have brought a lovely big house, the children are much healthier, even Naren Bhai is looking better. She was never good for you.'

"I have to go home," I tell him.

"You are home, Ree."

"Please, Nik … I can't do this. I see him everywhere in this house. I hear the conversations, the hurtful comments. I feel the pain. Let me go home."

"This is our home, Ree."

"Yes, it is … it was, but it isn't our home now." I lift myself off the sofa and walk back up the stairs to put on my clothes. I hear him climb up the stairs and he opens the door. His shoulders are slumped. In his hand he is holding a white leather photo album.

"I've ruined everything. I didn't mean to hurt you, Ree. I miss him, I miss you." He takes a deep breath and exhales. "I was waiting to find a way to give you this."

I take the album from him.

"I'll take you home." His voice is deflated.

"You don't need to, I'll get a taxi."

"No, I want to. I'll drop you outside, outside Dick's flat."

I wonder how he knows I am staying at Dick's. Then I think of the conversations my father and his father still have despite the breakdown of our marriage. One good thing that has come out of our union. My father has finally found someone he can truly talk to and call his friend.

＊

"IS THERE ANY CHANCE FOR US, REE?" His eyes plead as he holds the passenger door.

"You are the only man I have ever loved, Nik, but I'm not sure I … " I let my words trail off. I want to say I don't want to spend any time with your motaba, who has always believed I was the problem. The woman who thinks I'm the one who brought on the death of our child. *How can I come back into your life?* Should anything happen to you, I will be the one who will be blamed. A small piece of me believes that she might be right. What if he'd met someone else? If fate hadn't dealt us this card? He'd be happier. I can't bear to see those beautiful eyes that glinted and sparkled filled with dull ochre and brown. I want to see the sparkles dance in them once more. Even if I'm not the one to bring them back. My fragile heart disintegrates as I think of him with someone else.

I wrap my arms around him and cling to him, my body aching to stay with him forever. A little voice in my head tells me to give him up. When I do let him go, he waits and watches as I enter the foyer area of the modern three-storey building. I walk up to the first floor and open the door to the flat. I put on an old shirt of Dick's and lose myself in creating a true likeness of our son that has eluded me for so long.

Twenty Five

I AM POSSESSED BY THE URGE to finish the painting that has confounded me and had kept me up nights. To create a true likeness of Amar, the child that I grew inside me and held for eight weeks, eight glorious weeks, eight sad weeks, eight intense weeks. The light I was working with dims and the night draws in. I turn on the lights and walk to the window to close the blinds. I have to stare again. Nik is standing where I'd left him, his hands in his pockets, looking up; he begins to walk to the foyer. The intercom rings.

"Go home, Nik."

"I can't. Tell me you've seen the photo album?"

My eyes rest on the album I'd put on the side table with my handbag. "Okay, come up." I press the door entry button.

His eyes scrutinise my face when I open the door.

"You haven't looked at it." His voice is low.

"Sorry, I had to finish something."

His eyes drift to my paint-stained hands.

"Why are you still here?"

I step into the front room, picking up the photo album from the hall table, holding it to my chest with both hands. If he touches me, my resolve will melt away and I'll be in his arms once again.

He follows me slowly and halts at the door. His eyes glisten as he sees that every inch of the walls in the living room is covered with sketches of our son, drawings of Amar with our family and friends, pastels of him with us, depictions of his hospital stay. Memories of the cherished moments we had with Amar from the day he was born to the last day of his life. My life has been work and this, this urge to record everything I remembered. Lately, those memories have become faded. I haven't been able to see him as clearly as before. But the ache of losing him has come back again this morning. When I saw the photographs at our home, I knew I will never really forget him. He is unforgettable.

He clasps his head, his shoulders shake, and his legs fold as he slumps down onto the floor neither in nor out of the sitting room. A loud sob escapes from him. The album I am holding falls. I sit in front of him and take his hands. He stares into my face. "I've let you down. I shouldn't have let you go. I should have been braver and come to you sooner. Please forgive me."

He stayed the night; we slept in each other's arms, two souls mourning the loss of their child. I dreamt of my mother laughing and playing with our children, the same dream that I had the night before Amar died, but instead of waking up crying and screaming, I wake up feeling peaceful, knowing our children are somewhere better. I watch Nik next to me, his chest rising and falling in a deep sleep, his face serene, his hand holding mine. His eyes flicker; his expression changes. "Come back to me, my love. Come back, Diku," he whispers, and I see a tear trickle down from the edge of his eye. He is crying in his sleep, and I wonder how many nights he's done that since I left him. *I wonder why he stayed in the house full of sadness.*

After breakfast, Nik asks me to look through the photo album. He has filled it with pressed flowers, ticket stubs, receipts, a memento of every day we had met since the first day I'd dropped the tray. He watches me intently, sitting on his haunches as I turn the pages; his beautiful cursive handwriting noting what we'd done on that day. My heart aches. *How am I going to make him understand he has to let me go if he remembers so much of our time together?*

He dips his head and gazes into my eyes, "Now do you understand, my love? Every day I spend with you fills me with joy. Every day I'm away from you fills me with sorrow. My heart doesn't sing anymore. Please, come back to me." A tear descends slowly down his cheek and disappears under his jaw.

* * *

"HAPPY BIRTHDAY, REE."

He is holding a big bouquet of pink roses and pulls a small rectangular box wrapped in pink tissue paper from his coat pocket.

"Oh, I … I haven't got you anything … I forgot it was our birthday today," I apologise. I've been living each day as it comes. Some days are harder than others; most days the fact that I get out of bed is an achievement. A numbing fog has descended in my brain. I'm unable to function from the prickly ache that runs through every cell in my body.

He hands me the gift, and I follow him into the

kitchen.

"Fried egg on toast for breakfast?"

I nod and sit down at the breakfast bar to watch him make me breakfast. I love watching him cook, his actions graceful and leisurely.

"So, are you going to open it?" he asks as he reaches for the frying pan that's hanging above the hob.

I stare at the pink box. I pull at the bow and carefully remove the tissue paper. It is a black velvet jewellery box. I open it and inside is a gold chain with three heart-shaped pendants, two gold and one diamond encrusted.

He puts his elbow on the bar and rests his chin on his palm; his eyes watch me. I take it out of the box and read the engraved inscription on the first pendant. *Amar* on the front, and, on the back, *7th January, 1990 – 4th March, 1990. Our hearts are empty without you.*

On the other is *Greatest Mother and Wife* on the front, and on the back, *Love you always, Amar & Nik.*

"Thank you, Nik, it's beautiful." I close the lid.

"You don't like it?"

I wonder why I don't feel anything. *Should I cry? Should I be happy? Should I shout at him for the injustice of what has happened?* I have felt nothing but emptiness since the day after I finished the portrait. I have finally let my grief take over my life. I can't go to work and had called Tony and asked for some time off. For the first time in my life, I sleep a dreamless sleep. The new pills prescribed by my GP have enabled me to do that. Nik has come to see me every day. Most of my friends have popped by, checking to make sure I eat, wash and dress. I've allowed them to help with my basic care. Umi and Peter, Anne-Marie, Ravi and Rohini. Even

Dick calls me regularly to check how I am. My friends in England know Nik comes to see me; they know that I'm speaking with him. I'm worried about telling Dick. I remember how his body vibrated, his anger barely kept at bay when anyone mentioned Nik in our conversation before he left for South America. He was due to come back soon, his documentary finished; he has been delayed due to awards ceremonies and festivals he's attending.

When I had left Nik, my friends had found it hard to avoid mentioning him, after all, we had been together since our first year at university. In the first few weeks of our separation, my heart felt heavy, my chest ached. They avoided mentioning things from our past life together. But now it feels like a distant memory. Like a scene from a favourite film that you've watched over and over again. A life that didn't belong to me.

***

I OPEN THE DOOR TO HIM in my pyjamas. "Why are you here, Nik?"

"I'm here because I'm worried. You've hardly said a word since I gave … " He presses his lips, unable to finish.

"Nothing matters now; he's gone. Why do you keep reminding me?"

His eyes cloud over, and I see the hurt. "Shall we go for a walk after breakfast?" He heads towards the kitchen to cook my fried eggs. *Will I ever be able to eat fried eggs again without the memory of Nik cooking them?*

It's only when he pulls up by the gate that I realise where we are. I gasp, my heart races and I can't breathe. He takes my hand.

"Trust me, Ree. We're not going into the house. I want to go by the stream. You like it there. Breathe."

He parks the car by the garages. I sit in my seat, resigned. After all, I have given up control of my day-to-day life to Nik and my friends. He opens the passenger door and kneels down on the gravel. He asks me to swing my legs out, and he places my navy-blue wellington boots on the ground. He lifts me up out of the seat. "Do you want your sketchbook?"

"No, I won't be sketching anymore, Nik. I told you that before?" I frown at him. *Did I tell him?* I wonder. Sometimes my memory plays tricks on me.

He places my hand on his arm, and we walk down the winding path to Nik's favourite place in the whole wide world.

He has a blanket slung over his other arm and is holding a wicker picnic basket. We stop at the willow tree, and he lays the blanket under it. We are experiencing an Indian summer; the balmy, warm days are a sharp contrast to the cold, icy, foggy days when Amar was born. The sound of the water is calming, and I wonder about all the times we've spent here, just the two of us. I watch as the water skips and skirts the rocks hastening to join a bigger stream, eventually entering the vast ocean. I, too, want to join a greater force. My insignificant life is full of pain; *perhaps the water could carry me away to tranquillity and peace?*

"Do you remember the day of our wedding reception?" His voice interrupts my thoughts; his head is resting on his entwined hands as he lies on his back. I look down at him. I can't see his eyes; they are shielded by his aviators, and I wonder where this conversation is leading.

He starts to sing, "Mil jaaye is tarah," from *Yeh Vaada Raha*.

I feel hot and take off my cardigan. I remember every day, every hour, every minute, every second of time spent with him. Sometimes it feels like I'm watching a movie; the scene plays in my mind's eye as I recall a word, a place, a feeling, a smell. None of it is real. All of it is ephemeral from a life that didn't really belong to me, the role I played for a brief time. The role of Nikesh Raja's wife and love.

I stand up. "Can we go to the ruin?"

"Sure." He stands up and takes my hand, and we amble along the path that leads to one of the boundaries of Shakti Bhavan.

I sit down on the wooden bench that has been placed in what would have been the courtyard of the house, the house that existed here before it became toppled stones and overgrown grass.

"It is beautiful here." Nik is admiring the view. "I don't come often." He takes my hand as he sits down and kisses my knuckles.

"I can see why it's become your favourite place." Hot tears sting at my eyes, and I'm grateful my sunglasses cover them.

He turns towards me and lifts my chin up. My arms lash out at him, hitting his chest, thrusting him away as I scream and shout at him.

"Their life is a ruin! No one remembers them anymore! They've wiped them from their memory! They even built a house far away from them!" I point to the wall that obscures the view of Shakti Bhavan. He allows me to pound him with my fists. "They've abandoned them! There are no headstones, no memorial." Finally, I yelp through the sobs, "The people who lived here must have been happy, must have had dreams, hope for the future. No one cares, Nik. No one. No one cares about their life."

"My love, my love, they do have headstones. They were buried in the village churchyard."

He has enclosed me in his arms, and I wrap my arms around him and bury my face in his chest.

"I know it's painful to think about him, but you can't stop … I feel the pain, too, when I remember our son and our lost child. It's not our fault, my love. We had to make the decision. We weren't ready. I'm to blame for your decision to have the abortion. Come home, my love, you'll feel much better. Come and see him. Come and feel him. He's still with us."

It was then that I felt a little sad for Nik. He was also mourning for our children; his strength and belief kept him in our house and by my side, whereas all I want is to join them. It never occurred to me that if I left, too, he might not be as strong.

6th Day of Navratri

MY MOTHER'S DEATH ANNIVERSARY IS TODAY, and I've spoken to my father and told him I'm not able to come up to Leicester, using work as an excuse. This year I couldn't bear to go home to remember her, because remembering her would also mean we would have to remember Amar. I'm not ready to remember him. The pain is too sharp.

I haven't told my family that I've stopped working. My conversations are restricted to what the twins are up to and how Amit and Smita's new practice is faring.

I usually joke and laugh with them when I call, and they are none the wiser about how my life has changed.

Nik still comes to check that I've eaten something and spends most evenings with me. We watch TV, listen to music, play Scrabble. I sometimes ask him questions about the photo album and the keepsakes he has collected. Anything that doesn't remind me of our son. He stays to sleep with me when I ask him to and leaves when I don't. I like the comfort of his warm body next to mine when the days are full of sorrow. We have not made love since that time when I woke up in our bed. A small part of me smiles when I recall the day. The day my husband declared he and I were meant to be together, that we were soulmates. When I revel in his love, my mind screams at me for being selfish and tells me to let him have a happier life without me. Sometimes I lash out at him because of the guilt I hold, the guilt that I am responsible for his hurt, hoping for and dreading for the day that he'll leave me and never come back.

"We're going out for dinner today," he tells me as I open the door to him.

"Oh … I … it's … " I stammer unable to tell him what day it is.

"I know, Ree, but we're going to celebrate your mother's life."

"I … don't want to go home, Nik."

"No, it's just you and me," he shouts from the bedroom as he's searching through my clothes. "Do you want to wear a dress or trousers?"

"Dress," I say and start rummaging through my clothes with him.

"This one?" He's holding up a sixties-style green paisley-print dress. I shake my head. "I love this one." He's holding up a pale-yellow chiffon dress, grinning. I pull out a '70s dog-collared dark-navy dress with cream trimming and belt. His face drops for a second, but that lopsided smile comes back.

We are seated by the window at Osteria Napoli, a small, family-run Italian restaurant, that we used to go to when we first married. Nik has ordered a bottle of Bollinger and a platter of antipasti.

The waiter pours the champagne, and Nik raises his and says, "Usha Solanki, mother to Amit and Reena, wife to Naren, grandmother to Rishi, Rakhee and Amar. We remember you today and always."

My heart skips at the mention of Amar; the dream of my mother replays in my mind.

I bring myself back to the man who is sitting in front of me. He is telling me about the new contract they've negotiated with a Ugandan manufacturer and how so many people are going back to reclaim their properties and businesses. His face brightens when he talks about the legal framework of the deals he's involved with. I let my mind wander to how our life would have been if I hadn't got pregnant unexpectedly. Perhaps we'd still be leading a carefree life, discussing work projects, enjoying evenings like this.

"I spoke with Amit this afternoon," he says when our main course arrives.

I give him a thin smile, thinking about the day my brother had come to see me, and I had told him about seeing Nik. He had been angry at my decision to allow him back into my life. I had told him I needed to be in London with Nik as he understood what I felt. We'd fought until late into the night, and eventually, he'd relented, telling me that my stubbornness would get me into trouble. *Why did my brother ring Nik and not me today?*

"He's worried about you. He wants you to go see them."

"I can't go, Nik. It would be too difficult."

"I can take you. We could go for a day trip."

"Let me think about it," I reply, certain that my family would not welcome him back as easily as he thinks. I take another sip of champagne.

We eat our main meal in silence, and I finish a third glass of champagne.

"Want to share a tiramisu?" he asks, raising his left eyebrow.

We always share a pudding. It had become our thing. When we went out with our family and friends, when it came to desserts, they'd all shout, these two will share.

He feeds me tiramisu, his eyes focusing on my mouth as I open it and swallow the smooth creamy dessert. My stomach flips as I see those smouldering eyes.

When I woke up this morning, I'd thought it would be one of my unbearable days. Spent in my jogging bottoms, wallowing in my grief. But I haven't felt the pain that has gnawed at my being today. Everyone had called to see how I was today; even Dick had managed to find time for a call while on his tour of America. The anniversary of my mother's death has always been and will always be a sorrowful day, and they know that this year will be worse than most. Their love for me has helped with the ache; being with Nik has eased the pain of losing her. He always knows when I need him. He has a knack for being there when I can't cope. I feel a sudden yearning for the life we could have had. *Is it the conversation or the familiarity of the restaurant?* I wonder as I sit opposite him, surreptitiously stealing a look at his chiselled face.

The cold wind sends a chill through me as we leave the restaurant and Nik pulls me closer into his arms. He waits for me to strap myself into the car seat, and we drive home in quiet contemplation. Something has shifted between us. I can feel it in my soul. I have seen his eyes linger on my face all evening. I have felt him watch me intently as he sat down in the driver's seat before he started the car.

Aretha Franklin sings, "What a diff'rence a day makes."

As we pull up outside the flat, I wonder what is different about today that has made me feel this way. Our bodies are drawn together by a magnetic force as we walk up to the first floor. As soon as he closes the front door, I turn to him.

"Kiss me, Nik." My voice sounds breathless. Instead of kissing me, he takes off our coats slowly, his eyes drifting to my lips. His lips part a little and a slow sigh escapes as he leans in; his face is on my neck, and he lingers. My breath catches, and I wait for him to kiss me. The scent of sandalwood, musk and citrus fills my nostrils; the hairs on the back of my neck stand to attention. He pulls away and stares into my eyes. He walks into the sitting room, taking my hand and pulling me towards the sofa as he sits down. He takes a deep breath.

"You don't know how much I've wanted to kiss you these past weeks, Ree. It's taken all my strength to keep me from taking you in my arms and devouring you." He lets out a deep sigh.

He says nothing for what seems like an eternity. *So why isn't he doing it? Why is he waiting?* I've told him to do it. *Maybe he's found someone else?* That's why he's been so different tonight, so much happier. I even saw a glimmer of that lopsided smile dance across his face at dinner. My stomach is in knots. I've lost him. It has taken me too long. I have selfishly taken up all his time and energy and not once thought about his happiness. He clears his throat. "I've been thinking about this a lot." He pauses and takes a deep breath.

I brace myself for what I'm about to hear, my heart accelerates, an iron bar tightens across my chest. I've lost him, my one and only love. *How will I carry on with my life now?* I tell myself off for taking too long to tell him I love him.

"When I finally found you at Warwick, it was our third meeting. We got engaged three times."

How is this relevant to telling me he has met someone else? I ask myself. The bar around my heart tightens further. I hold my breath, willing myself not to cry. He sees the quizzical expression on my face.

"As far as I'm concerned, that Christmas cracker ring was the first time, the second was Brighton, and the third was in front of your family. We've even had three weddings so we can be together: the legal wedding, the seven steps we took on the day we were supposed to have married, and our wedding day at the Sanatan Mandir. I've been waiting for a sign. When Gino rang me, I knew it. We had to be separated to be finally together. This is the last time, from now on its forever. Three is our lucky number." *Did he say forever?* My mind cannot make sense of what he's saying. My heart stops. One, two, three, four, five, six. He lifts me to standing and kneels in front of me.

"Will you stay married to me, Reena Raja?" He pulls out a gold band and holds it up.

I burst out crying. I saw my world tumble before me in that moment. I thought he was leaving me. I want to be with him. He makes me feel safe. He is and will always be my only love. He fumbles in his pocket for a handkerchief and hands it to me.

"Is that a yes?"

I hold out my left hand, and he slides my wedding band back where it belongs.

I pull him up and kiss him, softly at first. His kiss tells me how much he loves me, wants to be with me and only me. I can sense the pain of our separation, the pain of the loss of our son. I want to possess him, I want my body and his body to be one, the longing and desires that have built up from our separation take my breath away. He pulls back, and I lose myself in those incredible eyes. The golden shards are back.

"Wait, we're only heavy kissing, my love," he whispers in my ear as he plants a kiss just behind it and works his way around my jaw, chin and neck.

Twenty Six

Diwali, 1990

I open the door with my key and shout, "Where are you, monsters? Come and give me a hug!"

Two boisterous children run down the long dark hallway full of twinkling tea lights. When they see Nik their eyes light up, and they rush and grab his legs.

"Neenufua, Neenufua," they shout in unison. Nik is smiling and holding a huge box of fireworks in his hands.

"More fireworks, Mummy. Neenufua's brought more fireworks," Rishi shouts.

Smita walks out of the kitchen wiping her hands on a tea towel.

She smiles up at Nik and gives me a hug. "Reena I'm glad you came." She squeezes me tightly. "How are you, Nik?" she asks as the twins scrabble to take the box off him.

"I'm good, how are you?" His expression is wary.

"That's far too big for you two to carry. Let Neenufua help you," she tells the twins.

His shoulders drop a little as the twins pull him to the back of the house to the family sitting room. She grabs me by the waist and we walk down the corridor, putting my coat over the newel post of the bannister as we pass. She informs me that my father has gone to get some mithai and Amit is on his way home.

My stomach is in knots; the thought of my father and brother meeting Nik again has made me anxious. My body is tense from the words that still haunt me.

'Let her go, Nikesh. Some people are unlucky, and Reena is one of them.'

When we had pulled up outside the house, Nik lifted me up from the car sensing my pain and said, "I'm the luckiest man in the world to have such a beautiful and courageous wife. Nothing can keep us apart, my love."

We hear the door latch turn and wait anxiously for whoever has come home.

"Smita, Beti, I've brought some barfi I made," the softly spoken words of Divya Ba inform us as we sit in the room. I walk out into the hallway. Divya Ba is taking off her coat, and my father is standing behind her. Her smile lifts into her eyes; her arms are outstretched.

"Oh, what a lovely surprise. You didn't tell me my Reena was here, Naren."

I rush to her and engulf myself in her arms. "Kem Cho, Divyaba?"

I glance at my father. His lips are thin, his eyes creased. He's seen the car and knows Nik has come too. He takes off his coat slowly, and then stands, his arms open.

"Come and give your daddy a hug, Reena."

I hug him, unable to keep the tears from welling up in my eyes and soaking his shoulders.

"Now, now. Did you miss me that much?" he teases as

he strokes my hair.

"I missed you so much, Daddy. Just couldn't bring myself back to you," I whisper.

We walk arm in arm to the sitting room. Divya Ba has gone ahead. Nik is hugging her, she releases him and plants a kiss on his cheek.

Smita Bhabhi's eyes dart to the door as we enter. Nik walks hesitantly up to my father. I am unable to gauge my daddy's emotions; his face is still and expressionless. Nik bends down and touches my father's feet. Instead of my father's usual reaction when anyone does that of pulling them up, his eyes drift to Nik's hand, and he slowly raises his right hand and rests it briefly on Nik's head.

It will take a long time for these two men to be as they were. My father still smarts at the injustice of the blame Sarladevi has thrown at me.

"Papa, look at the fireworks." Rakhee tugs at my father's hands.

"Goodness me," he says as she takes him to where they have collected them for tonight. "Your Neenufua knows how to spoil you two. This will last for hours!" he exclaims, his eyes smiling. "Where's Amit, Smita?"

"He should be here soon, Daddy. Can I get you a drink?"

"Yes, yes, something soft for us all, Beta."

I turn towards the kitchen, and she grabs my arm. "No, you sit with Nik." Her voice is low. "I think he needs you by his side."

I glance at my husband; of all the people he wants approval from my father is probably the most important. After all, he did promise him he'd protect me when he asked for my hand in marriage. He is standing where he had bowed down to my father, his arms hanging. I take his hand and guide him to sit on the sofa; his breath is shallow, his eyes are dull and glistening. I squeeze his hand tighter, and whisper in his ear, "Give him time, he'll come around."

He tries to raise a smile but fails.

"Hello, hello, I'm home."

The twins abandon sorting through the fireworks and rush to the hallway. "Daddy, Daddy, Fi and Neenufua are here," Rishi shouts.

"And they've brought a gigantic box of fireworks. It's the best Diwali ever," Rakhee adds.

"Oh ho, you are so spoilt. I don't know what we're going to do next year to make Diwali even better." Amit is holding his children on either side of him as he enters the family sitting room.

Nik stands up and approaches him, holding out his right hand, "How are you, Amit?"

My brother takes his hand, pulls him close and gives him a hug. My eyes search for my father who is sitting in his armchair by the fireplace. A small thin-lipped smile appears on his face momentarily. Some of the knots in my stomach loosen.

My big brother is generous and kind; he has always been and will always be on my side, no matter what decisions I make.

I stand up and run into his arms. "I love you, Bro. You're the best," holding onto him for a long time.

Diwali dinner at my house is a lengthy affair; we have starters, main course, dessert, mithai, tea or coffee. Then the fireworks display starts. Usually, it's Amit who lights the fireworks while we watch, but tonight, Nik has taken on the task, rushing back to the French doors to wait patiently as the twins argue amongst themselves for the next one. I'm enclosed in my brother's arms, watching as the rockets and fireworks light up the night sky.

My father has a protective arm around Smita Bhabhi and Divya Ba, and we observe the twins' faces light up as they ooh and aah at the colourful swirls and magnificent flowers in the sky. My husband's eyes sparkle just as much as the fireworks. He is relaxed with the children; at times like this he becomes the carefree man I used to know. His dazzling smile and his easy laughter permeate through my soul and I fall in love with him even more.

After the fireworks, we have hot chocolate and ice cream. The hot chocolate to warm us up from the cold winter winds and ice cream to remember the life my parents had in Kenya when they would go with their friends to the ice cream parlour after the fireworks.

Afterwards, the twins insist that Nik reads them their bedtime story and I sit with my bhai and bhabhi in the front sitting room waiting for him to finish before we go back to London. Divya Ba and my daddy stay in the family sitting room listening to the Diwali programme on Radio Leicester.

My brother reaches across from the armchairs and tries to pry my clasped hands apart. "Everything will be fine, Sis. You just need to give us time."

"I have to tell you something, Bro." I begin to tell my bhai and bhabhi that I haven't been to work since September, that some days I can't get out of bed. I tell them I have finally come to terms with the loss of Amar, and Nik and my friends have all taken turns to take care of me. Amit squeezes my hand tightly and nods.

"You know?"

He gives me a sympathetic smile.

"Yes, I've wanted to come and fetch you. That's why I came to see you." He pauses.

Smita moves closer to me and places her arm around my shoulders. "But Daddy wouldn't let him. You do know he talks to Kaka every day?"

"You've known all along that Nik and I are together?" My voice breaks as the relief floods over me. I hold my head in my hands and begin to cry.

The door opens. Nik rushes in and kneels in front of me, gently pulling my hands off my face. "Ree, my love." His eyes throw fiery darts at Amit and Smita. "What's happened?"

I pull my husband to me, holding him close. "I'm sorry. I should have come home sooner."

He laughs, "Oh, is that all?" and kisses my forehead.

***

"I'VE BROUGHT YOU A PRESENT FROM KAKI." Nik is holding a rectangular gift box.

I take it off him and open it. Inside there is a crimson silk chaniya choli with bandhani border and gold embroidery. I stare at his smiling face.

"It's my favourite colour on you," he whispers as he kisses me.

"There's a letter." I put the box on the coffee table and open the cream envelope. The sheets fill my nostrils with the scent of lavender. The writing is familiar from the notes left by his mother.

I read the letter slowly, making sure I understand what is written in it.

I don't know how to react. Should I be happy she has apologised for not supporting me or should I be sad that it has taken the death of our son for her to realise that her sister-in-law was manipulating her? Using her badge of betrayal and her fake act of kindness to get her own way?

"Are you okay, my love?" He lifts my chin with his fingers. I nod and close my eyes, not wanting to speak because I know I wouldn't be able to hold back the tears. He picks up the letter. "Can I read it?"

I wonder if I should let him, uncertain that the woman who wrote it would want him to, but I want him to know that the woman who he idolises isn't who he thinks she is. I take his hand and nod.

Pushpa Raja, Shakti Bhavan, Loudwater, England. UK
18th October '90

Dear Reena,
Forgive me for not being strong enough to defend you that terrible day. The day another piece of my heart was torn away from me.
Ever since I met you that March afternoon, I have loved you like my own child. I don't know what it is about you that draws me to you. Do you feel it too, Reena?
I'm so sorry to have subjected you to all the hurt. It isn't your fault. It is Bhabhi's prejudices and insecurities. When Amar arrived, some of her words brought back the memories of the loss of my children.
Yes, children. I lost three children before Niku came into my life. The loss still haunts me today. You are probably the only one who can understand how I feel. Women who have never lost a child don't feel or understand the all-encompassing sadness, emptiness, the guilt. Bhabhi has

*never lost a child, so will never understand our sorrow.
When I lost my first child, she said the same words to me.
I'm sorry to remind you of those words, I don't want to
cause you any pain. Enough, you will soon have other
children. The ache of hearing the words came back to me. It
is an ache that never leaves you. I should say to you that
everything will be fine, but I want to be honest with you.
You will remember the words, but your memory of Amar
and the time you spent with him will outweigh the hurt. I
wish I had the same time with my lost children, but it is
sorrow I carry with me.
When I lost my first child, she told me to do what she tried
to make you do, that's why Anant has been so cross lately.
He remembers the fasting, the prayers, the abstinence, to
conceive a child again.
At the birth of our Ritu, Anant and I were overjoyed. I'd
lost hope of getting pregnant again. We had dreamt of
having four children: two girls and two boys, a girl first to
help look after her younger siblings. But my happiness
didn't last long. I was made to feel inadequate that the only
child I could grow inside me was a girl. Bhabhi told me I
was cursed. I've never told anyone this. She said my bad
karma was visible as a shadow and, if I wanted to have a
son, I would have to keep away from my husband. So, she
made me stay in Kampala while Anant went to join
Motabhai in Nairobi. Watching you stand up to her has
given me the courage to think about what happened to me. I
realise now she must have resented the fact that Anant and
I were together. We went out to dances, hotels, and
restaurants. Her life has always been the house and the
mandir. It is what she has been brought up to do. Motabhai
tried to coax her out with us, but she would not let go of
her upbringing.
Not having Anant with me when Ritu was young was the
longest six months of my life. Bhabhi would not allow me*

to look after her. She would hand her over to the ayaa saying don't get attached Pushpa, eventually, she will have to leave us, and your heart will ache. When you have a son, you can use all your time and energy on him. I sometimes wonder what happened to her. My parents never made me feel inferior to my brothers. Perhaps it is because I am the youngest and only daughter, and she comes from a family of many daughters. It must be difficult when your family thinks of you as a burden to offload.

I was relieved when Motabhai sent Anant back to Kampala, and I fell pregnant again. But God was not on our side. I lost that child. He was born at five months, too early to survive. She took him away. I don't know where he is, just like my daughter. It's what they did then. We had no choice. She said the same words she told you that night, the night you left our family and my son. That it was my bad luck. My mind took me back to that day in Kampala, and I didn't even notice you leave. If I hadn't been in my own nightmare, I would have run after you, told you that you weren't to blame, to give my son a second chance. I know he would never cheat on you. He loves you more than life itself. I can see the pain when he is away from you. I'm sorry I wasn't there to defend you.

Eventually, I fell pregnant again, but this time Motabhai insisted I stay in Nairobi until the birth of our child. The day I lost our daughter in Nairobi was the hardest. I wept, and there were times I didn't want to live, then Bhabhi brought Ritu to me, our beautiful daughter.

I love Ritu more than life itself. We are lucky to have her as our daughter, just as we are lucky to have you in our lives, Reena. But, when I was told that I would never have children again, my heart broke, my life ended. How would I give my husband the family he'd always wanted? Bhabhi saw how we suffered. She saw my pain.

Then by some miracle of fate, Niku came into our lives. I

knew my son had come back to me, that the God I believe in had brought him back to me.

Niku is just like my Anant. Niku is steadfast, loyal and kind, and he loves you like my husband loves me. We are blessed to have found husbands who love us so much. Give Niku time, he has lost his way, but his love for you has never wavered.

I genuinely believe he is the son we lost, although Bhabhi reminds me that Nikesh is her son almost every day. She never talks of Raju or Suresh as my son, but with my Niku she always says my son Nikesh. It's her way of telling me that without their help, I would never have had a son. Reminding me of my inadequacy as a wife to provide my husband with an heir.

Since losing you and seeing my Niku suffer, I do not allow her words to control me anymore. You have done that, daughter. You have made me stronger. You have made me braver.

Come back to our family, Reena. If you find it hard to live in your house with Niku, we can buy a home for the four of us, anywhere you want to live, away from Shakti Bhavan. I miss you, my daughter, my son, misses you. I've seen his eyes dull and well up with tears when he remembers a memory of your time together. I want you to be happy, and I think you will be if you give him a chance to prove his love to you.

I've sent you this gift because red has become my son's favourite colour since meeting you. I have bought it for you because I see you light up when you wear red, knowing that my son loves seeing you in red.

I love you, Reena. Please forgive me for not being as courageous as you. Please forgive us for not protecting you, and come back to us. We want to prove to you that we are worthy of being called your family.

Love, Kaki.

I watch him as he reads his mother's confession; the hurt and pain she's felt all along. The devastation of never having a child again. The times when Sarladevi made her feel inadequate and reminded her of her bad karma. His eyes water and tears trickle down his cheek. I reach up and wipe them away.

"I never thought Motaba would be so ... " His voice trails off. I take him in my arms and hold him. His body shakes from the sobs. "I love Kaki, so much," he eventually says.

"I know, and she loves you just as much," I reassure him.

Twenty Seven

I DON'T KNOW WHO IS MOST SHOCKED, Umi or Peter, as their eyes dart from my ring finger to my face. I raise a thin smile.

We are celebrating Peter's birthday at Ketner's tonight. Usually, I would have met everyone in Soho, but this year Peter and Umi insisted we travel into the West End together.

Umi grabs my hand. "When did this happen?"

Umi has been, and still is, wary of Nik. I recollect all the times she's bumped into him at the flat. The way she is courteous to him, but the warm easiness with which she used to tease him has gone. I suppose we'll never be the same again after Amar; we all faced our own mortality when he died. We have assessed our lives and hewn new paths.

Peter, on the other hand, is a steadfast friend and has been in contact with Nik as regularly as he has with me. He was the only one who went to Nik after our separation to find out if what I'd told them was true. He had insisted I'd been misinformed and raged at Jay's underhandedness. He'd pointed out that Jay was jealous of me and in love with Nik. I couldn't accept it as an excuse. Nik had still spent a night with Julie, his childhood sweetheart. I recollect the conversation we had the afternoon when I told him that Nik was back in my life.

* * *

WE HAD SAT DOWN FOR A CUP OF TEA. Usually our conversation would be about how I was feeling and what he could do to help. But that rainy afternoon he told me of the change in Nik's work schedule, how they met weekly for a swim at Shakti Bhavan and how he was worried about him. He told me about his conversation with Julie.

"I wanted the truth from the horse's mouth. I spoke with her about that night. She told me everything. Nothing happened," his tone imploring that it was true.

"Nik was afraid he was losing you and drinking helped relieve his pain but also made his anxiety worse. They had gone to the nightclubs that Jay frequents and ended up at Julie's flat. She had taken him to her room, away from the party. He'd cried and told her he couldn't live without you. She waited for him to calm down and fall asleep. By the time she came back out, Jay had gone with someone he'd picked up. When he called her, Jay wouldn't believe nothing happened. You can call Julie, she's happy to speak with you." He'd taken my hand, his eyes urging me to believe him. "I have to tell you something else. You're not going to like it. I went to see Jay, too."

"It's okay, Peter. I don't want you to stop seeing Jay," I'd said.

"Umi will be upset, but I wanted to know ... I needed

him to tell me why. All those times you've bumped into Julie were arranged by Jay. He told her where you were and she played along with him thinking it was a joke."

What he'd told me confirmed what Nik had told me. My belief that Nik wouldn't have lied about something as crucial as an affair was justified. If I didn't believe it, I would not have let him come back into my life. *I was surprised at the lengths Jay went to to pull us apart.*

***

"NIK HAS ALWAYS LOVED YOU, there is only you.. I'm happy that you are back together," Peter hugs me.

"Is he coming tonight, Peter?" Umi asks angrily.

"Yes, my darling. I know you find it difficult. If Ree can take him back, you'll need to forgive him too," he tells Umi, kissing the side of her head.

"I'll reserve my judgment. All Nik needs is Jay to turn up and he behaves like a teenager again," Umi replies. "Sorry, Ree. I love you, but I won't welcome him back with open arms. Dick is going to be livid. Have you told him?" I shake my head.

"He'll be back soon, if you are sure that … " She waves her hand as if to swat a fly, "that this is what you want, you'd better tell him and tell him soon. He's bound to hear from someone," she continues.

I have been worrying about Dick and his reaction. All the men in my family haven't questioned my decision to leave Nik and have been my support. My brother and father have met him again, and the one man who has been through thick and thin with me is away. Telling Dick about Nik is going to be hard.

21st December, 1990

NIK HAS TAKEN ME HOME several times. Some days are hard and fill me with sadness, and some bring back happy memories. We have gone for lunches, afternoons and sometimes we go to hang out after dinner on our favourite sofa, watching television, listening to music and kissing, lots and lots of kissing. I have told him there's a part of me that wants to move back, but there are times when the memories of our son haunt me and the sudden sense of loss floods over me, wrecking the progress I've made so far.

I am disturbed from my sleep by the sound of the intercom and peer at the clock on the bedside table; the digits blink ten and thirty-five. The room is still dark, and I wonder if it's night or day. The intercom buzzes again. I pull myself up, and head to the hallway.

"Good morning, my love."

I let him in and wait by the door, hearing him take two steps at a time. A memory of an earlier life flickers through my mind, and I step out to wait at the top of the stairs.

He lifts me up as soon as he reaches the top of the stairs, dropping the bag he is holding and nuzzles his head on my neck and inhales.

He swings me around. "Happy anniversary, my love," he laughs.

It is the fifth anniversary of the day we took our vows. He had reminded me and asked if we could go to the mandir and home for lunch today. I told him that I didn't have a saree and he'd promised to bring me one to wear.

"Just got up, sleepyhead?" He put me down and

picked up the bag. I stifle a yawn and nod.

He takes my hand. "We don't have to go to the mandir if you're tired?" he adds.

I feel the need to go to the mandir today. I have only been once since Amar's death and listening to devotional songs does give me some peace. I rush towards the bathroom. "No. I want to go, Nik. I'll be quick."

The curtains are open and the bed made; the saree I wore on the day of our vows is laid on top. I pause at the door, my eyes drifting to the red cloth. I haven't worn any of my red clothes since the day of the telephone call. He turns to me, smiling, and then a frown develops on his face.

"You don't want to wear it?"

Hot tears form at the back of my eyes. "I can't. Not after ..."

He engulfs me in his arms. I sob into his chest until I have no more tears left to shed. He sits me down on the bed, pushing the saree away.

"That woman who told you not to wear red was a nasty old lady. You are stunning in red, my love, besides it's my favourite colour." Angry sparkles are dancing in his eyes, and then he pouts. "I brought another saree, as a backup." He pulls out a saree bag with my panetar in it. "Come and have breakfast while I iron it for you."

I'm standing at the dressing table, putting on my earrings when Nik walks back into the bedroom. He reaches for the filigree beaded necklace and fastens it around my neck. His hands rest on my shoulders, and his smouldering eyes rest on mine.

"I could lose myself in those intoxicating eyes," he

says as he picks up my mangalsutra and fastens it around my neck. "I've brought this, too."

He is holding a small pot, smiling. It is the silver sindoor pot Divya Ba had given me when we got married. He opens the clasp, lifts the lid and fills my side parting with sindoor. He turns me around and kisses the top of my head.

***

THE CAR APPROACHES Bhaktivedanta Manor through the long driveway, and we park in the car park. As we step up the wide entrance, we hear someone call our names. I turn to the voice. A tiny bespectacled woman in a printed grass-green saree is rushing towards us.

"Jai Shri Krishna, Reena, Nikesh. We've missed having you here." Her eyes twinkle.

"Jai Shri Krishna, Manju Masi," we both say, our palms placed together in greeting.

"So sorry to hear of your son." She takes my hand in hers. "Do you know only special people have such children born to them? You two must have done so many good deeds to have the privilege. Lucky you."

This is the first time someone has told us we were honoured and lucky to have had Amar instead of blaming our bad karma and past sins and we hug her. The darshan and kind words of the ladies who prepare the daily prasad has lifted the stone that has rested on our souls. They insist we take the sweet sheero with us, and, before we leave, we promise to come back soon to help in the kitchens. I think about how much we used to enjoy helping out in the kitchens on feast days and festivals.

* * *

AT HOME, NIK TAKES out the cooler bag from the boot and places it on the kitchen worktop. I join him, taking out the containers and finding pans to warm up our lunch. Every year we eat the same meal we ate on the day of our vows.

I don't have the headspace or the patience to make meals. Instead of relaxing me, they fill me with anxiety; it is another one of my favourite things I can't do anymore.

Reena & Nikesh's - Wedding Vows

Patra
steamed colocasia leaves stuffed with gram flour and spice masala

Crispy Bhajia
thinly sliced vegetable fried fritters coated in gram flour batter

Undhiyu
mixed vegetable curry speciality of Gujarat with fried fenugreek and gram flour dumplings.

Bateta nu shaak
potato curry

Chuti mug ni dall
lightly steamed split mung bean lentil cooked with mild spices

Mattar baath
pilau made with rice and peas

Kadhi
thick spicy broth made from gram flour and natural yoghurt

Dhudhpak
thin and creamy milk dessert with rice, sugar and cardamom

Puri
deep fried small rolled flatbread made from whole wheat flour

Ambli khajjur ni chutnee
tamarind and date chutney

Tameta ni chutnee
fresh tomato chutney

Kachumber
salad made with cabbage, cucumber, carrots, tomatoes and onions

Papad
fried thin crispy bread made from lentils flour

After lunch Nik brings a flowerpot with a wooden stem from outside. He grins. "Happy wood anniversary, my love. It's a pink rose. I was told it's too late to pot it up. But when spring comes, we can plant it. Do you like it?" He smiles shyly at me.

I lift myself up on tiptoes and kiss him on his cheek. "It's perfect," I tell him.

We spend the rest of the day in our home, listening to music and drinking. I worry Nik has substituted the cigarillo for whisky; he has had three glasses by the time I finish one. I wonder what is making him nervous. We have spent longer and longer at our home. I am going to make my mind up soon. Dick will be coming back in the new year and I want him to have his flat back. I want to live here with Nik, be with him when he suffers. I've seen his eyes flood as a memory comes to the fore. I've heard him crying in his sleep, always saying the same words, "Come back to me, my love. Come back to me, Diku." I want him to believe that I am back with him forever. My hesitation of moving back to our house must gnaw at his subconscious.

The house will always remind us of our son. I am hoping that I might be able to live with the happy and the sad memories. Amar will always be a part of our lives, just as my mother and Nik's papa are still remembered.

Barry Manilow melodiously sings, "Can't smile without you."

He stands up. "Dance with me?" He takes my glass away from me. He places my left hand in his right, and we glide along our narrow sitting room. We dip and twirl, and when the song finishes, he lifts my chin and

Saz Vora

kisses me, first softly and then longingly. I return the kiss telling him I want to be one with him, to be his forever. I walk up the stairs, pulling him. The door to our bedroom is open. I manoeuvre him to the end of our bed and push him back. I close the blinds.

His eyes are questioning, his lips part and a breath escapes from his mouth. My eyes tell him I want him. He licks his lips. I concentrate on the scar on his upper lip.

"Wait, we have no condoms. We were irresponsible last time." He is raised on both of his forearms. "I'll have to go get some." He lifts himself up to sitting.

"If three ... is our lucky number ... I don't think ... we should ... use a condom." The words escape as little breaths as I try to stop my heart from bursting through my chest.

He pulls me to him, his warm hands grabbing my exposed waist. "Are you sure?" His eyes sparkle like fireworks and the golden shards are back. He lifts me to sit by his side, and he frowns.

"Yes, one hundred per cent sure," I reply, reaching to take off the pin that holds my pallu.

"Are we having making babies sex?" He raises his wicked eyebrow and grins.

"Yes, instead of oh shit I'm pregnant sex," I reply and unbutton his jabo.

He pulls at my pallu and starts to unravel my saree.

The music player switches to the next CD and Amitabh Bachchan's voice travels up from the living room, the song from *Silsila*.

"Where have we have come, walking together for so long. In your arms, my love, my body and my soul melt."

Javed Aktar's words remind me of the day we brought Amar home; the same song was playing on the radio. I finally unite with my husband.

Epilogue

December 22nd, 1990

I CAN'T BELIEVE SHE'S HERE WITH ME, sleeping in our marital bed. My wife, my life, my heart has finally come back to me.

I keep pinching myself. I thought I'd lost her for good this time; this time, when she needed me the most to fight for her, to be on her side. I'd regressed again, lost in my self-pity like a spoilt brat. Not the strong husband she deserves. She has always deserved better than me. Sometimes I wonder what her life would have been like if I had let her go, after that terrible day in August. I was selfish; I wanted her, I needed her, she made me a better person, and everyone in my family told me that I was a better person with her than without her. So, I pursued her, persuaded her to take me back. I promised I would never hurt her. A promise I wasn't able to keep.

When Gino rang me, my heart squeezed. I have spent a lot of time waiting since March, waiting and watching, making sure she was safe. My life had become waiting at our home, keeping the memories of our son alive, and watching over Reena. My family come to see me and sometimes they take me back to live at Shakti Bhavan. But it isn't my home anymore. My home is this house.

The night I walked into Gino's Wine Bar and saw her slumped at the table, all I wanted to do was pick her up and take her home, join our hearts together, make my heart whole. But when she stared at me with her soulful eyes, I had to stop myself from gasping. They had turned into a dark pool of sorrow; they have always carried a sadness. That is what drew me to her. All I wanted was to fill them with joy, to make them shine. Instead, I have let her drown in the despair-filled pool. How did I let her live by herself, a lonely existence, with no one to help her heal? I was selfish; once again I failed her. I had promised to protect her, to be by her side in sickness and in health, support and comfort her in her hour of need. I hadn't kept the vows we'd taken in front of Agni Dev.

I waited and watched her. She needed to make the first move; she clung to me, she didn't push me away, my heart began to climb from its deep recess. She hadn't stopped loving me. Reena still loved me. My heart repeated the words back to me: Reena still loves you.

When she kissed me on my neck, every cell on my body ignited. I saw the desire in her eyes, the longing, and the look that made me want to be joined with her. I could never resist her when she looked like that at me. I wanted to kiss her and tell her how much I loved her, that without her my life means nothing. Without her I have no heart; it beats, the mechanics work, but it no longer sings. It did all the time when I was near her, with her. This heart isn't even the heart I used to take with me when I was away from her. The heart that would slow down and wait to return to her, the heart that counted the seconds, minutes, hours, days, quietly biding its time for when it would become whole again. Sometimes, when it's quiet, I hear it beat; the sound of it is muffled and drowned in the deep well.

I had thought about taking her back to Dick's flat that night but decided against it. It would be better if I took her home; she was far too drunk, and I wasn't happy to leave her alone. She stopped in the living room, her eyes filled with tears and she turned to me and said, "Why are you still here, Nik? How can you do this to yourself? I can feel him. Where is he? Can I hold him? Was it just a dream?"

I took her in my arms then, held her and told her it wasn't a dream, that it was true; he had left us. She kissed me, the way she used to kiss me, the way her body would meld with mine, and she pulled at her clothes, "Please ... Nik, I want you. I've missed you." She was in her underwear. I yearned for her body, to make her mine again. She grabbed at my clothes and then we were standing in the living room in our underwear and she started to kiss my chest, my neck, my jaw and I would have taken her there and then, made us whole again, made us one again. It took all my strength to stop myself. I wanted Reena to remember we'd joined as husband and wife. I wanted her to be sober when she made love to me again. I wanted her to remember when we became one again.

I picked her up and carried her to our bedroom and she whispered, "I miss the smell of you most. I wish I could die here in your arms, Nik, then I wouldn't have to remember Amar anymore, or you."

My heart tore in half; the woman who was a fighter,

who knew how much pain the death of her mother caused her father, had been thinking of taking her own life, of ending it all. And I had observed from afar. I hated myself then, hated myself for being a coward. I told myself waiting was not good enough; I was going to do all I could to make her realise she hadn't lost me, that I wanted her to come back to me.

I spent the night watching her. She woke up briefly, went to the wardrobe and pulled out one of my T-shirts, pulling off her bra. I loved that she would want to wear my T-shirt in bed when she was drunk. When she came back to bed, she saw me and said, "I love you, always and forever." She took my arm, wrapped it around her waist, tucked herself under my arm and fell asleep.

When I heard her stir, my chest swelled. I thought she'd smile, the way she used to when I would take her coffee and a glass of water in the morning. I thought she had forgiven me, but her eyes were full of pain and hurt. I couldn't understand what she was telling me. Her words didn't make sense to me. Why didn't I go see her and tell her about the night at Julie's? *Was I ashamed of what I'd done?*

Then she said the words, that I blamed her for what happened that day in August. I would never blame Reena. Never. If anyone is to blame, it's me: the fact I was too childish to take responsibility. I'm also to blame for what happened to Reena after the birth of our son. I was a coward and didn't protect her from Motaba and her superstitions. I understand now how she uses her faith as a whip to control the people in her life.

I couldn't bear to hear her cry. I saw the pain in her

eyes when she saw the photographs on the wall, the images I wake up and go to sleep with. My reminder of our loss; the only way for me to deal with the loss of Amar.

When we made love, my heart pounded in my chest; it was no longer at the bottom of the well. It beat loudly and I told her when my heart had filled. When the universe brought us together and it would only be whole with her by my side.

For a moment, I saw in her eyes the joy of recalling our first encounter. They shone like diamonds, but as suddenly as the joy had lifted her spirit, the windows to her soul drew down their shutters and she was gone again. The Reena Solanki I fell in love with retreated to how she was when we knew Amar was not with us for long. The hurt and pain were too much for her to carry; she fought to stay alive, she fought for our son, to ease his stay in this world, the only way she knew how: she shut down her soul.

I gave her the photo album that day, one of our lives together as a couple to tell her she hadn't lost us. Then I continued my vigil, but this time instead of observing from a hiding place, I made sure she knew I was there for her. I wanted her to understand I shared her heartache. I would help her deal with Amar's loss. I know I failed her. I hadn't protected her, like I promised Amit, Dick and her father. I'd left her to mourn the loss of our child and she'd never really dealt with it, how could she? She was mourning the loss of us first. She had no one to share the pain with. Only I knew how it felt to miss Amar. I have another album of our life as a family, Reena, Amar and me. I haven't shown Reena that yet, but I will when the time is right. I don't think it is yet; I'll wait for the day. I've become accustomed to waiting.

When I'm with her, my heart beats faster, like it did before, sometimes singing, sometimes skipping, but most of the time it is back into the habit of waiting quietly when we are apart. I have been to see her every day. I was there when she let the sadness overwhelm her, as she became an empty shell. I was there when she raged at the world. I was there when she hated me. I was there when fleetingly her soul would show itself to me, the soul that was partly mine.

She battled to come back to me; she fought to banish the words that have haunted her. I watched as the hurt engulfed her on the days she could barely live, but I hoped she would one day say she wanted me back in her life for good.

The day she agreed to be my wife again I told my parents their daughter was back in our lives. I told Amit and I told Dick, her protectors; they are both wary, how can they not be? I have hurt her before. I've abandoned her in her hour of need before. I know it will take time to trust me again.

Even my family berated me when Reena left. They, too, punished themselves for not supporting her. They smarted at the injustice of our actions and the words of Motaba. Kaki insisted I wait for Reena patiently, urging me to create the albums to give to my wife. Standing by me and helping me to build up the courage to fight for our love. I understand, now, how she must have felt when she heard the hurtful taunts from Motaba. My family have become Reena's protector, too; they are her rock, they stand by her decision without question, they tell me off for being weak, and when I despair she won't come back to me, they tell me I should have faith in the strength of my love. In the woman that is Reena Raja.

"Hello." She smiles up at me and her soft, luscious lips brush mine. "I missed you, Nik."

"Hello, my love. I've missed you too."

Her eyes are intoxicating. She turns to gaze at the wall of photographs.

"He's still here, isn't he?"

I hold my palm to her chest and hers to mine and say, "He'll always be here, my love, always and forever."

She nods and holds me tight entwining her leg over mine, trying to get as close to me as she can.

"When will the pain go away?" Her eyes are full of sorrow.

I want to say soon, but I know it would be a lie and say, "It won't go away, my love. It will ease. Some days are better than others. He is like the eternal flame; sometimes he comforts me and sometimes he scorches, reminding me that the flame that is Amar can do both. He is unforgettable, my love, and I wouldn't want it any other way."

She gulps back a sob, and I stroke her hair.

"Cry my love, cry as much as you want. I'm here, you're safe."

Spring, 1991

I SEEM TO BE DOING A LOT of this lately, waking up before sunrise to watch my wife, my heart, my life as she sleeps. I still can't believe she is here with me; the last six months have felt like our first six months at Warwick.

We spend all our time together, never being far from

each other. Even when Reena has to work later at the office, I go and sit opposite her with my work. We've been back to Shakti Bhavan, Leicester and seen our friends, but most of the time we've wanted to be with each other. Revelling in each other's company, cherishing the memories of our son in the home we have built for ourselves.

I run my finger over her cheek; I have to touch her when she's near me. The memory of when she left me still haunts me. How my heart skipped when an image of my love would appear at the edge of my vision, at the stove, on the sofa, sitting at the table, and as quickly as it appeared it would disappear, leaving me devastated and broken and my heart would dive back into the deep recesses of the well it had become accustomed to living in.

***

I waited with the lights off, in our living room. She leapt at me; her intoxicating eyes danced and her arms wrapped around my neck. She kissed me with longing and desire. We kissed as we used to when we first dated, slowly and sweetly, taking our time, savouring every moment. I pulled away. "I missed you, my love," my voice croaked.

"I missed you too, Nik." She smiled up at me.

I turned her around and pulled at her raincoat, still holding her around her waist. I kissed the back of her neck and she sighed. "I was going to meet you at the airport in your favourite dress," she said.

"Couldn't wait. Nothing happening tomorrow, except a group breakfast. You could always go and change into my favourite dress," I whispered as I worked my mouth along her jaw.

She took my hand and walked up the stairs to our bedroom. The blinds were already closed. I had anticipated what we would be doing as soon as Ree saw I was back.

The days we are separated have been difficult; the days leading up to my going away are strained. We argue about the smallest of things and then regret we've hurt each other and make love hurriedly to claim each other again.

This trip was the longest we've been apart. A week is a long time when your heart doesn't belong to you anymore and every waking and sleeping hour is focused on the person who isn't with you. I know Ree finds it difficult; she has voiced her concern about the women who are always present at these functions: the hostess, wives, and girlfriends. I can't seem to convince her that she is and will always be the only woman I ever want. Even though she believes me, a small part of her still recollects the memory of Jay's words, the lies he told her and how we had been apart because of them.

I lay on the bed, my arms crossed behind my head, and stared as she slowly and deliberately took off the pink print dress she was wearing. I gulped back the gasp that had released in my throat. She was wearing the black and red underwear I'd given her as a parting gift at the airport. I'd left a note in the box asking her to wear it for me when she came to pick me up.

"Did you know I was coming home?" I quizzed her. I couldn't help smiling from ear to ear.

"Nikesh Raja, you can't keep any secrets from me, after all, I am your heart."

She climbed onto the bed. I pulled her on top of me and we made love. At first it was fevered and intense, her fingers tearing at my shirt and trousers, the urgency of touching skin to skin, each of us claiming back the body we hated being apart from. I turned her on her back and then it was my turn to savour the feel and taste of her, and finally we made love unhurriedly. Afterwards, I wrapped my hand around her belly and I examined her intently. There is a glow around my wife; her features have softened, her hair has a reddish glint, she smells different too, freesias and roses mixed with another scent.

We hadn't bothered to get dressed and walked hand in hand downstairs in our dressing gowns. She gave me a quick kiss and stepped into the bathroom. I opened the fridge.

"What do you want to drink?" I shouted.

"Orange juice," she replied, and I poured it out for her in a glass, pouring myself a glass of Coke. As I returned the juice carton and closed the door, I saw a white stick in her hand.

"Nik." She smiled shyly at me.

"Is that what I think it is?"

I rushed to grab her; her head was on my chest, and she nodded.

"How long have you known?"

"I started wanting to drink gallons of orange juice on Wednesday," she replied, still clinging to me, unable to lift her gaze to my face. I don't blame her: the last two times she told me she was pregnant I overreacted, the first time using words like entrapment and betrayal and the second time thinking that her anger at being pregnant was because she didn't want a child with me, drinking to excess, misinterpreting everything we'd said to each other, and assuming the worst.

"Wednesday?" I lifted her face to look at mine, pushing back the fringe on her forehead. "And you didn't say a thing?"

"Wasn't sure … " She paused. "I wanted to wait for you to come back home," she gulped " … I thought I would do the test when you were here."

I hated how that made me feel. How unsure she was about my reaction. It was her eyes that gave her away. They were filled with an anxiety, even after we'd agreed that we wanted another child.

We both glanced down at the white plastic stick she was holding in her right hand. She lifted it up and in the centre of the window was a blue line and a plus.

"We're pregnant, Nik." Her voice was barely audible.

I swept her up and kissed her all over her face and then swung her around, shouting, "We're pregnant!" The joy of the news that we will be parents again filled me with happiness and Ree began to laugh, too.

"Fish and chips?" I am putting on my jacket.

"Yes, lots of vinegar," she nods, standing with her hands on her hips in her red silk dressing gown.

"Okay … " I grab her palm and lift it to my lips, " … This is new."

"I've been craving it all day. Hurry, Nik. I'm starving." She pushes me out of the door.

I run to the Fish Ahoy on Bond Street and wait impatiently for the man in front of me to make up his mind whether he wants cod or haddock.

I grab the vinegar bottle and start soaking the fish with vinegar. The dark-haired woman at the counter frowns at me as I continue to drench the chips.

"Wife's pregnant," I explain as she starts to wrap the paper.

"I see," she says, nodding, and she opens the jar of pickled gherkins, adding three to the package. "On the house." She smiles.

She sits at the table, a jar of pickled onions open in front of her, smiling at me as she pops a sour onion into her mouth like a sweet.

"Couldn't wait," she says, crunching it.

I take out the paper packages and open both, handing the one with the pickled gherkins to Ree. I sit down next to her with mine.

"Pickled gherkins." She smiles at me. "What else can we get that's pickled?"

She eats the fish and chips with her hands, licking her fingers with gusto, and I remember the last time Ree was pregnant and her strange taste in foods. The huge quantity of bananas and grapes she consumed and her sudden urges for Neapolitan ice cream and orange juice at the strangest times.

* * *

SHE LAUGHS, AND A SMILE develops on her face; she's dreaming. I'm confused. This dream doesn't seem to frighten her. It isn't one of her all-consuming anxiety dreams that results in night sweats and screaming. She still gets them. I'm usually holding her, comforting her; it is one of the reasons I don't like being away from her for too long. The build-up of adrenaline from our separation doesn't help the situation and I know the dreams are difficult to deal with, especially since she's stopped sketching.

She opens her eyes and then smiles at me.

"What did you dream about?"

Two lines develop between her eyebrows. "Why isn't there a swing on the tree on the hill?"

"The hill?" I ask.

"You know, at Shakti Bhavan."

"I don't know. I guess no one thought about it until you did," I reply. "Did you dream about the tree and the swing?" I ask, my words full of concern.

She turns on her side and lifts herself on one elbow.

"I dreamt of the children playing under the tree, taking turns on the swing."

"Children?"

"Yes, all of the children, Sammy, Anoo, Rishi, Rakhee … all of them."

"How many do we have?"

"Three, one girl and two boys."

"What are they called?" I ask unable to stop the smile developing on my face.

"Oh, I didn't dream of what they were called," she says earnestly. "I know we have three. You were running around as usual with our daughter in the baby sling."

"What else did you dream about?"

"We were living at Shakti Bhavan."

"Oh … in the house?"

"No, in our house in the stable block."

"You don't want to live here?"

She senses the disappointment in my voice. She leans in and kisses me softly.

"We don't have to move yet, but three children in this house isn't practical." She wraps her leg around my hip.

I smile. "You've put a lot of thought into this Mrs

Raja."

"I didn't have my husband to distract me, so I've been thinking."

"He's here now." I pull myself on top of my wife and slowly explore her body with my mouth.

While I'm making breakfast, I think about Ree's dream and I chortle, "Two older brothers huh, my little pari is going to be so protected."

Ree bristles. "No way. She can do whatever she wants, go wherever she wants. I won't allow you to stop her." Her eyes glare angrily at me as she collects the cutlery. I tuck her into my side and kiss her on her head. "Sorry, I'll take care not to be overprotective, my love," I say.

Her face softens. "I love you, Nik, always and forever." She smiles at me and then she wraps her arms around my neck and kisses me with her soft luscious lips.

The End

Want to find out how Reena and Nikesh met?
Read My Heart Sings Your Song Book One - University Series Reena and Nikesh

Glossary

Gujarati words

Agni Dev – God of fire

Ayaa – the name given to nanny or female attendant

Ba – mother or grandmother

Bapu – a respectable name given to a wise elder

Bandhani – specialist intricate tie-dye technique which originated in Gujarat

Ben – sister

Beta – child usually boy but can be used for either male or female

Beti – daughter

Bhabhi – brother's wife

Bhai – brother

Bhagavad-Gita – discourse between Arjun and Krishna in the Mahabharat

Bhagwan – God

Bhajan – Hindu hymn

Chaniya choli – traditional long skirt and blouse worn with a long scarf

Churidar – tight silk/cotton trouser worn under kameez or sherwani

Daba – a metal round tin

Dada – paternal grandfather

Dadima/Dadi – paternal grandmother

Dharma – one of the four objects of human pursuit in Hindu Scripture meaning moral duty

Darshan – an opportunity to see a deity at a temple

Dikri – a pet name for a daughter

Diku – a pet name for a small child

Divo – a lamp created using a cotton wick and clarified butter

Faiba – paternal aunt

Fua – paternal aunt's husband

Ganesh Prathna – prayers to Ganesh the god who removes difficulties and obstacles

Ganga – River Ganges

Gangajal – water from the sacred river Ganga and Jumana

Garam – hot

Gudiyaa – doll

Guruji/Guru – a spiritual teacher

Haan – yes

Hai Bhagwan – Dear God

Havan – a sacrificial ritual to Agni Dev

Jabo pyjamas – long shirt and trousers worn by men

Jai Shri Krishna – Glory to Krishna, a common greeting in Hindu households

Janam kundli – horoscope chart prepared at birth

Jijaji/Jiju – sister's husband

Jumana – also known as the River Yamuna

Kaka – paternal uncle

Kaki – paternal uncle's wife

Kameez – long shirt/dress worn over trousers traditionally worn by women

Katha – religious story

Kem Cho – Gujarati greeting meaning how are you?

Laxmi – Goddess of wealth

Mandir – Hindu temple

Mangalsutra – meaning sacred thread – gold and black bead necklace given to the bride by the groom

Masi – maternal aunt

Mataji – a term that refers to all Hindu goddesses

Motaba – eldest mother

Motabhai – eldest brother

Na – no

Nana – maternal grandfather

Nasto – savoury snacks

Navratri – nine-day festival to celebrate the divine power of the Goddess Durga

Pallu – The decorated end of a saree that is left loose or displayed at the front

Panetar – white and red saree worn by a Gujarati bride given to her by a maternal uncle

Pari – angel

Paath – recitation of a religious text

Parsi – a community of Zoroastrians who migrated to Gujarat from Persia

Prasad – an offering of food at Hindu temples and ceremonies

Ram Katha – religious tale of Ram from the Ramayan

Saree – traditional garment worn by Indian women

Sanskrit – ancient classical language of India

Shabaash – a form of praise meaning well done

Shakti Bhavan – home of divine energy

Sindoor – a vermilion red pigment used in Hindu ceremonies and worn by a married Hindu woman

Sunderkand Paath – recitation of the tale of Hanuman, the first devotee of Ram

Swami – a religious teacher

Tilak – auspicious mark on the forehead using vermilion or sandalwood

Tthoydi – white woman or girl

Foods

Aloo gobi – potato and cauliflower curry

Ambli khajjur ni chutnee – tamarind date chutney

Baath – plain boiled/steamed rice

Badam nu dhudh – milk with ground almonds, sugar and ground cardamom

Bajra no rotlo – thick, soft bread baked on griddle pan made with millet flour

Bajra ni rotli – thinly rolled bread baked on griddle pan made with millet flour

Bajra na thepla – thinly rolled bread fried on a griddle pan with ghee made from flour and spices

Barfi – sweet made with milk powder and sugar

Bateta nu shaak – potato curry

Bhaji – any green vegetables used to make a curry, e.g. spinach

Chaas – diluted natural yoghurt drink

Chai – brewed tea with milk, sugar and spices

Chevdo – a fried savoury snack made from gram flour noodles, nuts and potato chips also known as Bombay mix

Chora ni dal – split black eyes peas stew

Chuti mag ni dall – split yellow mung stew

Crispy bhajia – thinly sliced vegetable fried fritters coated in gram flour batter

Dal makhani – matpe beans (black gram) slow cooked stew with cream, speciality of the Punjab

Dall – split lentil soups and stews

Dhana marcha ni chutnee – fresh coriander and green chilli chutney

Dhudhpak – thin and creamy milk dessert with rice, sugar and spices

Gathyia – spicy fried gram flour noodles

Gaur – raw cane sugar also known as jaggery

Gaur keri nu athanu – sweet mango pickle using spices and raw cane sugar

Ghee – clarified butter

Idli – a steamed dumpling made from ground lentils and rice

Jeera chawal – fried rice with cumin seeds

Juwar ni bhakri – leavened thick bread baked on a griddle made from sorghum flour

Kaatlu – traditional snack for nursing mothers made from ghee, jaggery, coconut, gum arabic, course wheat flour and thirty varieties of herbs and nuts

Kachumber – a salad made with lettuce, cabbage, cucumber, carrots, onions and tomatoes

Kadhi – a thick broth made from gram flour and yoghurt

Kaju katli – sweet made with almond powder and sugar

Keera ka riata – cucumber and yoghurt sauce

Khaman dokla – a steamed cake made with gram flour and spices

Khichdi – steamed lentils and rice

Lassi – natural yoghurt drink blended with water and

spices

Masala chai – brewed tea with milk, sugar and spices like cardamom, cinnamon, ginger

Mattar baath – Fried and steamed rice and peas

Mattar paneer – peas and Indian fresh cheese curry

Meth murg– fenugreek leaves and chicken curry

Methi na thepla – griddle fried wheat flour, gram flour with fenugreek leaves, rolled thin bread

Methi nu shaak – fenugreek leaves curry

Mithai – generic name for traditional Indian sweets

Mug baath – rice with mung bean curry

Mug ni dall – yellow split lentil stew

Naan – leavened flatbread cooked in a tandoor oven

Parotha – Griddle fried layered flatbread made from wheat flour and cooked with ghee

Papad – thin crispy bread made with lentil or rice flour eaten either fried or dry roasted on flame

Patra/timpa – steamed colocasia leaves stuffed with gram flour and masala

Penda – traditional Indian sweet made with milk, sugar and spices

Phulli gathiya – fried gram flour shaped noodles with ridges

Plain dosa – thin rice and lentil batter pancakes

Pilau – fried rice

Quick naan – leavened flatbread made without yeast baked in the grill not oven

Raabh – hot drink made millet flour, jaggery, coram seed and water

Ringda matter nu shaak – aubergine and peas curry

Ringda no oro – roasted, mashed aubergine with dry spice and garlic

Rotla – thick soft unleavened bread usually made with grain flour, e.g. millet

Rotli – thinly rolled unleavened bread cooked on dry

griddle pan usually made with wheat flour

Shaak – any vegetable curry

Sheero – sweet dish made using semolina or wheat flour, ghee, sugar or jaggery

Tameta ni chutnee – fresh tomato chutney

Theekha gathyia – spicy chilli powder savoury fried gram flour noodles

Thepla – griddle fried wheat and gram flour rolled thin spicy bread

Tindora nu shaak – ivy gourd curry

Tuwar ni dall – thin broth made with pigeon peas, split lentils

Udad ni dall – matpe (black gram) beans split lentils stew

Undiyu – mixed vegetable curry especially eaten in Gujarat, made with a combination of root vegetables and green vegetables with fried fenugreek and gram flour fritters

Acknowledgement

The hospitals are fictionalised and used only for storytelling. I am grateful to all the doctors, nurses and support staff who work tirelessly for the NHS. Our words of thanks are not enough.

There may only be one author listed in this book, but I couldn't have written it without the support and constant encouragement of my family and friends. This book has been the story that I have wished to tell for a long time.

To my beta readers and my early support team, your feedback, support and constant friendship are more than I deserve. Thank you all for allowing me to fulfil my dream of writing this story.

To Marina and Sarah, thank you for reading through my drafts.

To Claire for your editing pen.

To our firstborn son, a day never passes without remembering you.

To my beautiful boys, I am proud to have you in my life. Without you, my life would really be empty.

To my husband, thank you for providing me with endless cups of tea when I was holed up in the study writing this book. Your cups of tea are the best. Look where we have come?

To all our friends and family who rallied around to support us when we needed it most, thank you for all your love and understanding that winter, so long ago, when our world fell apart.

To my parents, who supported us when we needed it most, I love and miss you both so much.

To my sisters, Bena and Gini, you are always there when I need you. I am so glad to have you in my life, and to Hassy, my sister from another mother, thank you for being who you are.

To Mita Gohel, your creativity blows me away.

To all the Bollywood films I have watched and loved for giving me inspiration for some of the dialogue, I have taken liberties with the translation of the lyrics in the songs that I've quoted.

To all the authors who have inspired me, I am a reader first and foremost.

To you my readers, THANK YOU so much for reading my story, I hope you liked it. I am always interested in connecting with you all.

Please leave a review; it will help other readers find new stories and help self-published author like myself to reach new readers.

To find out more about my books, free chapters, deleted scenes, recipes and much more please sign up to my **newsletter**

About the Author

Saz Vora was born in East Africa and migrated with her family to England in the 60's to the Midlands, where she grew up straddling British and Gujarati Indian culture. Her debut duet My Heart Sings Your Song and Where Have We Come is a story in two parts about love, loss and family, the second book in the series is based on true events that has shaped her outlook on life's trials and tribulations.

Before she started writing South Asian romance she held down successful jobs in Television Production and Teaching...But her need to write stories has led to what she is doing now – writing.

She lives in London, England with her husband in an empty house as her two beautiful sons have began their own life journey.

Saz's hobbies are listening to music, cooking and watching Bollywood, Hollywood and Independent films.

Please visit her website, where you can read her blog and sign up to her newsletter where she will share, missing scenes, recipes, playlists and all things book related.

Website www.sazvora.com

Lightning Source UK Ltd.
Milton Keynes UK
UKHW012101151120
373432UK00001B/54